# Mary Behan

Laurence Gate
Press

You can contact the author at mvbehan.com

Publisher's Cataloging-in-Publication Data

Names: Behan, Mary, author.
Title: A measured thread / Mary Behan.
Description: Mazomanie, WI : Laurence Gate Press, 2020.
Identifiers: ISBN 978-1-73449-430-3 (paperback) | ISBN 978-1-73449-431-0 (ebook) | ISBN 978-1-73449-433-4 (large print paperback)
Subjects: LCSH: Women--Fiction. | Immigrants--Fiction. | Wisconsin--Fiction. | Ireland--Fiction. | Secrets--Fiction. | BISAC: FICTION / Women. | FICTION / Family Life / General.
Classification: LCC PS5302.E33 M43 2020 (print) | LCC PS5302.E33 (ebook) | DDC 813/.6--dc23.

LCCN: 202093765



Cover image "Pastoral" by Gina Hecht
♦ ginahecht.com

Cover and interior design by CKBooks Publishing
♦ ckbookspublishing.com

Laurence Gate Press
6383 Hillsandwood Rd.
Mazomanie, WI 53560

For Tim

# *Chapter 1*

Maggie watched as the wall of flames approached. They licked upwards, shape shifting, clamoring for oxygen. Twenty feet in the air, their orange tips released a pall of smoke that spread upward and outward, obscuring everything in their path. Maggie wiped her nose with the back of her gloved hand and stifled a cough. She could taste the smoke in the back of her throat. The fire made a peculiar crackling noise, like a strong gust of wind plowing through a field of dry corn stalks. The wall of flames came closer, and the sound swelled. She watched, transfixed, as the fire demolished everything in its path with a tornado-like fury. It hissed, whined and roared. All other sounds were drowned out. The birds had left much earlier, alerted by the piercing calls from crows on lookout in the surrounding pine trees. Occasionally, a field mouse erupted from the leading edge of the fire, running haphazardly away from the inferno.

Standing at the edge of the prairie, her feet slightly apart, Maggie leaned against her fire swatter, a crude pole topped by a flap of thick black rubber. Glancing down, she considered how inadequate a tool it was in the face of the approaching flames. She reminded herself that she wasn't alone: to her left and right was a line of figures, many of them her neighbors, each of them alert and patient. A few carried fire swatters. Others were better armed, with backpack water pumps that weighed at least fifty pounds. In the early years, she too had carried a water pack, but those days were long gone. Had she chosen to watch the burn from the safety of her cabin, no one would have cared. But she was determined to play her part. After all, it was her prairie. Thirty years ago she had taken an exhausted corn field and transformed it into a kaleidoscope of color that changed with the seasons and over the years. When possible, she walked its perimeter, admiring its subtle beauty. That was her reward for being a good steward of her adopted home.

She held the fire swatter upright; its large rectangle of thick rubber would shield her face from the searing heat when the flames got closer. Her mind hopped to a silver-framed photograph of her grandmother on the mantlepiece in her parents' house. Seated close to a fireplace, the smiling face was protected from the heat by a tapestry screen. Maggie considered her own outfit: leather work boots, bib overalls, a heavy cotton shirt with frayed cuffs and collar, a sweaty kerchief and a faded canvas bucket hat. Smiling to herself at the contrast, she angled the flapper to scan the black ribbon of charred grass that separated her from the oncoming flames. This was the last stand, a magical barrier through which fire could not pass. It looked inadequate and yet, from years of experience, she knew it would work. The only danger was if an errant gust of wind propelled embers across the ribbon into the adjacent woods. They were tinder-dry after a long winter and the ground was covered by a thick carpet of desiccated leaves.

Her body felt old. She hadn't slept well the previous night, and the new feeling of discomfort, not quite pain, in her lower abdomen was a little disturbing. Scar tissue, she thought. All the same, it made her think: Would she be around for the next burn in three years' time? She'd be eighty-three by then, older than her parents when they died, older than all of her grandparents. But they had lived much harder lives in Ireland. It wasn't fair to use them as a comparison. Instead, she began to count the cousins who had survived past eighty, sticking out a gloved digit with each remembered name. A hand's worth. Not very encouraging. Ireland seemed to be featuring more frequently in her thoughts these days. Did every emigrant think about their country when they grew old, she wondered? Did they ask themselves how it might have been had they never left? And what if she had stayed in Ireland? Better not to go there.

The crew from the Aldo Leopold Land Stewardship Program had arrived shortly after breakfast and set about unloading equipment. This was the fifth time Ron, the fire boss, had been to Maggie's property, so he was familiar with the layout. He was accompanied by a group of six young interns, four men and two women, all of them eager to get started on the day's project. They followed him as he walked around the perimeter of the prairie, checking for flammable material on the fire break. Several of Maggie's neighbors arrived soon afterwards, and gradually everyone moved into place.

Walking briskly along one edge of the prairie, Ron had dribbled lighted kerosene from a drip torch onto the dry grass. As the dry stalks caught and flared, everyone held their breath, waiting to see what would happen. Too little wind and it wouldn't catch. Too much, or a change in wind direction, and the back fire could plow its way backwards into the heart of the prairie, out of control. This was the riskiest part of the burn, and it had gone smoothly, leaving a band of blackened grass that extended along the edge of the field. It contrasted starkly with tall yellow stalks of prairie grass on one side and a mowed, grassy fire break on the other.

Maggie waited patiently as the head fire made its way towards her. Smoke billowed across the ground, and for a moment she was enveloped in the choking swirl. Quickly, she pulled the kerchief up over her nose and mouth. Her eyes were watering uncontrollably, and she wiped away the tears with the back of her glove. She could feel the approaching heat and angled the flapper to shield her face. The clouds of billowing smoke made it impossible to see past a few feet in any direction. A patch of flame burst into color to her left, and she jerked the flapper down, snuffing it out. For a brief moment she relaxed, leaning on the shaft of the flapper, suppressing the urge to cough. As she straightened up, out of the corner of her eye she saw another patch of flame behind her, inching slowly towards the pine woods that bordered the prairie. The head fire had jumped the fire break.

"Water. Here. Now!" Her voice sounded weak and hoarse as she swatted at the flames. The circle of embers was widening. Just as soon as she snuffed out one segment, another would begin its malevolent crawl towards the adjacent woods.

"I need water now!" Maggie shouted at the top of her lungs. She could hear the panic in her voice.

Smoke continued to swirl around her and by now she had lost all sense of direction. Her chest felt tight and for a fleeting moment she wondered if she was having a heart attack. After all, it had happened to Aldo Leopold during a prescribed burn on his own prairie.

"Over here!" she continued to shout, in between ragged breaths.

A figure emerged from the gloom, lurching under the weight of a water pack.

"Where?" he shouted, pointing his brass wand in the direction of her flapper. She gestured to the growing circle of embers, and he pumped furiously, ejecting a strong spray of water onto the burning grass. The glow fizzled, sending up a puff of smoke. It caught again briefly, was doused with another jet of water and finally died.

They stood back to back, scouring the area around them for

new threats. Another patch of dead leaves was burning strongly a few feet into the woods. The water pack man shouted urgently for help as he pumped and sprayed. The stream of water sputtered and died. His tank was empty. Now he was screaming for reinforcements. He grabbed her flapper out of her hands and began to beat at the burning leaves in a frenzy. Two more figures appeared out of the gloom and rushed to the widening circle of flames, one with a flapper, the other a water pack. Close to exhaustion, Maggie retreated to the mowed strip of grass at the edge of the woods. She bent over and took a few tentative, shallow breaths before filling her lungs greedily. Behind her she could hear people shouting to each other as they continued to put out flames. At the sound of an approaching engine, she straightened and waved her hands in the air.

"Over here!" she shouted.

An ATV with a tank sprayer perched awkwardly on the back came to an abrupt stop beside her. Wordlessly, Maggie pointed in the direction of the three figures. The driver jumped off, flipped a switch near the tank, and an electric motor whined to life. Grabbing a hose, he ran into the woods in the direction of the shouting.

Maggie relaxed a little and leaned on her flapper, letting her mind wander. A week earlier she had called each of her neighbors to alert them to the burn, and most of them were here to help out. The notable exception was Bill Breunig. An image came to mind: a burly man in his late forties, well over six feet tall, a thick neck, and a shiny bald head below which a fleshy face radiated a permanent pink glow. He dressed like a new car salesman: crisp khakis, a cream-colored shirt and a blue blazer. Since her husband died, Bill had taken to dropping by Maggie's cabin, unannounced. Initially she was polite, but gradually Maggie came to resent these visits. The man had a predatory air about him and despite the thirty years age gap, he made her feel uncomfortable. Two years ago she read in the local newsletter that he had purchased a small piece of land adjacent to the north boundary of her property. His land was accessed from a different highway, and at the time she reassured herself their paths need never cross. Unfortunately, Bill used this property as an excuse to visit Maggie more frequently.

She thought back to the last time Bill paid her a visit, a month ago. That morning, coming back from her walk, she heard a crunch of tires on the driveway and watched as a shiny black SUV with tinted windows swept into view. On seeing Maggie, the driver slammed on the brakes, and came to a stop by the barn, leaving two deep skid marks in the gravel. The door of the car swung open and Bill stepped down. His gaze travelled first to the cabin, then the prairie, and finally to Maggie. He walked slowly to where she was standing in front of the barn. Ignoring the conventions of personal space, he loomed over her, his head and body blocking out the sun.

"Well Maggie. I see you made it through another winter unscathed."

He gestured towards the prairie.

"Are you still throwing money away on that land of yours?"

She looked up into his face to confirm the derision in his voice, and he returned her gaze with an inscrutable smile. Like all bullies, he reveled in verbal sparring, but Maggie was determined to keep her composure.

"How are you Bill? Did you get another new car?"

For a moment he was taken aback at the non-sequitur but recovered quickly.

"You know, you could put that land into corn and finally make some money off this place. It's the perfect time. The weeds haven't come up yet."

Maggie could feel anger growing inside her. She despised this man with his fake southern accent. He reminded her of all the arrogant men she had encountered during her career as a scientist. It was a well-kept secret that bullies thrived in academia, and she had experienced her share of them.

She kept her voice free of emotion. "They're not weeds, Bill. It's a prairie."

"Prairie, whatever. It's weeds to me. Corn prices are good right now, you know. Thirty acres would cover your property taxes."

Bill thrust his face down at her and demanded, "How much are they in any case?"

Maggie could smell his sweat. She took a step back from him and replied coldly, "It's none of your business."

He shrugged his shoulders. "So, when are you going to sell this place to me?" He was smiling now—a professional smile that ended at his lips.

Maggie was speechless. She opened her mouth to say something and found that her mind had gone blank.

"But we're neighbors, Maggie," he said in a conciliatory tone, pointing in the direction of his land. His voice took on a cold hard edge. "Didn't you realize? I'm planning to buy you out. It's just a matter of time."

An ATV engine coughed to life, jerking her back to the present. In the distance she could see Ron dabbing at the ground with his drip torch. Behind him, silhouetted against the hazy sun, was an old oak tree. On her morning walks, she had often wondered why this particular tree had been spared when so many others were cut down to build the cabin and the barn. Now, something about the tree triggered a memory: She had startled a hen turkey near there the previous week, the bird seeming to appear out of nowhere. Surprised, she watched it run into the neighboring field, its head bobbing awkwardly. But it hadn't flown off, and when she thought about the encounter later, she decided the bird must have its nest hidden in the prairie close by.

Without thinking, Maggie dropped her flapper and ran towards the line of fire. It was beginning to take hold, inching stealthily into the dry grass. By the time she reached the spot, flames were beginning to climb the desiccated stalks of last year's milkweed. In a panic she searched for the nest, aware the hen would have picked a well-concealed spot. The flames were more confident now, creeping towards the main body of the prairie and the oncoming fire. Maggie was oblivious, focused only on finding the nest with its precious clutch. Finally, she spotted them: nine perfect eggs nestled together under a swath of dry grass. Tearing her hat off, she knelt down and began to place the eggs, one by one, into their makeshift refuge.

"Maggie, what are you doing?" Vic shouted, grabbing her arm and pulling her to her feet.

She recognized the voice and was surprised by its harsh tone. Vic, a young man whom she had known since he was a child growing up in the valley, had never spoken to her this way before, and for a moment she was confused. The loud crackle of burning grass made it impossible to hear what he was saying, but the look of alarm in his eyes was unambiguous. He jabbed his finger towards the wall of smoke, and when she didn't move, pushed her ahead of him. She dropped her cap and the eggs spilled onto the ground. Instinctively, she stopped to pick them up, but the pressure of Vic's hand on her back didn't slacken. As he walked past the shattered eggs, he stooped to grab her hat and continued to herd her towards the edge of the prairie.

"What were you thinking, Maggie? You could have gotten seriously hurt!" He stared down at her, his eyes blazing. "Luckily, I saw you leave the line. I thought you were going back to your cabin, but you ran directly towards the fire. You scared the shit out of me." His voice cracked, and he looked away.

"I thought I could..." Maggie began to speak, but the inhale caught in her throat and she bent over, coughing. Vic unclipped the water bottle hanging from his belt and pushed it into her hand. Still bent over, she nodded her head up and down, unscrewed the cap and took a sip. Straightening, she ventured a deep breath.

"Sorry, Vic," she said, handing the bottle back, "I wasn't thinking clearly."

She looked back towards the prairie. A shift in the wind had cleared the wall of smoke, revealing blackened stubble where the nest had been.

"I saw a hen lurking around that spot last week. I should have shooed her off, made sure she didn't lay her eggs there. I knew we'd be burning the prairie." Her shoulders slumped.

"Aargh, Maggie. You're such a softie."

The worried expression on his face was replaced by a reluctant smile. He held out her hat and put his arm around her shoulder. She looked at the empty hat, and with a sigh, crammed it back on her head.

"Don't worry, Maggie. It's early in the season yet. She'll have time for another clutch."

They heard shouts from the direction of the fire break where Maggie had been standing earlier.

"Come on," Vic said, "We better get back to our places on the line." He began to run, and she followed as quickly as she could.

Suddenly, it was all over. An eerie silence descended. Maggie looked out across the prairie, a vast blackened landscape interrupted here and there by the still-smoldering stems of young willow trees and blackberry bushes. In the distance she could see figures moving slowly around the perimeter, checking for any residual hot spots. There was still one small segment of oak savanna to be burned beside the barn, but Maggie felt no compunction to help. She needed a little time to recover, especially as everyone would be coming back to her place for refreshments. The last thing she wanted to do was host a party, but it would be expected. She caught Ron's eye and pointed in the direction of her cabin. He nodded briefly and continued to give instructions to the interns, who were sprawled on the ground, their packs and flappers strewn around them. The young man who carried her flapper back from the fire break, jumped up and offered it to her. She shook her head.

"Thanks, but I'm done for the day. I'll see you all at the cabin."

Walking back along the fire break towards her four-wheeler, Maggie let her gaze travel past the scorched earth to an old log cabin nestled into a sandstone hillside, partially obscured by tall pine trees. Slightly downhill from the cabin stood a low-slung log barn, its sagging roof bearing witness to years of weathering. The guest house, which she called the Firhouse, was barely visible behind the barn. To the left, she could just make out the line of young willow trees growing by the edge of the pond. This view never failed to delight her, and Maggie indulged in a rare feeling of achievement. Not many immigrants managed to secure a slice of paradise, yet she had pulled it off single-handedly. As quickly as the thought came, it was replaced by the chastening reminder that everything comes with a price.

A familiar figure sidled up. Loren, one of the neighbors who shared the gravel road to her cabin, nudged her shoulder playfully.

"So, you abandoned us, Maggie. I saw you running away from the line when things heated up."

He grinned at Vic, who was walking over to join them.

"You saw her, Vic, didn't you? Leaving us alone out there." The rebuke was jovial.

Maggie swung around to face him.

"How *dare* you, Loren Zander!"

Loren scrutinized Maggie's face for any sign of levity.

Her eyes were blazing. "How dare you say I abandoned you. I was doing my best..." Her voice broke, and she turned away.

"Maggie, I didn't mean to...." He put his hand out to touch her arm, but she jerked it away. Vic looked at Loren who responded with a shrug.

Without a backwards glance, Maggie strode towards the Gator, climbed in, and drove off.

# Chapter 2

Waking was a painful reminder to Maggie of her frenetic efforts during the prairie burn just twelve hours before. The anti-inflammatory tablet she took before going to bed had worn off, exposing the true state of her aging joints and muscles. Her shoulders felt stiff, her wrists hurt and there was a dull ache at the base of her spine. The clock face showed three-fifteen. These were the worst times: waking in the middle of the night, knowing that sleep would evade her for three or four hours. During these pre-dawn hours, her mind took her on journeys into the past she would rather avoid. It had been easier when her husband was alive and when she was still working at the university. In those days her life had purpose. She could focus on endless to-do lists: entertaining, holiday planning, house projects, lab experiments, journal articles. Some of her best thinking was done during those private, middle-of-the-night hours, but now she dreaded them. Try as she might, her brain always managed to tear free of her carefully-maintained narrative and lead her down memory-filled rabbit holes, at the bottom of which, too often, lay guilt and regret.

A hint of wood smoke lingered in the air, mixed with the

smell of food. She sniffed at her arm. It smelled of wood smoke, and her mind switched immediately into list-making mode. She would have to launder the sheets, together with the clothes she wore yesterday. The kitchen was a mess. People had offered to help with the post-burn party clean-up, but it was well after dark when everyone finally left, and besides, she preferred to be alone. It would be so much easier to do it by herself, she thought. That way she could decide what to keep and what to throw out. Her cleaning lady was coming in a few days and everything would be back to normal after that. She made a mental note to send a generous check to the Aldo Leopold Foundation. It would guarantee a return visit by the burn crew if she was still around in three years.

Her mind went back over the previous day and evening. Overall, it had been successful; the prairie was safely burned, and to her surprise, she had enjoyed the party. One of the pleasures of these prairie burns was watching the expressions on the interns' faces when they walked into her cabin. Few, if any, had ever been inside a settler's log cabin, and their curiosity was palpable. She had ended up surrounded by a group of eager young faces, telling them the story of how she found the place. A colleague in her department at the university who knew Maggie was looking to buy a place in the country, told Maggie there was a place for sale near where she lived. As a new assistant professor, Maggie felt she should live closer to work. But this woman was a senior colleague, and Maggie was too polite to refuse an invitation to lunch, followed by a visit to the property. They had walked over afterwards, approaching the property through the same colonnade of red pines. From the moment Maggie caught sight of the cabin, she knew she wanted to live there for the rest of her life. Die there too. That was fifty years ago, she reminded herself. Half a century. In their future careers as land stewards, she hoped they would recall an 1850s log cabin in the Driftless

Area of south-western Wisconsin and the Irish woman who lived there.

She remembered the look on Vic's face when he pulled her back from the turkey nest, a mixture of alarm and dismay. She knew he worried about her, and she felt badly for giving him yet another reason to be concerned. He probably wonders if I'm starting to lose it, she thought. Lashing out at him and Loren afterwards had been inexcusable, and during the party there had been no opportunity to apologize to them. But even now she wasn't sure how she could explain her outburst. The accusation that she might have let them down, even in jest, clearly hit a nerve. Of course, she hadn't abandoned them. But she had abandoned her parents all those years ago. And there was another time... She forced her mind to return to the present. Maybe Vic and Loren would forget the incident.

She made a wry face, tensed her muscles and swung her legs over the side of the bed. A grunt escaped as she took the full weight onto her legs. They were sore too. She checked the time again. It seemed too bright for the middle of the night. Pulling up the edge of the drape, she looked out. To the left the sky had a reddish hue. From this angle she couldn't see exactly where the glow originated, but she was certain there was no town in that direction. Opening the window she stuck her head and shoulders outside as far as she could without losing her balance. The smell of smoke was stronger outside, but of course it would be after burning thirty acres of prairie. Out of the corner of her eye she saw something move. Her first thought was a deer, the white round on its rump contrasting against a dark body. But the shape was wrong. It looked more like a human. Without her glasses she couldn't be sure, and by the time she retrieved them from the bedside table, the figure had disappeared.

The glow was brighter now. She frowned, considering the possibilities. Had someone left a light on in the barn? The single bulb that hung from one of the cross beams wasn't strong enough, she reasoned. A terrifying thought crept into her mind. The two acres of oak savanna they had burned late in the day was just beyond the barn. Could an ember from that have started a new fire? And if so, where? Her mind raced through the possibilities. There was a pine plantation on the far side of the oak savanna. If those trees caught fire, it would burn until it reached the highway on the other side of the hill. She struggled with a mental imagine of the surrounding topography, searching for any houses or buildings nearby. There was none. The fire would be devastating, but at least no one would be hurt and no structures damaged. She craned her neck around the thick wooden frame again. The red glow seemed to be localized, as if a discrete structure was the source. Could her barn be on fire?

She pulled on her shirt and coveralls, repelled now by the smell of smoke that clung to them. Her mind was racing. She needed to call the fire department, but they would want to know what was burning. She decided to run down to the barn and find out before making the call. This was one of those times when she wished there was cell phone service in the valley; she'd have to run back to the house and use the land line, wasting precious time. After calling 911 she would call Vic and some of her other neighbors. She'd need all the help she could get.

The previous evening she had left her boots by the basement door. The basement, a low-ceilinged root cellar under the cabin, was accessed by a steep stairway off the kitchen. A single forty-watt bulb hung at the bottom of the stairs, casting a pale pool of light on the rough fieldstone walls. Someone had left a crate of mostly empty beer bottles at the top of the stairs, blocking the narrow doorway completely. Without thinking, Maggie gripped it awkwardly and began to maneuver it down the narrow steps. Towards the bottom she thrust her right foot out, expecting to feel the solidity of a concrete floor. Instead, there was nothing and she stumbled forward, trying to hold onto the crate while flinging her arm out to break her fall.

The first thing she became aware of was the smell of beer.

I don't drink beer or even like the stuff, so this must be a dream, she thought. She opened her eyes and tried to focus, but her glasses were askew. For some reason she couldn't get her right arm out from behind her, and she raised her left arm to straighten the frames. It made no difference; things were still out of focus. Her left hand was wet and she licked it. It had a smoky, metallic taste. Definitely not beer. Slowly, her brain began to function, and she realized that she must have taken a fall. She was lying in a crumpled heap in the space between the bottom stair and the bare stone wall. Looking around she could see a few bottles lying on their sides; a pool of beer had leaked from one of them where the neck had shattered. Breathing was painful, and she tried to take small shallow breaths. Everything hurt. For a moment she considered the possibility that if she just closed her eyes tightly, things might go back to normal.

How long had she lain there? A stab of panic made her try to move, but the ensuing pain overwhelmed her and she almost passed out. This was serious. Gradually some clarity returned to her brain. The fire. That was it, the reason she had rushed downstairs. She was going to pull on her boots and go outside, see whether it was the woods or the barn, then come back and call for help. How long ago had that been? Minutes? Hours? She looked around at the windowless room. What was happening outside? Did she still have time to do something about it?

Tentatively she wiggled her toes. She could feel them move—a good sign. At least she wasn't paralyzed. Her left arm worked, although it was smeared with blood. Her head hurt dreadfully. She must have banged it against the stone wall when she fell forward. Touching her forehead, she found the tender jagged area from which blood was seeping out and dribbling into her eyes. With her left hand, she felt around for something to wipe at it. A dirty dishtowel she had thrown down the basement stairs the night before was lying on the ground, and she pressed it against her forehead.

She knew the next part was going to be excruciating: trying to move her body and assess the extent of the damage. The concrete floor felt cold as she tried to shift to a less awkward position. Her right leg was pinned underneath her. She attempted to free it as gently as possible but found that any movement of her ankle caused an intense stabbing pain that radiated up her leg. Something must be broken, she thought. She looked across the room towards the basement door. Her boots stood neatly beside it, and she realized that even if she managed to stand up, there was no possibility of pulling them on, let alone walking to the barn. She concentrated on not passing out. Still hunched over, taking careful shallow breaths, she began to straighten her legs. Each tiny movement elicited a grunt.

Her right arm was still pinned behind her. Trying to move it, she took a deep breath and immediately realized her mistake. It felt as if someone had dug a hot iron into her ribs, and she held her breath, waiting for the pain to subside. Once again, she willed her shoulder and elbow to move. Her right hand brushed against the rough stone wall and a wave of agony pulsed through her wrist. Slowly, she twisted around, cradling her right forearm in her left hand and bringing it to where she could see it. The wrist was at an odd angle. She hunched over, still cradling it tenderly, and began to cry. She wanted to blame someone, if only to feel less angry with herself. If she hadn't picked up that stupid crate...

The initial surge of adrenalin passed, leaving Maggie shivering and feeling sick to her stomach. With a rising sense of panic, she realized that if the barn went up in flames, the cabin could be next. Surely someone would see the fire before that happened and call the fire department. Someone would come looking for her. But what if she had been mistaken about the glow. Maybe there was no fire after all. In that case she might not be missed for several days. She turned her head, wincing a little with the movement. She could just see the door at the top of the stairs. Somehow, she was going to have to crawl back up there. The nearest telephone was in the kitchen.

Her headache had built to a crescendo, threatening to obliterate any rational thoughts. Taking the dish towel away from her forehead, the flow of blood seemed to have slowed a little. She shifted her position slightly and reached up with her left hand for the hand rail. Her plan was to push off with her good leg, while pulling up with her left arm. If she could get six inches of elevation, she thought she might be able to balance sideways on the bottom step. This awkward maneuver would have to be repeated twelve more times. The first attempt was so painful that she crumpled onto the floor, tears streaming from her eyes. She found herself saying aloud, "Maggie O'Connor, you have no choice. If you don't do this, you are going to be found here in a few days, dead." An image of her dead body lying in a pool of stale beer was sufficient impetus to try the maneuver again. This time it worked.

She had lost all sense of time, although a dim light at the top of the stairs suggested it must be daytime. Her world had shrunk to a single measure: one stair, six inches. Whether it took one minute or twenty to gain another step, it didn't matter. She had entered an eternity of agony, all thoughts of a possible fire pushed aside for now.

She was resting on the fourth stair when she thought she heard something. It was difficult to concentrate but it could be a vehicle. Then she remembered. Last night Vic said he would come by and make sure all the tools had been put away after the burn. If he came inside, she could shout to him. Then again, he might just drive around the prairie and leave, in which case he would have to pass by the basement door. For a moment she considered giving up her four hard-won stairs and crawling back down towards the door. But that might take her an hour, by which time he would have left, and then she would be back at square one, or worse. She decided to wait and listen. The cabin was silent. Maggie felt herself drifting back into unconsciousness. Her hand loosened its grip on the railing and she began to slip. She slid down to the next stair, jarred into alertness by the knife-like stab into her wrist when she put her right hand down to steady herself.

There were footsteps overhead. She could hear the floor-boards creaking.

"Help," she called out. Her voice was weak, barely audible. She grabbed at the railing with her left hand and pushed up with all the energy she could muster. The scream of pain that sprang from her mouth shocked her.

Vic's footsteps were directly above her now.

"Maggie, where are you?" There was a hint of alarm in his voice.

Suddenly, his face appeared at the top of the stairs. He rushed down to where she was slumped on the stair, holding herself tightly, rigid with pain.

Stepping carefully around her, he squatted so that he could see her face.

"Maggie, what happened?" he asked gently.

"I slipped and fell down the stairs. I've hurt myself...badly."

She began to slide off the stair and he put his arm out to steady her.

"Can you stay in this position for a minute while I go upstairs and call 911?"

"I think so," came the weak reply.

He guided her left hand to the lip of the stair so that she could steady herself. He was about to do the same with her right hand but she tensed involuntarily.

"Don't touch it," she said, wincing. "It's broken."

Stepping around her again, he ran upstairs. Maggie closed her eyes and concentrated on not moving a muscle. It seemed a long time before he returned and squatted on the stair below her.

"They'll be here in ten minutes. What can I do for you right now?"

"I don't know. Turn the clock back." It was barely a whisper.

"I know you don't feel like talking, but I want to make sure you don't pass out. I'd get you a glass of water, but I'm afraid to move in case you slip again."

She lifted her head and looked into his worried face. "Something was on fire. I saw the glow in the sky and rushed downstairs to get my boots. What happened? Is the barn gone?"

"It's okay, Maggie. Everything's all right. The barn is fine. The fire must have caught again during the night. Fortunately, Loren spotted it from across the fields and came over. He said a hollowed-out tree stump had caught and was burning like a firecracker, but with everything around it already burned, there was no real danger. Even so, he stayed for a while just to make sure. He called me this morning and I said I'd come over to check on it. I didn't know if you were still asleep, but I decided to come up to the cabin and see if there was a free cup of coffee going."

"What time is it now?"

He looked at his watch. "Noon-ish."

They could hear the wail of a siren in the distance, followed by the sound of a heavy vehicle on the gravel driveway.

"Can you hold on to the stair and try not to slip? I need to show them where you are, so I'm going to have to stand up."

He eased himself carefully upright, opened the basement door and ducked outside. A few minutes later two EMTs came in carrying a stretcher. Maggie thought she recognized one of them, a retired electrician who had worked on the cabin several years earlier.

"Don't worry, Maggie. Everything is going to be all right," he said.

Maggie wanted to believe him, but she knew he was lying.

# Chapter 3

Maggie had little memory of the ambulance ride to the university hospital in Madison. Vic sat beside her, filling the silence with a one-sided conversation, his voice reassuringly calm as he stroked her arm, carefully avoiding the plastic line tethered to the back of her hand. The admission process was slow and cumbersome, but things moved quickly once the ER doctor learned Maggie had hit her head on a stone wall and might be concussed, or worse. People kept asking about her level of pain, insisting that it be a number between one and ten. At some point in the afternoon she replied "Forty!" but that was when a first-year resident attempted to reduce her wrist fracture manually, tugging on the damaged joint. Her animal-like howl echoed around the small examination room, shocking everyone within earshot. The young resident left hurriedly and was replaced by a more skilled physician.

Maggie felt adrift. Nurses and doctors came and went. When she asked to see Vic, someone told her not to worry; he had gone home but would be back later. For the first time in years, she was scared. A litany of potential outcomes from this misadventure clawed for her attention, each more terrifying than the last. What if she couldn't stand or walk, couldn't use her right hand? How long would it take before she could climb stairs or drive? She wouldn't be able to wash herself, cook, do laundry, mow the grass, work in a garden...the list grew ominously. Throughout her life Maggie had always prided herself on being a superior problem-solver. "That's what being a scientist is all about," she used to say to her students as she guided them through challenging research projects. Now, facing a dozen or more insurmountable problems simultaneously, she felt overwhelmed. Her mind was still fuzzy, but even taking that into consideration, she couldn't see how she was going to be able to get back to her old life.

"This time yesterday, life was perfect," she muttered to herself, "And now look at me."

A tear made its way down her cheek. Unable to wipe it away, she felt it on its slow journey to the collar of the hospital gown. Lulled by the steady hum from the monitors, she closed her eyes. For a moment she was back in time, when she had surgery for bowel cancer fifteen years earlier. That time she had spent two weeks in hospital, her recovery complicated by a herniated intestine that necessitated a second surgery. Alan had been with her throughout that ordeal—her steady, loving and endlessly patient husband. When she heard the door open, Maggie opened her eyes, expecting to see his smiling face. Instead, it was a young nurse.

"We need to take a look at that wrist of yours, Maggie, and your foot. Let's get you ready now and we'll wheel you down to Imaging."

The nurse bustled around, unhooking the saline drip in Maggie's left hand and adjusting the warmed cotton blanket draped over her chest and legs.

"I'll put your purse on your lap so that you know where it is. Careful now. There might be a little bump as I wheel the bed around."

Maggie resented being treated like a helpless old lady, but

this was the new reality. This time there would be no Alan, and for the foreseeable future she would be completely dependent on other people. Her lips tightened as she fumbled to locate her purse, laying her left hand on it protectively.

Over the next two hours, she was wheeled from test to test, each more uncomfortable than the preceding one. They had given her something to dampen the pain, but nothing could mitigate her despair. Besides a severely sprained ankle, the x-rays of her right foot showed two broken bones. She had three fractured ribs. Her right hip was badly bruised, and it wasn't clear whether the damaged ligaments in her knee joint would require surgery. Her wrist had a displaced fracture and would need to be stabilized with a metal plate and screws. There might be other issues—her scans were still being analyzed—but for now, wrist surgery was the priority. Every few minutes some doctor or nurse pestered her with a ridiculous question: Did she know the name of the President? Could she count backwards from ten? What day of the week was it? She understood why they were doing this, but their constant questions did nothing to help with her throbbing headache.

The hospital's routine seemed much the same as she remembered from fifteen years ago. The machines and monitors surrounding her looked more complicated but they did the same job as before: fluids in, fluids out. On the wall facing her was a white board with the names of her doctors in large black letters. By now Maggie was beginning to recognize and remember the names of her nurses, who seemed to turn over with dizzying frequency. She made a point of asking new arrivals to update their names on the board, insisting they use a green marker.

"That way, you'll remember I'm from Ireland!" she said each time, giving them as warm a smile as she could muster.

The request always started a conversation about a parent or grandparent who had emigrated from Ireland, their lifelong wish to visit the country and their surprise that Maggie hadn't lost her accent. These tiny personal interactions helped to dispel the anonymity she felt.

Loren's wife, Julie, dropped in to see her most days around lunch time, as the Credit Union building where she worked was located near the hospital. Perched on a chair at Maggie's bedside, she munched on a sandwich and sipped at a cup of coffee while describing the comings and goings back in the valley at Maggie's cabin. Everything was being taken care of, she insisted. Maggie's cleaning lady had dealt with everything: dirty dishes from the party and the broken beer bottles in the basement. Sally, another neighbor, had taken charge of watering Maggie's plants, and Julie said she would make sure nothing spoiled in the refrigerator. Word of Maggie's injuries had circulated rapidly, and Julie and Loren were fielding calls from neighbors who wanted to know if they could visit. Julie had two young children and her husband traveled during the week, so Maggie was reluctant to ask her to fetch things from the cabin. Still, she desperately needed her spare pair of glasses, so when Julie stopped by she made the request anyway.

"If you're going to the cabin, could you get my computer please? I feel lost without it. Not just e-mail or the news but all the questions I have, like how long is it going to take for my wrist and foot to heal? They never give me a straight answer here, and I could just look it up if I had the internet."

Interruptions were endless from dawn onward, and Maggie welcomed the early evening when dinner was cleared away and the sound of people and carts passing her door finally stopped. Listening to the muffled sounds of televisions in the adjacent rooms, she idled away the evening hours in unproductive daydreaming. She had no interest in watching a movie or reading, and there seemed little point in making lists or plans for the future.

"Something to help you sleep, Maggie?" The nurse's question brought her back to the present.

"Well...I'm not sure...perhaps half a tablet?"

This might guarantee a few hours of oblivion. When sleep eluded her, inevitably she found herself thinking about what lay ahead. That topic exhausted her, and with the hours still crawling by, everything else in her life became fodder for critical appraisal. Whereas, at the cabin she might be able to redirect her thoughts, distracted by the distant howl of coyotes or the chittering of flying squirrels in the attic, here there was no possibility of escaping them.

She found herself thinking about the time her mother suddenly became ill and had to have an operation, after which she went to a nursing home to recuperate. At that time her mother was a widow, living alone in the town where Maggie was born. It came as a shock to Maggie, who was not married at the time, to hear that she was expected to come home and care for her mother. As the only daughter, and with no children, it was her filial duty. Maggie was incensed, knowing full well that this sacrifice would never be asked of a son. She refused, explaining that she had a career and students who relied on her; she had no intention of throwing it all away. In the end, her mother's siblings and neighbors took on the task, checking in daily, buying the groceries, making sure the lawn was mowed, and keeping up appearances—so important in a small, rural Irish community. At the end of the semester, Maggie grudgingly made a trip to Ireland, where she was made to feel selfish and ungrateful. None of her accomplishments in America mattered; she had failed as a good daughter.

~

It was mid-morning on the day before Maggie expected to be discharged from the hospital. A plump, middle-aged man— his name and the type of medicine he practiced stitched on the pocket of his white coat—pulled up a chair to her bedside and sat down.

"Hello, Maggie. My name is Dr. Carney. I'm your oncologist."

Maggie looked past him, squinting as she scanned the doctors' names on the white board. His wasn't among them.

"I haven't seen you before, have I?" she asked.

"No. We've not met. How are you feeling today?"

"I'm fine." It was a safe answer. She didn't want to have a conversation with this man.

"Maggie, we've taken a closer look at your scans and there are a few issues I'd like to discuss with you. We compared the images with the ones taken a couple of years after your colon surgery, and we've noticed some changes."

Before he could say anything more, Maggie thrust her good hand towards him, the palm out.

"I know what you are going to tell me, and I don't want to hear it."

Dr. Carney readjusted his position in the chair and opened his mouth to speak.

Maggie shook her head vigorously from side to side. "I said NO." Her voice was shrill.

He looked at her, his eyebrows raised. "I could come back later, if you like."

"No. I don't want to discuss this now, or later. Please leave."

Her face was impassive as she looked past him, fixing her gaze on the white board. He sat for another minute without speaking, waiting for her to acquiesce. Finally, with an audible sigh, he got up from the chair and left the room.

She slumped back on the pillows. Her defiance made absolutely no difference in the long run, but for a moment she felt she had taken back a fragment of control.

Eight days after she was admitted to the hospital, it was agreed that Maggie should go to a rehabilitation facility. As she waited for the patient transport that would take her to the next phase of her life, she gripped the handle of the large leather purse on her lap. Her possessions were minimal: a wallet, cell phone and computer, together with a comb, a stick of lip salve and a pen, none of which she could manipulate easily. She glanced down at her small overnight bag, which looked as forlorn as she felt. She gave a deep sigh. The red-jacketed volunteer who had wheeled her to the lobby, touched her gently on the shoulder.

"It's going to be fine. I hear they take very good care of you at Cherrywood."

Maggie turned her head and looked into the eyes of a gangly youth, who, she assumed, was volunteering with an eye towards medical school. She smiled and said nothing. Going to Cherrywood was a little like going to boarding school for the first time. But then she had been buoyed by curiosity and innocence, whereas now she was filled with dread.

# Chapter 4

"This is *not* how I planned to spend my eightieth birthday!"

Maggie pursed her lips, which made the corners of her mouth turn downward. Her frustration had been building gradually during the hour-long occupational therapy session and had reached a boiling point. She knew she was being difficult, but she couldn't help herself. It wasn't the pain that annoyed her, although since she had stopped taking prescription opioids, she dreaded doing these exercises. What irritated her most were the daily reminders of her limited strength and mobility. There was a time when she could do wrist curls with a ten-pound weight, but now she could barely lift the brightly colored dumbbell with a single "1" inscribed on it. Side by side her hands looked the same: thin, creased and age-spotted, but now one of them was a cripple, all the more apparent when compared with its healthy twin. Turning them over, palms upward, she examined the raised, red scar on the inside of her right wrist. Daily massage had failed to flatten the three-inch-long rope-like bulge, although the therapist assured her that eventually she would be left with nothing more than a thin white line. Right now it looked like evidence of a botched suicide attempt.

"How long is it going to take before I'm back to normal?" Maggie asked in a petulant voice.

"Oh, it depends...a few months for most people." The woman sounded upbeat. Maggie wasn't mollified. She knew this was just part of a therapist's job. It was so easy for patients to slide into depression.

Maggie had spent hours searching websites and chat rooms for information about wrist and foot fractures and how long it took to recover. The consensus seemed to be somewhere between six months and three years but it varied. Age was definitely a negative. Some people reported that their injuries hurt more in the winter and that moving to a dry and warm climate had helped. Maggie didn't want to move to a dry, warm climate; she just wanted to go home.

"What have you planned for your birthday, Maggie?" The therapist asked, unperturbed by her patient's ill humor.

Maggie sighed. "Not much, but definitely not this. We used to make a big deal of the zero birthdays. That's what my husband and I called them—you know, fifty, sixty, seventy..."

She stared balefully at her scar.

"The Galapagos was the next trip we had planned for my seventieth birthday. But then he died. Instead, I did the Camino in northern Spain. I needed to get away from everything." She looked up at the therapist and shook her head from side to side. "I didn't do it as a pilgrimage, just a long walk, where I could get my head around his being gone. Funny, but as I was walking, I used to imagine him there beside me and I'd talk to him. I'm sure people thought I was praying out loud or maybe just losing it."

Smiling at the memory, she allowed the therapist to manipulate her hand into a new sequence of movements.

"What did you do on your sixtieth birthday?"

Maggie's eyes lit up as she remembered that milestone. For

a moment she felt like her old self: an intrepid traveler, independent, energetic and full of life.

"On my sixtieth I was hiking in Patagonia. It's a magnificent place."

Her voice was animated now. "I spent my fiftieth birthday in southern India. It sounded so romantic: to wake up on the Coast of Malabar, like the words in the Ry Cooder song. The reality was quite different, of course. Not at all romantic. Still, I loved Kerala, loved the whole experience. And you cannot help but be changed by India."

She gave a short gasp of pain. "Ouch! That hurts," she said, pulling her hand back.

The therapist adjusted the angle of Maggie's wrist slightly and continued with her manipulation.

"Tell me more. Where else have you been?"

For the next ten minutes Maggie entertained the woman with stories from all over the world, and for a time she forgot about her situation.

"Maggie, you are so lucky." The young woman smiled. "I wish I could travel like that."

Maggie almost said, "Why don't you?" But the therapist probably had a husband and children and would never consider putting herself first. With a flash of self-awareness, Maggie acknowledged that she was indeed lucky; she had always done exactly as she wanted...until a few weeks ago. Strapping the plastic support onto her hand and wrist, she apologized for her grumpiness earlier in the session.

"You're very good at what you do," she added, "and incredibly patient."

The young woman smiled and began to put away her equipment.

"I'm sure you'll get to the Galapagos. After all, there's still three hundred and sixty-four days left in the year."

Maggie pushed herself upright with her good hand. She

held her breath, waiting for the sharp pain in her ribs to settle back to a steady ache. By now she was using a walker, having graduated from a wheelchair a few days earlier. It took some time to get back to her room, and she paused to rest every so often at one of the conveniently located armchairs scattered throughout the complex.

The rehabilitation facility was part of a continuum-of-care campus located on the west side of Madison. Maggie was already familiar with Cherrywood, as the university retirement association frequently hosted lectures in the auditorium there, many of which she had attended. Some of the residents' faces were familiar: living out their golden years, she supposed, moving inexorably from independence to assisted living and finally to memory care. She could see the attraction of these communities, especially if you lived alone. You were guaranteed comfort, exercise, entertainment, good food and, most importantly, people to socialize with.

Daily life in the rehabilitation wing was strikingly similar to her old boarding school in Ireland, and she wished her sister was still alive, for they would have howled with laughter at the comparison. Every minute of the day was structured: waking, washing, dressing, feeding, physical therapy, occupational therapy, assessment, recreational activities. Repeat. The only thing that was markedly different, Maggie thought, was the absence of prayers. At boarding school, each day included morning Mass, prayers before and after every meal, reciting the Angelus, Chapel in the evening and Benediction added for good measure on Sundays and Holy Days. She was surprised to find herself thinking fondly about those six years at Loreto Abbey. It seemed so normal at the time: to be sent away at age eleven, returning home briefly for holidays at Christmas and in the summer. Her parents were allowed a visit on Sunday afternoons and would sit with Maggie and her sister in a draughty parlor, talking in hushed tones among the other family groups. Despite its strict environment, the Abbey had been good for her. She left with a great education, a firm moral compass and a strong sense of independence and self-worth. These had served her well up until the accident, but looking to the future, she wondered if they would be sufficient.

~

Each week Maggie met with her rehabilitation team to discuss her progress. She dreaded these encounters. They felt like parent-teacher conferences, with the added complexity that she was both parent and child.

"We want you to resume your normal life as quickly as possible," was always the opening sentence, delivered with sincerity by someone on the team. But their ideas as to what was normal for an eighty-year-old woman, who lived alone in a settler's log cabin on a farm in the most remote corner of the county, varied considerably. The occupational therapist was concerned with basic functions such as personal hygiene and being able to go to the toilet unassisted. The physical therapist wanted Maggie to be ambulatory, with her wrist recovering its full range of motion. The respiratory therapist emphasized deep breaths to avoid getting pneumonia, while the pain management specialist insisted that Maggie choose a number between one and ten with the expectation that it would gradually decrease. The staff doctor appeared infrequently, but when he did, Maggie rebuffed his efforts to discuss her other health issues. Those could wait. For now, she had one goal and would not be distracted from it: to go home.

In many ways the social worker was the most challenging member of the team. She was a thin woman in her late forties with a pinched face. Maggie wondered if the woman was dealing with the infirmities of her own aged parents, wishing they would agree to move to a retirement community where someone else would look after them. She made it clear that she didn't approve of Maggie returning to her solitary lifestyle in the country. There was even a suggestion that, by insisting on returning home, Maggie would become a burden to the already-stretched county services. Their mutual dislike simmered at every meeting.

The woman went so far as to arrange for Maggie to tour the independent living facility. Confined to a wheelchair at the time, and thoroughly bored, Maggie agreed to the distraction. A pleasant young sales representative pushed her wheelchair expertly around the facility, pointing out its numerous advantages. The single bedroom apartment was easily as large as her cabin, bright and airy, with hardwood floors and large doorways. The apartment had an outstanding bathroom, a far better kitchen than she was accustomed to and everything was positioned within easy reach for someone with limited mobility. Reluctantly, Maggie admitted it was well thought out. Nonetheless, the view from each window of identical concrete buildings reminded her of what she would be giving up: the endlessly changing rural landscape she had enjoyed for the last fifty years.

"Above all, you'd be safe here with us," the sales representative said when she had wheeled Maggie back to her room.

Maggie swung the wheelchair around and glared at the young woman.

"What is it with you Americans? The whole notion of safety is an obsession in this country. I'm sick of it. I don't need to be protected from the world!"

~

The small chapel at Cherrywood was one of the few places where Maggie could sit and not be disturbed, and she had taken to spending a few hours there each day. Two heavy wooden pews faced forward in the room, one in front of the other, and it was Maggie's custom to sit in the back pew where her head was visible through a small glass panel in the door if anyone should look in. The staff and residents were familiar with her routine and respected her privacy. Consequently, she was surprised when the door opened one afternoon and Bill Breunig's shiny head appeared around the door frame.

"I'm not disturbing you, am I Maggie?"

Before she had a chance to respond, he stepped into the chapel and closed the door. Bill slid into place beside Maggie in the back pew, blocking her exit.

"I heard about your accident." He made a tut-tutting noise. "Such a pity. You might have been killed."

He picked up her cane and twirled it in his fleshy hand.

"I guess you won't be able to manage at your place anymore?" His cocked his head slightly and stared down at her, his eyes moving from her bandaged wrist to the plastic walking boot. She shifted her position, sliding along the bench until her back came up against the tall wooden frame of the pew.

"Look, Maggie. I'm still willing to help you out. I'll take the place off your hands. You wouldn't even need to pay a realtor. I'd give you a fair price—in cash. Now, what do you say to that?"

He looked down at her, waiting for her answer. She remained silent, refusing to meet his gaze. His hands tightened on the cane, as if he were trying to bend it, but the aluminum was unyielding.

"What other options do you have? You're going to end up in a nursing home one way or the other. With the money you'd get from me, you could stay here. The whole deal could be done in a couple of weeks. What do you say?"

"It's not for sale. Now leave me alone," Maggie said through gritted teeth.

He paused. Then, with a deliberate move, he placed Maggie's cane on the bench beside him and gave it a shove. It slid along the polished surface, hit the end of the pew and clattered to the floor. Maggie refused to respond. Looking towards the front of the room, she clasped her broken wrist with her good hand and sat perfectly still. She could hear his breathing and out of the corner of her eye, saw his hands clenching and unclenching rhythmically. Finally, he stood up, and with a look in her direction, stepped over her cane and stomped to the door.

"Let me know when you're ready to talk business," he snapped, pulling the door open roughly. It slammed closed. Maggie waited for a few minutes, every sense on alert, before she moved. She struggled along the pew, limping towards her cane. She was trembling and could feel her heart thumping in her chest. As she left the chapel, the words of the Cherrywood sales representative came to mind: "You'll be safe here with us." She gave a derisory snort.

# Chapter 5

Few days passed without someone coming to visit Maggie: neighbors, friends, and even a few colleagues from the university, who were already living at Cherrywood. As she became more mobile, she spent the early part of every evening sitting in a small garden near the memory care facility. It was the quietest spot in the campus grounds and few people went there. It was here that Vic found her one evening in May.

"How are you, Maggie?" Vic asked, taking a seat beside her on the sun-bleached wooden bench in the small garden.

"I'm grand. But I'll be a lot better when I get out of this place."

Vic nodded.

"You know, I've been meaning to apologize for shouting at you and Loren that day of the prairie burn. It's been on my mind."

"Don't give it a thought, Maggie. I'd forgotten all about it, and I'm sure Loren has too."

She patted his hand, and they sat in silence for a few minutes. Maggie was accustomed to his quiet demeanor. Vic grew up in the valley. His father, a carpenter, worked on innumerable projects at Maggie's place, often bringing the boy with him. Vic quickly learned to bring a fishing rod, as Maggie kept her pond stocked with bluegill and largemouth bass, and she grew accustomed to seeing his bicycle leaning against the barn on summer evenings. He was shy and rarely came to the cabin, so she made a point of waving to him as he walked towards the pond and occasionally interrupting his fishing with a glass of cold lemonade and cookies. The boy always thanked her formally, but he was reluctant to make eye contact, let alone have a conversation.

"I'm sorry that I didn't come to see you before now, but I've been swamped with work."

Maggie knew he was feeling guilty. She hadn't seen him since the day of her accident. "It's great you have the work, Vic," she said reassuringly.

He gave a tentative smile, and Maggie could see his shoulders relax a little. Vic was in the building trades. Unlike his father, who had learned on the job, after high school Vic enrolled at a technical college in northern Michigan, keenly aware that to be a success in the construction industry, you needed a head for business as well as solid engineering skills. Four years later, with his degree in hand, he returned to the Driftless Area like a homing pigeon and found a job at a local construction company. Five years after that, he started his own business, taking over from his father, who, by then, was ready to retire. Nowadays, Vic's father sometimes helped him with projects at Maggie's house, and she took enormous pleasure in watching the two men work together.

"I've been over to the cabin a bunch of times," Vic offered. "I mowed the grass and did the fire breaks. They've grown a lot since the burn."

"That was very kind of you. I know it was needed. It's been four or five weeks now...I lose track of time in this place."

Maggie sensed he had something on his mind, something else he wanted to tell her.

"Putting away the mower, I noticed water on the floor of the barn," Vic said with an apologetic look. "Maggie, I'm afraid you've got a leak in the roof."

"How bad is it?"

"Well...I think it must've been leaking all through winter because the plywood is damaged."

Maggie gave a sigh. She hated dealing with problems like this.

"Dad and I could go over at the weekend and patch the roof, if you like. It'll work for a few months. But you're going to need a new roof before winter."

There was an apologetic expression on his face, and for a moment Maggie felt a ridiculous urge to make the sign of the cross with her hand like a priest offering absolution. Her wrist was still in a splint, and she kept her hands in her lap.

Nodding her head, she said, "I suppose I should have been expecting this...kept a closer eye on it. Still, it's over thirty years since the roof was last done. Did you know that your Dad worked on it that time? I don't think you were even a twinkle in his eye."

She chuckled mischievously. "Look. I know you're busy right now, but I'd like you to reroof the barn this summer. So, put me down on your list. Whatever it takes, I want that barn and its roof to last for at least another thirty years."

"I should be able to fit it in next month if you don't mind us working weekends. Dad might be able to help too. I'll see him tomorrow evening and ask him."

The corners of her eyes creased into a smile as she shook her finger censoriously at him.

"Be careful you don't criticize the last roofing job or he'll not help you with this one."

Vic grinned, and for a moment she caught a glimpse of

the shy teen who used to fish in her pond. She reached for her cane. The temperature had dropped and she was beginning to feel the chill.

"There's one more thing, Maggie."  His voice had dropped half an octave. "I met someone down by the pond yesterday when I was mowing."

Frowning slightly, Maggie waited to see what he was going to say next.

"It was Bill Breunig."

She kept her expression neutral, but inside she could feel her stomach turn over.

"I didn't think much of it—just presumed you had given him permission. We got to talking, and he said he'll be hunting on your land in the fall."

Maggie saw that the expression on Vic's face was now a mixture of confusion and hurt. He had hunted at Maggie's since his teens. He knew every inch of the property and felt a strong sense of stewardship towards her land.

"Is it true?" he asked, and for a moment she thought he might begin to cry.

She looked directly into his face. Her voice was firm and insistent.

"No. It's not true." Her mouth tightened into a thin line. "I can't believe he said that. How dare he. I never gave him permission—not to fish or to hunt. I loathe that man. If you see him on my land again, you can tell him from me: he's trespassing!"

This outburst prompted a look of shock, followed by relief on the young man's face.

He nodded solemnly. "That's good to know. Thanks Maggie."

Standing up to take his leave, Vic put a hand out to help Maggie.

"Thanks, but I'm going to stay here a while longer. Don't worry—I'll be able to make my own way inside."

She watched as he walked across the courtyard towards his truck. He turned to wave before rounding the corner of the building. Maggie stayed seated, cradling her wrist in her left hand, stroking her scar absentmindedly.

"The sooner I get out of this place, the better," she muttered.

She got up awkwardly from the bench and began to walk towards the building, her cane thumping on the concrete path.

# Chapter 6

Conversation stopped as Maggie made her way to an empty chair at one end of the Formica-topped table in the dining room. The sitting room, where they usually met, had been commandeered due to an unexpected death at Cherrywood. Some attempts had been made to soften this room: a few plants, vases of artificial flowers and cheerful paintings on the wall. But these small touches couldn't dispel the feeling of being in a cafeteria with its lingering smell of breakfast mingled with the odor of bleach. Maggie could hear noises from the adjacent kitchen. The staff must be already preparing for the next meal, she thought.

A young intern who had recently started to attend Maggie's weekly meetings with her rehabilitation team jumped up and pulled the chair out for her, but she waved him away with her cane. Rebuffed, he poured water carefully into a glass and placed it on the table in front of her, within easy reach. She took her time sitting down, conscious of the six pairs of eyes focused on her every movement. Settled at last, she looked around the table at the four women and two men who, by now, she had come to realize were her adversaries.

"I intend to go home this weekend," she said, an authoritative ring in her voice.

Her statement was met with a constrained silence. Maggie looked around the table from person to person, mildly amused at their reluctance to meet her gaze. With the exception of the intern, everyone's body language betrayed what they were thinking: It was too soon for her to leave Cherrywood. She reminded herself that she was not their prisoner, and she braced for the argument that had been brewing for the past two weeks.

"Maggie, you know we all want what's best for you."

The social worker had taken it upon herself to open the discussion. She sat facing Maggie, flanked by the physical therapist, the occupational therapist, the staff doctor, the intern and an older well-dressed woman, whose role Maggie wasn't quite clear about but who had recently begun to attend these meetings. Whether intended or not, Maggie detected condescension in this statement, and her irritation with the social worker increased. After Maggie's wheelchair tour of the retirement community, this woman had made a point of highlighting the advantages of Cherrywood's resident campus every time they met.

Maggie rapped on the table with her good hand. She thrust her head towards the social worker as she spat out the words, "Can't you get it into your head? I am not moving to your retirement community!"

The woman gave a little sniff but didn't reply. Instead, she glared at Maggie, who met her gaze with a defiant smile.

The room fell silent. Maggie glanced around at the circle of faces; everyone's eyes were averted. She felt ashamed of her outburst. This wasn't like her at all. She had prided herself on never raising her voice in anger with her students. But as she thought about it now, her patience had worn thin in recent years, and these outbursts of hers had become more frequent, especially since Alan died. Was it just because of growing old, she wondered? She thought back to her lashing out at Loren and Vic in the prairie. That hadn't had anything to do with growing old. Instead, for a split second she had felt the carefully constructed narrative of her life being undermined.

"I'm sorry. That was unnecessary." She sighed. "I know you are trying to help me."

The occupational therapist spoke first. "Why don't we go over some of the challenges you might have when you go home. That way we're all on the same page." Her voice was calm as she looked around the table. Most heads nodded in agreement.

"Your mobility has improved greatly," she went on, "but I think stairs might be a little hard for you right now." She looked down at her notes. "You mentioned that your bedroom is up a flight of stairs. What do you think?"

"I'll manage." Maggie's response was terse.

"And the bathroom? It's on the same floor as the bedroom, isn't it?"

"I said I'll manage."

The questions continued. Did she have an accessible shower with grab bars? Were there steps between the living room and the kitchen? What about cooking? How would she get to her physical therapy appointments? With the exception of the intern, they were relentless as they dissected her living arrangements, each one striving to make her see things their way.

"Can I say something here?" The social worker's voice was brittle and precise. "There's no cell service where Maggie lives. No possibility of panic buttons. How is she going to be able to contact anyone in an emergency? Yes, there's a land line, but what if she can't get to it...like the last time?" She sat back in her chair and folded her hands across her chest.

The questions hung in the air.

A wave of irritation passed over Maggie. The social worker had spoken as if she weren't in the room.

Maggie gave a sigh. "I checked online: the county community services are said to be very good," she said in a tired voice.

"That's all very well," responded the social worker, "but they are overwhelmed. The most they could manage would be an hour-long visit a couple of times a week. That's not going to solve the emergency problem."

For several minutes they argued over whether Maggie should employ a live-in nurse. At least some of the expenses would be reimbursed by the county, and there were grants available. Names and agencies were swapped around the table.

"Could I say something?" The staff doctor had rarely spoken at these meetings, so when he broke into the conversation, everyone stopped talking and turned to look at him.

"We haven't talked about your scan results yet, Maggie. I think we need to factor them into our discussion. There needs to be some follow-up, and the sooner the better, in my opinion."

"I will follow up in my own time," Maggie said, looking at the man pointedly. Before he had a chance to respond, she turned to the social worker.

"As for your last comment, money is not an issue. I can afford a nurse. I just don't want one."

Maggie was exhausted by now and wanted nothing more than to go back to her room, close her eyes and pretend she was somewhere else.

"Look," she said with an audible sigh, "my neighbors will help me. Someone will drop by every day, and I'm sure they will do anything I ask." It sounded weak, even to her own ears.

"That's a lot to expect from your neighbors," snapped the social worker. There was an uncomfortable silence around the table, and in a slightly more conciliatory tone she added, "Another few weeks here at Cherrywood would make such a difference, Maggie. You really should consider it."

Maggie turned her back to the woman and reached for her cane, which she had propped against the back of her chair. It fell to the floor and the intern leapt to retrieve it.

"I think I might have a solution." Everyone turned to look at the older woman.

"I know you want to go home, Maggie. Everyone does. Frankly, I hoped you might consider moving next door, to the retirement community...and perhaps you will change your mind in the future. But we have to respect your wishes too." She looked around the table.

Up to now Maggie had considered this woman to be another adversary, so she was taken aback by the change in attitude. Maybe she had won the argument after all.

"We have a volunteer group here at Cherrywood. These are people in the local community whose family members have stayed with us in the past. They understand the challenges that we all face." She gestured to everyone sitting around the table before fixing her gaze on Maggie. Her voice was calm and reassuring.

"They are a wonderful resource and can be surprisingly helpful. Last week I met with a few members of the group. I described the problem...the situation...in the broadest of terms. Naturally, I didn't mention your name, Maggie. They wondered if you might consider employing a companion for the next couple of months? I'm using the term companion in the loosest possible sense. This is not a nurse; the individual wouldn't live with you. You could just as easily call her a personal assistant or a secretary."

She paused briefly, but it was clear she did not expect anyone to interrupt her.

"There's a young woman who one of our volunteers knows through her daughter's school. This person has been working at the school for the past two years—she's a school counselor. It appears that she's decided on a career change and mentioned that she was looking for some work for the next couple of months. Let me emphasize once again: she is not a qualified nurse. But she sounds like an intelligent and responsible young person."

Everyone looked at Maggie. She took a drink of water and replaced the glass on the table slowly. Maybe it was the quiet, reasoned way that it had been presented, but she had to admit, there was some merit in this proposal. True, she would have to put up with someone sharing her living space during the daytime, but the hours would be up to her to decide. It might be like having a graduate student again—someone young, eager to please and not yet set in their ways. It could even be interesting. Her mind darted back and forth, considering the logistics. What would the girl do all day? Maggie reminded herself of all the things she was not yet able to manage: grocery shopping, meal preparation, doing laundry in the basement... The more she thought about it, the more the idea appealed to her. And if it didn't work out, she'd tell the girl to go away.

"I'd be willing to meet with her," Maggie finally said, her tone cautious. "At the cabin, of course," she added, in case anyone had forgotten that she was leaving Cherrywood in three days.

Despite the unpleasantness of the meeting, Maggie understood the competing desires and needs each person brought to the table. There was pressure on everyone for a successful outcome. Nobody had any personal or financial interest in prolonging her stay. They had to argue with insurance companies, who demanded justification for every day Maggie spent at Cherrywood. No, they were just doing their jobs. Nonetheless, the last few weeks had given Maggie endless time to consider the remainder of her life, and she didn't want to waste one minute more.

"I'll be leaving at the weekend then," she said, struggling to get up from her chair. The intern leapt up from his chair and rushed to help. Maggie allowed him to take her arm and guide her to the door.

# Chapter 7

The following Saturday morning Maggie sat in the brightly lit foyer of the rehabilitation facility, waiting for Julie to arrive. In the lull after breakfast, only a few visitors came through the large sliding doors that opened onto a covered portico and the parking lot beside it. The outside temperature was already in the seventies and Maggie wore a light cotton shirt and blue jeans. Beside her sat the director of Cherrywood, Caitlin McGuirk. By now they were on excellent terms, for Caitlin had visited Maggie each day since their meeting earlier in the week, ostensibly to discuss the paperwork that was needed before Maggie could leave. The two women quickly formed a bond, partially based on their shared Celtic origins, although Caitlin was clear that her heritage lay farther to the north and east, in Scotland. The director had an easy way with words, though not quite the gift of the gab, Maggie thought. Nonetheless, she enjoyed their bantering.

"You know you don't have to wait with me," Maggie said. "I won't be offended." She smiled at the director.

"I have to see you off the premises," came the jocular reply. "Otherwise, how would I know that you weren't getting a free lunch?"

"That's a typical response from a Scot! Always minding their money."

Maggie cocked her head sideways and asked innocently, "Did you know the Irish invaded Scotland once? Seriously. It was called Dalriada."

"Well, it looks like they didn't succeed," came the reply, and they both laughed.

A maroon-colored Subaru station wagon turned into the driveway, and the two women watched its slow progress towards the portico.

"Maggie, if you change your mind about Cherrywood, call me. I've put my card in with your paperwork," Caitlin said, gesturing to the large brown envelope tucked into the black roller bag beside Maggie's chair.

"My cell number is on the back. Call me at any time, even if you just want to chat." She looked knowingly at Maggie.

"Thanks for everything, Caitlin. I really appreciate it."

Maggie pushed herself up with the help of her cane and walked towards the entrance, with Caitlin at her side pulling the roller bag. They waited in the portico while Julie's car came to a stop. With her usual fuss, Julie ran around to open the passenger door and hovered as Maggie lowered herself into the passenger seat. Reassured that everything was in order, she got back into the driver's seat and, with an aimless wave of her hand above her head and a slight screeching of tires, drove off. For an instant, Maggie experienced a sensation of childlike excitement, as if they had made a dramatic escape, and she laughed out loud. She was going home.

For the next hour, Julie talked incessantly.

"We've got everything organized. Yadira came to clean the cabin yesterday. She called me last night to say she changed the sheets on your bed and did the towels too. Loren did a little grocery shopping, so you've got the basics: milk and butter, cheese and eggs, bread, bananas. Who knows what else he thought of.

I gave him a list, but he probably forgot to take it with him. He's like that. Whatever. Just let us know what else you need and we can pick it up the next time we're going to the store. I popped some home-made soup in the fridge for this evening so you don't have to cook. Oh, and there's a cold bottle of wine there too." She glanced over at Maggie. "I doubt they offered you anything to drink at Cherrywood."

Barely pausing to take a breath, she continued with the litany of accomplishments. "Vic was over last night to get the grass cut, but he ran out of time so he couldn't finish. He called and left a message at our place. It was late, so we didn't answer the phone. He said to tell you not to worry; he'll mow around the prairie on Monday evening. I think he was heading up north for the weekend to his father's cabin."

There was another pause for breath. Maggie looked around her as if seeing the countryside for the first time. The journey brought back a visceral memory of coming home from boarding school at the end of a school year. The sky seemed bigger and brighter, the grass greener, the trees taller and the future promised happiness with endless time to enjoy it.

"Oh yeah. I almost forgot, Sally said she'd stop by the cabin tomorrow afternoon. She wants to see about putting in a garden for you."

Maggie gave her a skeptical look. Managing a garden was not one of her priorities for the summer.

"Yeah. It's a bit late to plant the usual stuff, but her idea is to plant some tomatoes and herbs and maybe lettuce and arugula in those half barrels you have outside the back porch. Sally's got green fingers or thumbs, or whatever, so it'll work out just fine. Besides, she and John have a huge garden and are always trying to give away vegetables. They'll be delighted to share with you."

Julie continued to talk, bringing Maggie up to date on everything that had happened in her absence. Six weeks. This was the longest she had been away from the cabin, except for a sabbatical over thirty years ago. Maggie let the words slide past, not paying much attention. She wanted to savor this journey home, every moment of it. They turned off the state highway, took another turn and drove up a long steep hill. Piles of small round stones marked the crest, testament to a retreating glacier. Looking to the west, if you were lucky you could just make out a glint of sunlight on the Wisconsin River in the distance. The road was called Katzenbuckel, a German word that perfectly described its similarity to the curve of a cat's back. Who had decided on that name, she wondered?

They drove down a long winding hill into a valley bordered by open fields on one side and dense woods on the other. The corn was already knee-high. Looking up to where a hay field bordered the woods, Maggie was delighted to see a flock of wild turkeys. The females pecked industriously at the soil while the males ambled around them. Julie was still talking and didn't notice Maggie wiping her eyes. The car slowed and they turned onto the gravel road to her cabin. There must have been a heavy rain in the past few days, she thought; the creek is flowing swiftly under the narrow bridge, and the water looks muddy.

One final turn and they arrived at the colonnade of tall red pine trees that led up to the cabin. She noted with satisfaction that the sign was still there, a small board with "Tír na n'Óg" carved into it. Roughly translated from Gaelic, the words meant "land of youth," a perfect name for the place she and her friends had enjoyed for many years. She shifted in her seat and winced at the sudden stab of pain. Right now she wasn't feeling particularly young.

The cabin with its alternating horizontal stripes of brown log and grey chinking, topped by a green shingle roof, came into view. A myriad of emotions swirled in her chest: relief, joy, comfort, reassurance. How had she ever been lucky enough to find this place? Luck, and maybe destiny.

Her thoughts were interrupted by Julie's strident voice announcing, "We're home!"

The prairie had changed utterly. An uninterrupted carpet of green extended in all directions with no hint of the well-worn deer paths that crisscrossed it. The only evidence there had ever been a fire was an occasional telltale blackened stem emerging from the depths. For a moment Maggie felt as if she had died and been reborn.

They drove up to the cabin. Julie rushed around the car to open the passenger door. While she was busy getting the roller bag from the back of the station wagon, Maggie stepped into the kitchen, breathing in the familiar, slightly musty smell. She looked around approvingly. Yadira had done a fine job: everything was spotless, everything in its place. A vase of flowers stood on the kitchen counter and beside it a card with the message, "Welcome home from all of us." It was signed, "Your Neighbors."

"Shall I take it upstairs?" Julie said, gesturing to the suitcase.

Without waiting for a reply, she walked past Maggie, up the few steps into the living room and disappeared in the direction of the bedroom. Within a minute she returned.

"All done," she said with satisfaction. "Now, how about a cup of coffee?"

It was churlish to refuse, but for the past six weeks Maggie had endured an endless barrage of noise. Now all she wanted was silence.

"Thanks very much, Julie, but you've done more than enough for me. You're wonderful. You all are. To be perfectly honest, I just want to sit here and luxuriate in being back in my own home."

Seeing the look of concern on Julie's face, she continued, "Don't worry about me. I'm fine. Honestly. I just need a bit of time to adjust."

Julie's face relaxed. There was genuine kindness in her voice when she spoke. "I understand completely. You just call us if you need anything—anything at all. Loren and I will be at home for the rest of the weekend."

"Thanks Julie...for everything. I really mean it. You've been wonderful—both of you. I'm lucky to have such great neighbors."

She listened to the sound of Julie's car on the driveway, becoming fainter by the second, for Julie was always in a hurry, her life filled with the endless demands of children, a husband and a large extended family, all of whom seemed to live within a ten-mile radius. The silence of the cabin was uncanny and Maggie strained to hear anything, for a moment wondering if she was going deaf. Then the refrigerator began its plaintive whine and she laughed, reassured.

It took some time to make a simple cup of tea, each step of the process an exercise in minimalism. Finally, carrying a mug of hot liquid carefully in her left hand, she stepped out onto the deck and sat down on a dusty metal chair that Yadira had not thought to clean. That was the next job, Maggie thought: to open up the screen porch for the summer. She wouldn't be able to manage it herself. Perhaps she could persuade Yadira to come for an extra few hours this week. Her mind churned with all the other things she would not be able to do for several weeks or months. Maybe her hasty departure from Cherrywood hadn't been such a good idea after all? She looked down at her hand resting on the dusty metal table, noting the mottled dry skin stretched over thin bones. She pressed her palms together in a gesture of prayer, measuring the asymmetry: her right wrist didn't bend as fully as the left. Closing her middle finger and thumb around each wrist in turn, the right wrist was thicker than the left. Bending her wrist backwards as far as it would go, she scrutinized the raised scar flanked by tiny red marks from the metal staples. Her body would never be the same again, never as good. Never.

She looked towards the prairie and the pond, her gaze unfocused. What now? What was she going to do with the rest of her life? Could she really manage out here in the country by herself? Not for once in fifty years had she doubted it, but the accident and the weeks of recovery had hijacked her confidence. Her thoughts strayed back to Cherrywood.

From the pond came a loud honking noise, accompanied by much splashing and flapping of wings. Geese. There were six at least, all adults, aggressively defending their rights. Each year they returned to rear their families on her pond. Fortunately, the numbers were kept in check by coyotes and foxes that found an equally hospitable home in the valley. Maggie smiled and could feel her mood begin to lighten. Savor this moment, she reminded herself. Whatever happened, she was not going to give up this place.

# Chapter 8

The meeting was scheduled for eleven on Monday morning, and it was now ten after the hour. It wasn't a good sign. For the past two days Maggie had brooded over this first meeting with a young woman who might become her personal assistant. One question kept nagging at her: What sort of relationship would they have?

Her eyes roamed around the room, into which the sunlight was pouring through tall windows on three sides and skylights in the sloping roof. The room had been added onto the cabin thirty years earlier with no attempt made to hide the rough exterior of the original walls. As a result, the weathered oak logs with their dull grey chinking formed a striking backdrop to the contemporary space. Against the wall stood a massive fieldstone chimney that had endured well over a hundred years of hot summers and freezing winters. Books dominated the room, filling the gaps underneath the window seats. Even more were piled above, leaving little space for sitting. A few ornaments dotted the window sills, each one with its own unique provenance and accompanying story. The furniture was minimal: a leather sofa and arm chair, a round pine table with a couple of chairs, three old cheese boxes that served as coffee tables. A sepia-tinged photograph of Maggie's mother looked down at the room, an inscrutable expression on her face. After her mother died, Maggie hung the photo as a reminder of what...she was no longer sure. Looking at it now, she wondered if the gesture had been driven by guilt.

What would happen to all of this stuff? What happened to possessions when the possessor no longer needed them? In the past if the subject came up in conversation with friends, Maggie would have made some glib comment to the tune of, "Well, it won't be *my* problem. I'll be dead." But thinking about it now, she realized that it was going to be someone's problem and a rather large problem if you considered all the buildings on the property, every one of them filled with the accumulations of fifty years. She hadn't been totally neglectful. When her husband died, she had made a new will, giving everything to her few remaining cousins in Ireland. But by the time they sorted it all out, the place would be a shambles. Mice and flying squirrels would have set up permanent homes in the cabin, unchecked by the traps she diligently set out each week. If she was found dead in the cabin, would anyone think of emptying the traps...or the fridge? An image of Julie popped into her head. Julie would surely think about something like this and make sure anything that might smell would be thrown out. She'd probably reset the traps too and return to empty them until a new owner took over.

Maggie shook her head from side to side. "Not my problem," she said aloud and listened for the uncertainty in her voice. A thought struck her: Getting rid of stuff could be the perfect solution to keeping the girl busy. She corrected herself: the personal assistant. "Girl" was not the right word to use these days, the same way "maid" was not politically correct in her mother's time. Maggie and her sister were warned to refer to Alice, who functioned in every way as the family maidservant, as the "girl." She smiled at the memory: Alice, who came from a family of seventeen and was just glad to get away from an impoverished farm and drunken father. Alice didn't care what she was called.

Glancing at the clock again, Maggie's irritation returned. The girl was twenty minutes late. Something must have happened, or perhaps she herself had made a mistake about the time. Out of the corner of her eye, she caught a hint of movement. A small silver car emerged from the pine alley and made its way tentatively up the gravel driveway. It came to a stop in front of the barn. Maggie watched as a young woman stepped out of the car. She looked to be in her early twenties, tall and athletic, with shoulder length blond hair tied up in a ponytail. She hesitated briefly, looked around her, then walked up to the cabin. The expression on her face seemed to say: I'm curious, a little apprehensive but totally capable of doing this job. Maggie realized that, had their roles been reversed, she would have worn the exact same expression.

"Hello," Maggie said, opening the kitchen door. She was still irritated by the girl's tardiness, and her voice was sharp. "I'm Maggie O'Connor."

"Hi," the girl said, "I'm Isobel Babić."

Maggie shrugged her shoulders at the proffered hand. "Sorry. My wrist is still healing. I'd give you my left hand, but unfortunately I need that one for the cane."

The girl stepped into the kitchen and closed the door behind her. Turning to Maggie, she said, "I'm so sorry I'm late. I didn't realize how long it would take to drive out here. It's quite a ways from Madison, isn't it?"

Maggie ignored the question, only marginally mollified by the apology.

"Let's go through to the front room," she said, stepping past Isobel through a deep crooked doorframe that separated the kitchen from the rest of the cabin. From habit, she pointed to the top of the door frame, adding, "Mind your head. It's low and lots of people have banged their foreheads on it. As you can see, it's a very old house. I think people must have been shorter then."

She could sense Isobel's curiosity as she led the way through the main cabin and another low doorway, and into the front room. The transition from the dark wood, low ceilings and tiny windows of the original cabin to the light and airy front room generally drew comments from first time guests, but Isobel was silent.

Maggie sat down carefully in the armchair, placing her cane by her feet. She gestured towards the sofa. "Please, sit down."

She looked appraisingly at the young woman who met her gaze with a even expression. The girl was dressed in beige Capris with a peach-colored short-sleeved top. She wore sneakers and carried a small satchel. Maggie presumed that it contained the inevitable iPhone and perhaps a tablet too. She didn't appear to be wearing any make-up, nor did she have any obvious piercings or tattoos, although each fingernail sported a different colored polish. Maggie wondered if this was some sort of fashion statement.

"Where would you like to begin?" was all that she could think of saying when Isobel remained poised and quiet.

The girl smiled. Her voice was hesitant when she replied. "Well, I was told that you had an accident and that you need some help for the next few weeks...." Her voice trailed off.

"You're correct. I had an accident." Maggie could hear the resentment in her own voice, and she made an effort to soften her tone. She continued, "And yes, I need some help, at least for a little while."

There was a brief pause as each of them considered how to proceed.

Isobel broke the silence. "Actually, I'm not clear what the job is, Maggie." She hesitated for a moment, then added, "Is it okay if I call you Maggie or would you prefer something else?"

"Maggie is fine."

"Mrs. McGuirk—she's the person at Cherrywood who contacted me and arranged this meeting—she didn't say anything much about the job. So I suppose I need to ask: What is it exactly you want me to do?"

The girl looked around the room as if the piles of books might provide an answer, before returning her gaze to Maggie, who was massaging her wrist.

"Well, right now I've got a broken wrist that's healing. But it's very weak and I can't do much with it. I can't drive, can't carry anything heavy, can't do laundry, can't cook..." Her voice became increasingly querulous as she enumerated each shortcoming. She looked at the offending wrist before returning it to her lap, where it lay like a discarded tool.

"What happened?" asked Isobel, her tone sympathetic.

Maggie let out a long sigh. "I tripped on the basement stairs. I was in a hurry and not paying attention. Oh. I should have said, I was carrying a crate of beer bottles at the time. Despite appearances, I'm not decrepit or even clumsy. I've gone down those stairs thousands of times and never had a problem." She shook her head ruefully. "They do say that one false move can change your life."

Isobel nodded in agreement.

"The upshot is that I broke my wrist, broke three ribs, broke my right foot, twisted that ankle, messed up my knee, and...oh yes, I got a concussion. I spent a week in hospital and five weeks at the rehabilitation center. They weren't at all happy last week when I insisted I was going home. It was their suggestion that I get someone to come here each day for a few weeks. And that's where you come in."

"You don't have any family around?" Isobel looked surprised.

"No. My husband died some years ago. Neither of us had children. I have great neighbors, but they have their own lives to get on with. I can't expect them to babysit me."

"So...what exactly would each day involve?" Isobel said.

Maggie tried her best to answer the question succinctly. "Well, I can get around the house: get out of bed, get dressed, wash...although I'm afraid to take a shower unless there's someone in the house in case I slip and fall. There's grocery shopping and preparing food. That's a bit of a problem right now. For example, I can't use a can opener and all my saucepans are too heavy. Even eating can be awkward because I can't use my right hand to cut anything. Then there's getting around. I have physical therapy twice a week in Madison and various doctor's appointments there too." She ran her left hand through her hair, pushing it back from her face. "Oh, and I'd really like to get my hair done."

Isobel listened intently, nodding her head every so often.

"There are probably more things I haven't thought of. I've only been home a couple of days. Oh yes. I can't kneel or squat, so if I drop anything, it has to stay on the ground until Yadira comes. She's my cleaning lady, and she comes for a morning every other week."

"So, how many days a week would you need me to come out here?"

"Well, right now I'd say five days a week, let's say from ten in the morning til five or six in the evening."

Maggie could see the girl's eyebrows lift a fraction of an inch.

"Don't worry," she said with a brittle laugh, "I'm not looking for a companion. I've lived alone quite happily for the last ten years. I just need you for meal preparation and driving. Maybe a little housekeeping and laundry, of course. The washer and drier are in the basement and I'm not ready to face those stairs yet, especially not with a load of sheets and towels in my arms. And if there's nothing that needs to be done, you could read a book... or go outside for a walk. I have good internet service. You could even watch movies."

Maggie stopped talking. A minute passed, then another while she waited for Isobel to respond. For several hours the previous night she had lain awake, worrying about this interview. Now, listening to her own admission that she couldn't manage by herself, she hoped fervently that Isobel wanted the job. If not, what alternative did she have? Find someone through an agency? Could she tolerate someone whose clothes and breath smelled of cigarettes and who didn't listen to her instructions? By contrast, here was an educated young woman, who, at least on first inspection, smelled clean. The girl might not be a good time-keeper, and maybe she couldn't cook, but she was young enough to learn. If I had been in a similar situation at that age, would I have taken this job? Maggie thought. The demands were minimal, the hours good and the pay... All of a sudden she realized that she hadn't mentioned pay.

"Of course, I'll pay you whatever you were earning in your last job. And travel expenses." She waited for a response, looking at the girl intently.

Finally, Isobel spoke. With a brief nod of her head she said, "Okay. I think this will work."

# Chapter 9

Isobel's hands were covered with flour, and she held them up like a surgeon as she leaned against the door frame of the front room.

"Is there something you'd like done? I'll finish rolling out the pastry dough in a minute."

Maggie looked up from where she was sitting, a book in her lap and a cup of tea within easy reach on the cheese box.

"Let me think for a moment," she said, taking a sip from her mug.

The past three weeks had been more of a challenge than she expected. There were definite advantages to having Isobel at her beck and call, but at times she felt uncomfortable with the loss of privacy. The cabin was a small space to share with a relative stranger. On Isobel's first day of work, Maggie insisted they open up the screen porch, giving her another room to retreat to when she needed privacy. It was a ritual that involved buckets of soapy water, followed by a thorough hosing down to remove the accumulated grime of winter. Dust covers were removed, rugs and cushions beaten, and the furniture arranged precisely as it had been for decades. This year she watched from her armchair in the front room, feeling somehow deprived, as if by not participating she might be excluded from summer too.

Isobel was always five or ten minutes late to arrive in the morning, but Maggie learned to accept this. In the larger scheme of things, it hardly mattered. She made her own breakfast each morning and with a second cup of tea in hand, sat out on the screen porch and waited for the familiar sound of a car on the driveway. Isobel was a cheerful presence in the cabin most of the time, and she tried to anticipate Maggie's needs. Early on Maggie was shocked to discover that the girl had no idea how to prepare a meal from scratch. This soon became the creative outlet of her day: menu planning and teaching Isobel the basics of making each dish. Each evening before Isobel left, she set the table and presented the meal, carefully plating a serving for Maggie. To the delight of the girl's roommates in Madison, Maggie insisted that she take the leftovers home with her.

Despite Maggie's inquisitiveness, Isobel was reluctant to talk about herself. The picture that emerged was of a somewhat neglected child whose immigrant parents had struggled, often working two or three jobs at a time, in their adopted city of Toronto. Their only daughter had a talent for tennis that eventually resulted in a four-year scholarship to the University of Wisconsin. There was little indication that the girl had a close relationship with her parents since leaving Canada.

"There's a project that I've been meaning to get around to for a while," Maggie said, replacing her mug on the cheese box.

Isobel cocked her head to one side. "Yeah. What is it?"

"Well, I need to do something about the Firhouse. That's the building you see behind the barn," she added by way of explanation. "I might need to rent it out or at least clean it up so that someone could stay there."

Isobel wiped her hands on her apron. Stepping into the room, she sat down on the sofa, facing Maggie's armchair and looked at her.

"The thing is, my husband died there. That's why I don't go there. I've not been inside it for several years."

Maggie could see Isobel's eyebrows rise a fraction.

"Oh, I get Yadira to go in every so often to check on things. The heating is on in winter, and she airs the rooms out in summer. Sometimes I have guests who prefer to stay there instead of the cabin. But I haven't wanted to spend any time there since he died. It was his place."

"What was he like—your husband, I mean?" Isobel's voice was gentle.

Maggie gazed out of the window towards the Firhouse and let out a long sigh before speaking. "He was a lovely kind man, and he adored me." She rubbed absentmindedly at her wrist. "We met when I was in my mid-forties. He had just turned fifty and had been divorced for a few years."

She looked at Isobel and chuckled, her eyes lighting up with remembered pleasure.

"We were on the same committee—at the university— trying to decide who would get an honorary degree that year, and I disagreed with him. It was all very civilized, but I thought his arguments were weak. The committee itself was a lot of fun because you worked with professors from all over the university whom you would normally never meet. He was a professor of history, about as far from zoology—my line of study—as you can get, and we had absolutely nothing in common. But maybe that was why it worked. Timing too. Timing is so important. After the meeting we went for coffee and continued to argue. But there was something about him that I really liked. I was ready for a long-term relationship, and I suppose he was too. It still took a few years before we decided to live together. After all, we each had fully-formed lives, personalities, habits, and merging those was quite a challenge. I didn't want to leave the cabin, and he was equally reluctant to leave his house in Madison. The Firhouse was our compromise. The word "fir" in Gaelic means "man.""

It was a sort-of man cave—he could have his own space, and more importantly, bring his library. By then he had about ten thousand books. So that's what we did. It all worked out, and we had twenty-five great years together. Oh, it wasn't perfect all the time. No marriage is. But the thing is, right from the beginning I knew I was the most important person in his life. To be loved that much is a small miracle."

The smile lingered on Maggie's face.

"What was his name?" Isobel asked in a quiet voice.

"His name was Alan. Alan Webster.

"When did he pass?"

Maggie thought for a moment. "It's been almost ten years."

She looked away, as if searching for the memories. Turning back to Isobel she said, "We played tennis that morning."

Seeing the surprised look on Isobel's face, she said, "Yes, tennis," nodding for emphasis. "It was the one sport that we both enjoyed doing together, I suppose because we were more or less equally matched. We used to play a couple of times a week." She looked out the window again, her gaze unfocused.

"That day I walked down to the Firhouse to tell him lunch was ready. He was sitting in his armchair, and at first I thought he was dozing. But all the color had gone from his face, and when I touched his cheek, it was cold."

Maggie looked down at her hands, as if they could remember that feeling.

"He was older than me, and I suppose I always thought he would die first. Still, I hadn't expected it to happen so suddenly. One day he was here and life was good. Then he wasn't, and I had to adjust."

The two women sat in silence, each alone with their thoughts.

After a few minutes Maggie said, "Let's go there tomorrow instead."

# Chapter 10

The following afternoon Maggie and Isobel made their way to the Firhouse. Walking was easier for Maggie now, although she moved slowly, especially on uneven ground. The pain in her foot was barely noticeable, but she still didn't trust her ankle or knee. A hiking pole was a constant companion outside, and she jabbed it into the sandy ground as she walked past the barn and up the grassy slope, Isobel following close behind in case she stumbled.

The two-story building sat at the base of a terraced hillside. A hipped roof with broad eaves cast a generous shadow over the band of windows that wrapped around the upper story. The wooden siding had faded to the color of gray lichen. White stucco walls on the ground floor had also mellowed over the years and were now a dusty tan making them almost indistinguishable from the sandstone hillside. The overall impression was one of harmony—a prairie-style building thoroughly at home in its surroundings. A gravel driveway curved around the side of the house to the upper floor, but Maggie followed the grassy path to a door on the lower level, the only feature in the blank stucco wall. She slid a key into the lock, turned it and pushed open the door. Straightening her shoulders, she stepped over the threshold into a small vestibule and stood aside to let Isobel into the small space. Light poured down on the two women from the upper story and reflected off the white walls and tiled floor. A wide wooden staircase led to the upper story where floor-to-ceiling windows covered the south and west-facing walls of a perfectly proportioned room. Against the east wall was a large built-in desk, above which yet another row of windows looked out onto a terraced sandstone hillside. To the north side of the room, a small galley kitchen was hidden behind a wall of glass blocks, and past the kitchen, a short hallway led to the bedroom and bathroom.

"Wow! This is an amazing place," Isobel said, circumnavigating the room and stopping at the central windows to examine the view.

Maggie lowered herself onto one of the wingback armchairs that flanked the stove. She closed her eyes and listened. The house was utterly silent. It had always been this way: a place of stillness and calm and contemplation. Opening her eyes, she looked around the room, trying to see it as a stranger might. The overall design was of Scandinavian minimalism, softened by comfortable furnishings and warmed by a dark red enamel stove in the center of the room. The walls were covered with an eclectic collection of art work that only her husband had understood. She had loved some of these pieces and loathed others. But this was his space, so she made no comment when he had excitedly produced each new treasure, telling her in detail how he had acquired it. Surfaces were dotted with pieces of art and sculpture, items he had collected throughout his life, each with its own story. She caught sight of a familiar piece: a whimsical pair of birds made from repurposed metal that had always made her smile with their devil-may-care attitude. Looking past the birds to her husband's desk, where a computer screen sat forlornly, she saw that her photograph was still there, propped up just below the screen. It was Alan's favorite photo of her, and he had placed it there so that he could look at it throughout the day. She remembered the day he took the photograph, the texture of the polka dot blouse she wore, how it felt crisp against her skin, its dusky blue color highlighting her eyes. Her gaze wandered back towards the stove and hesitated for a moment before resting on the other armchair. She tried to see her husband's face there but couldn't.

Isobel inspected the bathroom and afterwards, wandered into the bedroom. Maggie followed after her, noting a rim of evaporated water on the toilet bowl and making a mental note to ask Yadira to give the room a thorough going over the next time she came to clean. In the bedroom she looked around thoughtfully, taking in the furniture and the pictures hanging on the wall. The room had an impersonal feel, like a well-appointed hotel bedroom. She and her husband used it infrequently, preferring to sleep at the cabin. She opened one of the built-in closets and sniffed. It smelled a little musty, and she left the door open.

The two women returned to the main room and Maggie walked over to the windows. The ground dropped away steeply, and the upper branches of pine trees filled the view. Maggie beckoned Isobel to join her and pointed to a small gap in the foliage.

"You can barely see the pond at this time of year because of the leaves, but this is a wonderful view in winter. I always think of a tree house when I look out."

She turned to face the room and gave a deep sigh.

"This was my husband's favorite place in the whole world. He used to sit here with his books and magazines strewn all around him," Maggie said, gesturing to the large glass-topped coffee table in the center of the seating area. She sat down again and rubbed her finger idly along the surface of the table, leaving a clean line in the thin layer of dust.

"What happened to all the books?" asked Isobel.

"The books were never in this room. He kept them in the basement. It was climate controlled, you see. He used to haul them up in the dumb waiter. It's in that cupboard over there," Maggie said, pointing to a door facing the bathroom.

"Several years before he died, he made arrangements to donate his collection to the university library. They were delighted with the gift—it was a superb collection. A few months after he died, someone from the university took the books away. I was relieved at first. After all, it was what he wanted. But the place felt empty without them."

Maggie made a wry face. "After sorting through his papers and getting rid of clothes, I ran out of steam. Once the books were taken, it was easy to just close the door and walk away."

She fell silent and Isobel waited for a few minutes before asking gently, "What would you like me to do?"

Looking around the room once more, Maggie considered the question. When she replied, her voice was decisive. "I'd like you to help me make the place into the perfect, furnished apartment. Think Airbnb or a rental...or somewhere for a housekeeper or a caretaker."

The last few words were out of her mouth before she had time to think. Listening to them hanging in the air, she could feel her heart racing. This seemingly intractable dilemma, what to do with the Firhouse, had been lurking in the back of her mind since the accident. Isobel's arrival had provided her with a solution. It would be available whenever the time came for her to get live-in help. Otherwise, her only alternative would be to go back to Cherrywood. She forced herself to sound upbeat.

"You haven't seen the basement yet. The books are gone, but my husband was a bit of a hoarder. He couldn't bear to part with pieces of furniture he grew up with, even his mother's Royal Doulton china. It's all still there. I have no idea what to do with the stuff. It seems a shame to throw it all in a dumpster. I suppose I could donate everything to charity or try to sell some pieces, but I have no idea how you go about that."

Isobel looked at her watch. "I should be getting back—the dough'll be ready. But I can come back here on Monday and make a start. I'll bring my tablet. I can catalog everything with an App, or perhaps you'd prefer to work with an Excel spreadsheet. I'll take photos too. We'll need those if you plan to sell stuff on Craigslist or eBay."

Maggie heard the enthusiasm in Isobel's voice. This was a project that could occupy the girl in the long hours between grocery shopping and cooking. With a small grunt, she pushed herself up to a standing position, steadied herself and turned towards the stairs. Pausing, she looked around the room one more time, taking in its smell, its memories.

They made their way down the stairs where Maggie opened the door off the vestibule and flipped a switch. Light from long fluorescent tubes hanging from the unfinished ceiling bounced off the concrete floor and walls, giving the impression of an industrial warehouse. Rows of empty metal shelving lined the walls and filled the large room. A small pile of paperbacks lay discarded on one of the shelves. In a corner of the room, a well-worn leather armchair sat on a plush Persian carpet, the only color in the otherwise stark space. A lamp arched over it protectively. Maggie pointed to a door at the opposite side of the room.

"His hoard is in there."

Just before they stepped back into the vestibule, Maggie noticed a heavy-duty cardboard box lying on the floor.

"Those must be more of his papers. Like I said, I ran out of energy. We might as well take it back with us."

Obediently, Isobel lifted the box and carried it back to the cabin.

# Chapter 11

Later that evening Maggie sat in the kitchen nursing a glass of wine. The comforting smell of freshly-baked bread hung in the air. Isobel had prepared a cold leek and potato soup for dinner followed by a salad. With Maggie's urging, she had taken some soup and most of the loaf of bread with her when she left. Maggie imagined Isobel's roommates waiting patiently to see what their dinner might be that night. Perhaps her leftovers were the highlight of their evening. She smiled, remembering the meals from her own college days in Dublin: an endless series of cheese on toast, shepherd's pie and mutton stew.

Despite her initial reservations, Maggie was beginning to like Isobel. The girl reminded Maggie of students she had taught, although the age gap was larger. Maggie calculated she would be the same age as Isobel's grandparents if they were still alive. Did the girl get along with her grandparents, she wondered? Did they even live in North America? It had always surprised her how students seemed to fall apart when a grandparent died. As their professor, her role was to be sympathetic and accommodating, rescheduling class assignments and exams, but she found it irritating. After all, these were only grandparents, not parents or siblings. Her own grandparents had died before she was old enough to get to know them, so that unique relationship remained a mystery to Maggie. Nonetheless, it was important these days. Most of her contemporaries were absorbed by the lives of their grandchildren, and Maggie had learned to recognize, if not fully appreciate, the joy it brought them. Not just joy, but a reason to continue living. For a fleeting moment she thought of what it might be like to have a grandchild—Isobel for example—but the thought dissipated quickly. Her wine glass was empty. She stood up and carried it over to the sink. Isobel would look after it and the other dirty dishes in the morning.

It was still relatively early and Maggie wandered into the living room to watch the approaching sunset. She noticed the cardboard box on the window bench. The lid was sealed and she debated whether to go back to the kitchen to get a knife or wait until the following day. Curiosity won, and a few minutes later she settled herself comfortably beside the box and slit open the heavy-duty tape that secured the lid. A pungent smell of old books burst from the box when she pried it open. Her first thought had been that the box was left behind when her husband's books were moved. Looking inside, however, she saw a sheet of paper with the words, "Thought you might want these," written in large block letters, followed by a scribbled name, Maureen. Underneath was a layer of yellowed newspaper, which she lifted up cautiously. The box was filled with letters, some loose, some in packages held together with perished rubber bands, some stuffed into clear plastic bags. She picked up a blue airmail envelope from the top of the pile and was shocked to see her own handwriting. Postmarked Amherst, Massachusetts, USA, the letter was addressed to her parents in Ireland. She sat for several minutes, still holding the envelope, her mind racing. Very deliberately, she returned the letter to the box, closed the lid and went upstairs to her bedroom, knowing that there would be little chance of sleep that night.

~

*I've been thinking about how that box ended up at the Firhouse. I suppose it must have been sent after the house in Ireland was sold. When was that? Fifteen years ago? I went back when Mummy died and cleaned things up a bit. The place was on the market for a few years and when a buyer finally came through, I was too sick to do anything about it. Cancer does that. The neighbor helped out—what a saint she was! I remember her calling me here and asking if there was anything I wanted kept of my parents' things. I told her she could throw everything out. She must not have believed me.*

*The surgery was bad enough but the six months of chemo almost killed me. I lost so much weight and was completely exhausted all the time. I'd be in the middle of doing something and suddenly feel as if a hole had been punched right through me. I'd have to stop what I was doing, sit down, try to recover. The last thing I cared about was memorabilia from Ireland. I'm sure Alan told me about the box being delivered, but I just don't remember. There's an awful lot I don't remember from that time. Chemo-brain, I suppose, or maybe I just chose to forget.*

*There must be over a hundred letters in there. I can't believe my parents kept them all. What were they thinking? And there's Daddy's spidery handwriting on some of the bundles: Massachusetts, Germany, Wisconsin. Every letter I wrote home, from when I left Ireland until they died. God! Every week of my life is there, fully documented. The diary of their prodigal daughter who left them behind but in the end didn't come home. Did I hide the reason well enough from them, or did they manage to find it between the lines?*

*Isobel is coming tomorrow. I know she's going to ask me about the box, what's in it. I honestly don't know what I'm going to tell her. The truth, I suppose. But what is the truth?*

# Chapter 12

Rain thundered on the roof and streaked the west-facing windows of the cabin. Sitting in the living room, Maggie watched Isobel run from her car, holding a satchel above her head in a futile attempt to stay dry. The girl radiated health and vibrancy, and Maggie tried to remember that feeling of buoyancy and excitement, when life presented limitless possibilities. Her gaze dropped to the box on the window bench. It was closed but the genie had already escaped.

"How are you today, Maggie?" Isobel called out cheerfully from the kitchen. A few seconds later, her face appeared in the doorway. A strand of blond hair was plastered against her wet cheek, and she wiped it away with the back of her hand.

"Shall I put the kettle on?" Her voice sounded a little out of breath.

"I'm grand." Maggie's voice was flat. "A cup of tea would be nice."

Over the past three weeks, Isobel had learned that Maggie's use of the word "grand" could mean mediocre, all right or something far worse; it all depended on the tone in which it was delivered. "Nice" was another ambiguous word. But regardless of what today's utterances really meant, a cup of tea was always a reliable remedy. With a nod of her head, she disappeared back into the kitchen.

A few minutes later she returned carrying a tea tray.

"I see you've opened it up," she said, gesturing towards the box on the window bench, a note of approval in her voice. "What did you find in there?"

"Letters. A lot of old letters."

"So...what are you going to do with them?" Isobel cocked her head to one side.

Lying awake in bed last night, Maggie had asked herself the same question. One part of her was curious. Who was the young Maggie O'Connor who wrote so religiously to her parents each week? It might be enjoyable to find out. Yet, somewhere in the back of her mind was a feeling of reluctance: Did she *really* want to know? When she finally fell asleep several hours later, she was no closer to an answer.

"I'm not sure. Maybe I'll just burn them."

"You can't do that!" Isobel said, a note of censure in her voice. "I mean, there might be something important in them. Are they from anyone special?"

"Actually, I wrote them. All of them."

Isobel gave Maggie a puzzled look.

"Take a look," Maggie said, with a nod towards the box.

Isobel opened the lid, lifted up the yellowed newspaper and looked inside.

"*You* wrote all of these!"

Maggie could hear the incredulity in her voice. She watched as Isobel lifted out one of the packages, turning it around so she could read the address.

"Mr. and Mrs. Michael O'Connor, Greenhills, Navan, County Louth, Ireland. Are they your parents?"

Maggie nodded. "I used to write a letter home every week."

"How many years did you write to your parents?"

"Twenty years or thereabouts...until they died."

"I'm sorry," Isobel said quickly.

Maggie acknowledged the girl's expression of sympathy with a weak smile, adding, "They were old."

"The return address on this one is Amherst, Massachusetts," Isobel said, placing the bundle of letters beside Maggie's mug of tea on the coffee table. Wrapping her fingers around her own mug, she settled into the armchair facing Maggie, tucking her feet up under her.

"What were you doing there—in Amherst, I mean?"

Maggie was surprised. She hadn't expected the girl to be curious about her early life, and she wondered if this new-found interest stemmed from Isobel being entrusted with a project: to organize Maggie's life. Over the next hour, she found herself telling Isobel about why she chose to emigrate. Ireland in the sixties was backward and repressed—the antithesis of Isobel's North American world. Job prospects for women with PhDs were limited, as contemporary mores ordained that men were given high-level jobs. After all, they had families to support. A woman, even a highly educated one, was expected to marry and have children. Failing that, her PhD in science would be frittered away as a technician in a government laboratory with no prospect of advancement.

As she reflected on her male professors at the university in Ireland, by today's standards most of them would be forced into early retirement for sexual harassment. Fortunately for Maggie, at that time sex wasn't traded for grades. Nonetheless, male professors expected their students to be deferential and sycophantic. Her only chance of establishing a successful career in science was to emigrate to Europe or America. A year as a postdoctoral fellow at the University of Massachusetts-Amherst had been a first step along that road.

"You're an emigrant too, aren't you?" Maggie said, moving

the conversation away from herself. "What age were you when you left Canada?"

"Eighteen. It was easy for me, though. I came on an athletic scholarship, so the university took care of everything. My tennis coach picked me up at the airport and drove me to my dorm. Our coaches looked after everything: housing, meals, even signing me up for classes. It was pretty mindless."

"What did you study?"

"I majored in psychiatry with a special emphasis in child behavior."

"And afterwards?" Maggie probed. All she knew was that Isobel had worked as a school counselor in Madison.

"I wasn't sure if I wanted to go back to Canada. Then my parents decided to move to New Zealand. So I stayed and looked for a job here."

"It's not that easy to get a job if you're a foreigner. I remember having a terrible time trying to get a green card. What sort of visa did you have?"

"I got a green card in the lottery. Pretty lucky, eh?" Isobel smiled triumphantly.

Maggie was surprised to find herself enjoying this conversation. The fact that they were both immigrants to the United States gave them something in common, even if their arrival was separated by almost half a century. Leaving Ireland, she had no idea as to what her future might hold, so she was curious as to whether Isobel had a clearer sense of her path. She continued with her inquisition.

"What are you planning to do next?" Although she tried to make the question sound innocent, Maggie could hear the ring of mother superior in her voice.

The look that crossed Isobel's face was difficult to decipher. The girl seemed to be collecting her thoughts before venturing an answer. Maggie waited.

"Yeah. Well...I'm at a bit of a crossroads right now." Isobel took a sip of her tea, which, judging by the expression on her face, was now cold.

"I'm pretty sure I don't want to go back to working at a school. Don't get me wrong. I like kids. But a lot of them are insufferable, and the ones with real problems are awful. As for their parents...geez!" She made a face.

Maggie laughed. "That's what every generation says about the next one. Mind you, I tend to agree with you about parents. These days they seem to be overly-involved or the opposite—downright neglectful."

"You wouldn't believe what some of the kids were like." Isobel threw her hands up in a gesture of despair. "I mean, all their lives they've been the center of attention. In the end, I couldn't handle it. They have no idea what's happening to the world they're going to be living in." There was a genuine passion in her voice.

"So...I've been thinking about applying to Veterinary School."

It was Maggie's turn to look surprised.

Isobel nodded her head vehemently. "Yeah. In undergrad I had a part-time job in the Vet School. I used to clean out cages in the evenings. I didn't mind, really. The residents and technicians let me hang out with them, watch what they were doing; they even asked me to help sometimes. So I decided to look into the entry requirements. I'm missing a few courses, but my GPA is good enough, and best of all, I'm a Wisconsin resident. They get in much more easily than out-of-state applicants."

"It sounds a bit irresponsible—starting all over again."

As soon as she said it, Maggie wanted to take the comment back. It was something her own mother might have said. Nevertheless, she didn't approve of Isobel's plan. The girl already had a career, a good one that she could take anywhere in the country. It paid a living wage. She didn't have to take work home with her in the evenings, and her summers were free. If she was ambitious, she might find a job in school administration where she wouldn't have to deal with children at all. Best of all, she'd be able to retire early with a decent pension.

"Why do you say that?" Isobel uncurled her legs and sat upright in the armchair. She folded her arms.

A wave of despair swept over Maggie. How could she explain to this young woman that life was too short to fritter away on dreams?

"You know, a job with a pension is nothing to sneer at. You are lucky. You have a good career that can provide for you for the rest of your life. There will always be troubled school children."

"But I'm not happy...." Isobel's voice trembled.

"Oh. For heaven's sake! Your generation is obsessed with being happy."

For a brief moment their eyes met. Maggie saw that Isobel's were filled with tears. She moderated her voice somewhat, adding, "All I'm saying is, don't delude yourself. You *can't* have it all. Life isn't that generous."

Isobel stood up abruptly, picked up the tray and carried it to the kitchen, leaving Maggie to consider how much damage she had just done to their nascent relationship.

# Chapter 13

That evening, when Isobel had gone back to Madison, Maggie sat on the screen porch and stared out into the darkness. The purr of insects filled the air, interrupted occasionally by a deep, throaty croak from the direction of the pond. Fireflies sparked over the lawn. She went over the day in her mind, trying to reconstruct her conversation with Isobel. They had been getting on so well, but then she had allowed her own prejudices to emerge. Instead of listening as the girl tried to sort through her plans for the future, Maggie had behaved like a parent. It was something she had no experience with and clearly had little natural talent for. The remainder of the day Isobel had been withdrawn, but at least she hadn't stormed out. Maggie admitted to herself that something had changed in their relationship, and she wasn't sure if it could be repaired. Fortunately, they both had a weekend to think about it, and perhaps by Monday it would be forgotten. There I go again, she thought. I'm becoming a crotchety old lady. Going forward, she would try to hold her tongue and be less critical of Isobel's plans.

She walked slowly through the house, turning off lights before going to bed. In the living room she glanced over at the window bench. The package of blue aerogrammes lay next to the box where Isobel had left them. It might be interesting to read them, Maggie thought, perhaps re-live the excitement and novelty of her early immigrant experiences. But she wasn't sure if she had the stamina or indeed the time for such a project. In the weeks since her accident, she had become increasingly aware of how quickly time was passing.

Absentmindedly, she picked up the package of letters and sat down on the sofa. Raising the package to her nose, she inhaled deeply, closed her eyes and allowed her mind to drift back to her first day in America.

~

*It was early in January when I left. I have an image in my mind of the scene at Dublin airport, but I'm not sure if it's accurate. I've watched too many Irish plays and movies about emigration, so perhaps it's them that are in my memory, muddled with my own. Always the stoic, my mother didn't cry, but my father did. I just wanted to get it over with, the goodbyes. I was free, with a wonderful unknown ahead of me. If everything went terribly wrong, I had enough cash to buy a ticket home. But the possibility of failure never crossed my mind.*

*My one-way ticket was for Bradley International Airport where I would get a bus to Amherst. I'd never heard of Bradley International, but fortunately, the word Boston was typed on the thick paper ticket, a reassuringly familiar destination for Irish emigrants. It was already getting dark when the plane finally took off, and I watched the blinking lights of Dublin become smothered in the wintry cloud bank over the city. It was a long flight, yet, I hardly slept with the excitement. Aer Lingus airhostesses in their elegant green uniforms and pert pillbox hats glided up and down the plane, serving fresh sandwiches and tea.*

*Strange, but I have no memories of landing in Boston or of the connecting flight to Bradley Airport. What I do remember, vividly, is that America was a lot colder than Ireland. Dragging my suitcase from the terminal building to the bus stop through deep snow was bone chilling. When I finally spotted the bus for Amherst, the driver let me get on immediately. He put my suitcase in a compartment underneath the vehicle, leaving me to worry if he would remember to take it out at the right stop or give it to someone else by mistake. It was warm inside the bus, and I must have fallen asleep because I woke in a panic when we began to move.*

*Snow was everywhere. It's not as if I hadn't seen snow in Ireland. The Dublin mountains were often dusted with it in winter, but it rarely stayed around more than a couple of days. Looking out the bus window I could make out trees, endless trees lining the highway. I kept hoping to see a road sign that would reassure me we were going in the right direction, but I couldn't make out any names through the fogged-up window pane. It grew dark. The road narrowed to a two-lane highway. Occasionally, through a haze of yellow neon light, I could make out shops, some houses, a lonely petrol station. I was tired, and with the initial excitement long since gone, I began to worry. What if the man whose lab I was going to work in didn't show up to meet me? How would I find a hotel?*

*We pulled into a pretty New England town square, still festive with Christmas decorations. The door of the bus opened with a hiss. "This is your stop, miss," the bus driver said as he pulled on a jacket. I stepped down to the pavement, bracing myself against the arctic chill and looked towards the group of people waiting nearby. A small, wiry white-haired man in his fifties, wearing a tweed overcoat and a muffler, was peering at me inquisitively.*

*"Maggie O'Connor?" He said my name tentatively, and I had to hold back my tears. All the pent-up fear and exhaustion of the days and weeks leading up to this moment dissolved, only to be replaced by a new set of worries. Would I be able to live up to his expectations? Would I end up going home with my tail between my legs?*

*Nodding to the bus driver, he lifted my suitcase into the trunk of an old station wagon and we drove to their house. I was too tired to be curious. All the same, I remember that the house felt strangely old fashioned, as if I had stepped into Louisa May Alcott's book* Little Women.

*"You must be exhausted from the journey," his wife said, taking my coat and hanging it on the hall stand. She ushered me into the colonial-style sitting room, where I perched on the edge of an uncomfortable chair.*

*"The boys will be down in a minute. We'll have dinner and then Vince will drive you to the hotel."*

*I remember being a little surprised. He hadn't mentioned a hotel in our correspondence, and I just assumed I would be staying with them until I found an apartment.*

*Dinner that evening was brief. My advisor and his wife kept up a polite conversation during the meal, but neither of the teenage sons said much. I was glad when the evening came to an end. It must have been around nine when he finally drove me to the Jeffrey Amherst Manor Hotel. That name has stayed with me all through the years; it sounded so posh. Looking around the unfamiliar room before undressing, a wave of loneliness and nostalgia swept over me. Pushing those thoughts aside, I climbed into the large bed and curled up tightly under a comforting weight of blankets.*

*The following morning the enormity of what I had done hit me. Lying in bed, listening to the unfamiliar sounds of the hotel, I realized that I was completely on my own. For the first time in my life, everything I chose to do would be my own decision, with nobody to weigh in on the pros and cons. It was a heady feeling, and at the same time terrifying. Finding a flat was going to be the priority, as I couldn't afford to stay at the hotel for more than a couple of days. I wasn't sure how to go about it but reasoned that Amherst was a college town with thousands of students in the same predicament as me. There was bound to be a solution. Putting on all the winter clothes I had brought with me, I stepped out into the picture-perfect snow-covered street and walked towards the town center.*

*There's nothing like going to an American diner for the first time. You look in the window and the place oozes warmth and welcome. Once inside the door, the stools at the counter are inviting and anonymous. Soon there's a mug of coffee in front of you, with thimble-sized containers of milk, so different from the ubiquitous milk jug on an Irish restaurant table. Just like the bar in an Irish pub, it's easy to get into conversation with the person sitting beside you at the counter. In this case it was a tall, lean, shaggy young man whose dark hair was tied loosely in a ponytail.*

*The menu was staggering, with a whole new lexicon of unfamiliar choices. Before I had a chance to read it, the waitress came back to top up my coffee cup. She looked at me expectantly, the pad and pencil in her hand poised for my order. Looking around for inspiration, I pointed to my neighbor's plate, which had the remnants of eggs, potatoes and rashers on it. Her questions came fast and furious.*

*"Howdya want yer eggs?"*

*"Fried, please," I answered, enunciating each word carefully.*

*"Yeah, but howdya want them? Over easy? Sunny side up?"*

*I had no idea what she was talking about. Once again, I pointed to my neighbor's plate.*

*"The same as he has, please."*

*She nodded, scribbled on her pad and strode briskly towards the kitchen where she clipped the slip of paper to a rail above the delivery hatch.*

*The man with the pony tail smiled and asked where I was from.*

*"I'm from Ireland. I arrived yesterday."*

*"Geez. I've never met anyone from Ireland before."*

*He went back to eating, and I noticed that he held his fork with his right hand, turning it upside-down and scooping up the food into his mouth as if it were a spoon. Mummy used to say you could always tell someone's breeding by how they held their knife and fork. This man would not have passed muster. He must have noticed me looking at him, for he said, "They're over easy. The eggs. Sunny side up means that you see the yellow."*

*"I've never heard of that. We only get them one way in Ireland... sunny side up. Unless someone messes up and spills the yolk."*

*"What brings you here?"*

*"I'm going to do a postdoc in the Department of Zoology."*

*"Cool." He held out his hand. "Pleased to meet you. My name is Jeff—Jeff Fitz."*

*I offered my name and for the next few minutes we went back and forth, sharing bits of information about where we grew up. His parents lived on Long Island, which he explained lay to the east of New York City.*

*"I'm a junior, majoring in Botany."*

*"I'm sorry but I don't know what that means."*

*He laughed, explaining that this was his third year at the university and that he planned to get a BS degree in Botany. I was starved for conversation, and we chatted easily.*

*"Do you know how I might find a flat? Is there a board or something where people put up notices?"*

*"A flat?" He looked perplexed.*

*"A place to stay. A bedsitter, or I could share. Either would be okay."*

*"Oh. You mean an apartment." He smiled. "And the other thing you said—that must be an efficiency. Yeah. There are a couple of rental agencies in town. I can point them out to you on a map, if you have one. The campus newspaper advertises rentals too, but some of them are a bit sketchy."*

*He cocked his head to one side. "You know, my roommate quit after last semester and I'm looking for someone to sublet. You wouldn't be interested, would you? It's a two-bedroom apartment close to campus. There's only one thing: I have a dog. He's called Ari, after Aragorn in Lord of the Rings. He's a shepherd, kinda like Aragorn. But then again, some people don't like dogs." He shrugged.*

A nagging voice in my head insisted that he could be a rapist or a murderer, but I chose to ignore it. After all, he liked dogs.

"That would be brilliant. The thing is, I don't have any furniture—no bed or sheets or towels or anything. Just one suitcase. I can get all those things, but it'll take a little time."

"That's no problem. I've got an extra bed and linens. Everything for the kitchen too. My Mom keeps on bringing me all this stuff from home." He laughed.

Jeff scribbled his address on a napkin, together with his phone number, and we agreed that I would move in the following afternoon. Looking at his watch, he jumped up and said he had to go to class, leaving me at the counter with my bottomless cup of coffee to marvel at the ease with which it had all fallen into place. I felt on top of the world: I had a place to live, a job and a future waiting for me.

# Chapter 14

Maggie rarely answered her landline, especially on weekends. Calls were invariably from strangers who would try to persuade her to support an organization or political cause. She reasoned that anyone who wanted to talk to her would leave a message. On those rare occasions when she grabbed the receiver out of frustration, only to discover it was yet another sales pitch, she took pleasure in pretending she was dying. By the time the caller recovered, she had replaced the receiver. The ruse gave her considerable satisfaction, although occasionally she wondered if it might be tempting fate.

Sitting on the screen porch on Sunday afternoon, she heard the telephone ring four times followed by a click, and someone starting to leave a message. Something in the timbre of the voice made her get up and limp into the living room as quickly as she could. She picked up the handset and heard Isobel's distraught voice. The girl was sobbing as she spoke.

"Maggie, I'm sorry but I can't come tomorrow. Oliver's been hit by a car. He's at the hospital and he looks awful. He was hit hard...there was a lot of blood, and he kept yowling and someone came out with a blanket and we wrapped him in it, and they drove me here. They've taken him to surgery, and I don't know what's going to happen. It's all my fault. I let him off his leash and he ran out onto the road."

At first Maggie was confused. In her mind she saw a young man flying through the air like a rag doll, landing heavily on the road in front of a stopped car. Wrapping him in a blanket and taking him to hospital seemed a little strange. Why hadn't they called for an ambulance? It was only after she processed Isobel's last sentence and the word "leash" that it dawned on her: Isobel must have a dog. The angst and misery in the girl's voice sounded heart-wrenching, and Maggie tried to reassure her that everything would be all right. Gradually, Isobel calmed down and her choked sobbing slowed. Maggie continued to talk, her voice calm and authoritative.

"Don't worry about me. I'll be just fine. If there's anything I need tomorrow, I'll call one of my neighbors. Meanwhile, I want you to let me know how Oliver is doing. Promise me that. Otherwise I'll worry."

There was an audible sniffle before Isobel replied. "Okay. I'll call you tomorrow. I promise."

Maggie could hear someone speaking in the background. Isobel came back on the line a moment later.

"I know some of the people at the hospital from when I used to work here—that was one of them. Sorry, Maggie. I've got to go now. I'll talk to you tomorrow."

The line went dead. Maggie put the phone down and returned to the porch. She thought about Isobel, sitting alone in the waiting room at the veterinary hospital, blaming herself for what had happened. Her heart went out to the girl, but there was little to be gained by worrying. By the sounds of it, Isobel had planned to come to work tomorrow, so she must have put aside the disagreement they had the previous Friday.

Maggie returned to the screen porch and placed the phone within easy reach in case Isobel called again. From where she sat, she could see the oak tree that marked the grave of her own dog, Cara. When they buried her, Maggie and her husband planted a sapling to mark the spot, and over the years watched as it grew into a healthy tree, now over forty feet tall. In another hundred years, someone will sit here and admire the tree, she thought, unaware of who had planted it and why, let alone what had nurtured it.

Maggie first noticed the dog late one afternoon in March when she came home from work at the university. The animal circled the cabin at a safe distance, apprehensive, and at the same time curious. It was undernourished, with matted hair and no sign of a collar. She offered a bowl of water and, as an afterthought, some left-over stew that the dog wolfed down in seconds. She called around to all her neighbors and the local veterinarian, but nobody had heard of a lost dog in the township. Everyone said the same thing, that it was probably dumped. This part of the county, with its remote valleys and secluded roads, was a convenient place for someone to abandon an unwanted pet. As the temperature dropped below freezing that evening, Maggie found herself making a rough bed of straw in the barn, covering it with an old blanket. She couldn't see the dog but felt that her every movement was being watched carefully. She propped the door of the barn open with a log, left a bowl of warm water that would inevitably freeze and went back to the cabin, trying to put the animal out of her mind. The following morning the dog was still there and eyed her suspiciously as she got into her car and drove away. She didn't give it a thought during her busy day, but when she returned that evening, the animal emerged from the barn and followed her part way to the cabin. She relented and put the remainder of the stew outside in a bowl, arguing with herself that she could do with scrambled eggs.

This pattern continued for several days, during which she bought a large bag of dog food. Gradually, the animal insinuated itself into her life, and she looked forward to seeing it at the end of the driveway each evening. The animal chased after the car, following it up the driveway to where she parked, then stood at a safe distance watching while she walked to the house. Once inside, she could sense it hanging around the kitchen door, waiting for some food. Unlike a real pet, this animal didn't come with responsibilities. If she chose to stay in town overnight or returned home very late, she didn't worry that the dog would starve, reasoning that it must have survived for weeks on its own before fetching up at her doorstep. Moreover, the woods were full of rabbits and squirrels, and deer hunters didn't always take their kills, leaving the meaty bones to be discovered with the spring thaw. After a month, she decided to call the dog Cara, the Gaelic word for friend.

Within a year, Cara had become a member of the household. She still slept in the barn but occasionally came indoors and allowed herself to be petted. The socialization had begun when Maggie invited Alan to the cabin for the first time. For some strange reason that Maggie could not understand, Cara was drawn to him. The dog's native wariness disappeared completely when he visited, and it followed him around like a slavish pet, happy to play fetch with a ball or frisbee. Maggie often thought it was Cara's affection for Alan that solidified her own relationship with him. If this fiercely independent animal could accept him in her life, maybe she could too. The next twelve years were a joy. She and Alan wept at the end, which was mercifully swift. Afterwards, neither she nor her husband wanted to chance fate by getting another dog. They used to joke that the dog's ghost wouldn't tolerate another animal in her territory.

Isobel called late on Monday morning. She enumerated Oliver's ailments and went into some detail as to what the surgeon had done. The prognosis was good: Oliver would recover fully, although he might have a slight limp, as one of his rear legs was badly broken and required several pins and plates to stabilize it. Isobel thought he should be able to go home by the end of the week. She sounded relieved and went on to describe her visit to the intensive care ward earlier that morning and Oliver's attempts to wag his tail and stand up despite the cast on his leg. She reassured Maggie that she would be back to work the following morning, adding that she was looking forward to keeping busy and having her mind occupied.

Isobel normally prepared extra meals for the weekend, and there were still some leftovers. Nonetheless, her absence presented Maggie with a perfect excuse to try driving for the first time since her accident. Her wrist was healing well, its strength and range of motion increasing gradually, and she felt confident she could manage the steering wheel and gear lever. Her right ankle was still sore, but if necessary she could use the cruise control. On her way back from the store, Maggie pulled into the gravel road leading to her cabin where a cluster of mailboxes marked the junction. As she walked to her mailbox, a pickup truck approached and she waved absentmindedly to it as it passed. The pickup stopped abruptly and reversed towards her, coming to a halt beside the mailboxes. The tinted window rolled down revealing Bill Breunig's shiny bald head and ruddy face.

"So you came back?"

Maggie ignored him and continued to empty her mailbox. Behind her she could hear the door opening followed by a grunt as he heaved his bulky frame down from the vehicle.

"I thought you were going to stay at Cherrywood. Seems like a real good idea to me. You'd be a lot happier there. Safer too. You wouldn't need to worry about falling down the stairs again."

Listening to his smug tone, Maggie began to tremble. She held onto the mailbox to steady herself and turned to face him. Bill looked her up and down slowly, his eyes taking in every detail. He continued to speak in his faux southern drawl. "I'm still willing to make you a fair offer on that run-down cabin of yours."

"I'm here and I'm planning to stay. You can take your offer and get out of my sight!"

She began to walk towards her car, but Bill moved quickly, blocking her way.

His body tensed as he spat out the words. "The cabin's a worthless piece of shit, and the barn's a fire trap. The whole place should've been condemned years ago. Mark my words, you'll regret not selling to me."

Maggie clung to a mailbox, determined not to show any sign of weakness. Finally, with a snort he stepped aside.

"You should have stayed at the nursing home," he shouted over his shoulder as he climbed back into the truck. He slammed the door loudly, and as the window rolled up, she heard him mutter, "Stubborn old bitch. You'll see. Just you wait." The engine roared as he drove away.

Maggie made her way back to her car and, sitting down heavily on the seat, gripped the steering wheel to stop her hands from shaking. Once she was back at the cabin and had carried her groceries into the kitchen, for the first time ever she locked the door. A range of scenarios raced through her mind, each more disturbing than the previous one. Was he capable of hurting her physically? Would he be crazy enough to set fire to the barn or perhaps the cabin? Nobody would suspect arson; they'd blame a faulty electrical connection in the ancient wiring. The same thing had happened to a neighbor of hers some years earlier when his old dairy barn burned to the ground. Even though the fire engine got there within an hour, there was nothing they could do to stop the blaze. She considered her options. There was no point in complaining to the local police. They would dismiss her fears as typical of an old lady living alone in the country. For a fleeting moment, she considered buying a gun. There were at least three shops that sold firearms within a ten-mile radius of the cabin, including the local hardware store. But she hadn't grown up with guns and knew that she would never be able to raise one in threat, let alone fire it. She considered calling Bill's wife but dismissed that idea. If he was a bully with Maggie, he was equally likely to be a bully at home. From now on, she decided, she would have to keep her guard up.

Although Maggie was reluctant to admit it, having Isobel around each day provided not just practical help but a measure of security. Bill would be unlikely to try anything if there were people around, she reasoned. But going forward, would Isobel want to continue working for her? After all, the dog was going to need a lot of care and nursing over the next few weeks. The thought alarmed Maggie, and she racked her brain for a solution. Isobel must realize that Oliver's surgery and hospital stay would be expensive, so she'd need to continue working to pay those bills. Perhaps the girl could be persuaded to bring Oliver with her when she came to work? Maggie spent the rest of the afternoon fleshing out the plan and considering how best to present it to Isobel when she came back to work the following day.

# Chapter 15

To Maggie's surprise, Isobel agreed to the plan readily. On the first morning of their new arrangement, Isobel thrust a bunch of yellow roses into Maggie's arms before returning to her car to retrieve the dog. She lifted a large crate from the back seat, maneuvered it carefully into the kitchen and placed it gently on the floor. Kneeling down, she opened the door and eased a small brown dog from the crate.

"This is Oliver," she said, sounding for all the world like a proud parent. "I know he looks terrible right now, but he's very well behaved and he never barks."

Isobel shook her head from side to side, as if her gesture could convey the importance of this pronouncement to Oliver. Looking down at the dog, Maggie's first impression wasn't particularly favorable. The animal was a runt with short wiry hair that emphasized his skinny body. He was about fifteen inches tall, with a terrier-like head that tapered to a dark muzzle. One of his rear legs stuck out awkwardly from his body, the bright blue bandage contrasting with a white one that encircled his belly. He wore a plastic cone around his neck that emphasized the numerous fresh pink scabs on his face. One ear seemed to be stitched in place with thick black sutures. The dog balanced on three legs, and looked up at Maggie with a doleful expression.

"Do you mind if he doesn't wear his leash?" Isobel asked. "It rubs against his neck, and he has a raw spot there."

"He's a right mess," Maggie muttered as she opened a cupboard to get a vase for the flowers.

Isobel undid Oliver's collar. Free at last, the dog took an immediate interest in his new surroundings. While she filled the water bowl she had brought, the dog clumped awkwardly across the kitchen floor to the garbage container in the corner and sniffed. From there, he made his way around the perimeter of the room, checking each corner in turn. Without warning there was a snapping sound, followed by a yelp from the dog, who retreated from under a small wooden table next to the stove.

"Sorry. I forgot about the mouse traps," said Maggie. "You better snap the rest of them shut before that poor creature ends up with another bad leg."

She chuckled, despite herself, at the abject look the dog gave her. Isobel made her way around the cabin, snapping mouse traps shut. With each sudden noise, Oliver immediately shuffled over to investigate. As she watched the dog's clumsy efforts, it was hard for Maggie to keep a straight face. An old cabin like this must present an endless and irresistible feast of exciting smells for any dog, she thought.

Isobel unpacked some groceries and set about making coffee for both of them. This was a habit that she and Maggie had recently adopted at the start of the week. It was their 'business' time. First, they discussed what needed to be done that day and what new tasks Maggie had lined up for the rest of the week. After that, they focused on the Firhouse project, which was beginning to show progress. Isobel had a knack for showcasing each object to its maximum potential and had already made some surprisingly lucrative sales on Craigslist and eBay. She had a considerable incentive: Maggie proposed that the girl could pocket fifty percent of any sale she made. The "sold" column on the spreadsheets was filling up nicely.

The Firhouse had changed considerably in the space of three weeks. On the one hand, Maggie thought, it was wonderful to see the transformation. The musty smell was gone, surfaces gleamed, and all sense of clutter had been banished. On the other hand, the place had lost its personality. Maggie could almost see the ghost of her husband walking off into the woods, his shoulders slumped, a sad expression on his face. She wanted to call out after him, "But don't you see, I have to do this." She needed to move on with her life, or however much was left of it.

As soon as Isobel sat down at the kitchen table, the dog tried to jump up onto her lap. Bending over, she gathered him carefully into her arms and helped him up. Oliver sat awkwardly on his haunches, facing forward and stared intently at Maggie. Isobel absentmindedly petted his head and fondled his good ear and a look of drowsy bliss descended on the dog's face. Stretching towards her coffee cup, Isobel shifted slightly in her chair. Suddenly off balance, the dog tried to jump down but instead slipped awkwardly to the floor. There was a yelp of pain, and a stream of urine escaped from his underbelly.

"I'm so sorry," exclaimed Isobel, leaping up from her chair. For a moment, Maggie wasn't sure if Isobel was apologizing to the dog or her. Isobel cleaned up the puddle of urine and apologized again, this time clearly to Maggie.

"It's hard for him to pee with his leg in a cast, so he holds it in," she explained.

"Don't worry," Maggie said with a reluctant smile. "Yadira comes to clean tomorrow."

~

In contrast to the Firhouse, Maggie had made no progress with the box of letters.

"I could help you sort them, you know," Isobel offered one morning as she handed Maggie a mug of coffee. Nodding in the direction of the box, she added, "You said they're from the first twenty years after you left Ireland. I could sort them by year, if you like. Put them into separate zip lock bags. Then, when you wanted, you could just pull out a bag and be reminded of where you were and what you were doing that year. It could be fun, eh? The story of your life in weekly installments."

The enthusiasm in the girl's voice was palpable. She loved projects like this where she got a chance to bring order to chaos. Maggie wondered if this was why she left her previous job as a school counselor. There was no way to bring order into the chaos of children's lives. She gave a tired sigh. Sometimes Isobel's energy overwhelmed her. It was one thing to make the Firhouse habitable—a project that would pay off if she needed a housekeeper in the future—but the letters were different. She hadn't been ignoring them. She was afraid of them. They were a Pandora's box, brimming with ghosts. Whoever said that emigrants leave with a single suitcase but carry a lifetime of emotional freight was right on the money, she thought.

Minutes passed. Meanwhile, Isobel waited with all the patience of a school counselor.

"You're right. I should do something about them," Maggie said finally, walking purposefully towards the box. Opening it, she inhaled the musty smell that wafted into the room.

"Let's begin." She lifted out packages of envelopes and laid them in a neat row along the bench. Isobel joined her, and over the next hour they sorted the letters into a chronological sequence. Isobel brought some zip lock bags from the kitchen and repackaged each year's collection of envelopes with an index card. On each card she noted the year and the addresses from which the letters were sent. When they were finished, even Maggie had to concede it was an impressive collection.

Maggie began to replace the packages in the box, ignoring the disapproving look that Isobel gave her.

"Don't you want to read them?" Isobel asked, as she selected one of the zip lock bags and offered it to Maggie. "Didn't you say that you went to Amherst when you left Ireland? You could start with these—the first year."

Maggie felt torn. Isobel's eagerness meshed with her own curiosity as to what she had got up to all those years ago. But deep inside there was another feeling she couldn't quite identify. A mixture of fear and apprehension. That year in Amherst was at the core of her life. Reluctantly, she took the zip lock bag from the girl, opened it and pulled out the contents.

Each letter consisted of a single sheet of blue paper, folded into the shape of an envelope. The outline of a small airplane and the words "Aerogramme, Via Airmail, Par Avion" were printed on the front, together with an eighteen-cent stamp in the top right corner. The paper was tissue thin, and pressure from typewriter keys had penetrated its fabric, creating a form of braille. Maggie ran her fingertips over the impression, lingering for a moment, lost in thought. She squinted at the postal code.

"Postal Service, PM..." Her voice trailed off. "My eyesight has gone to hell since the accident. I see two of everything and end up having to close one eye or the other. I can't read this date—even with one eye. Get me the magnifying glass from the desk, will you?"

While Isobel went in search of the magnifying glass, Maggie unfolded the envelope gently. The musty smell clung to her fingers. A date was neatly typed in the top right corner of the blue sheet of paper and below it the greeting, "Dear Mummy and Daddy." For a moment she was overwhelmed by an unexpected wave of emotion.

"Can you get me a glass of water please, Isobel?"

By the time Isobel returned from the kitchen, Maggie had composed herself.

"We'll put these in order. You take half of them," she said, handing Isobel a stack of blue envelopes. "Write the date on the front of the envelope in pencil, and if you can't make it out, open up the letter; there'll be a date inside. I seem to have been very organized," she added with a derisory laugh.

They worked in silence for a while, eventually assembling an orderly stack of forty-eight letters. Getting up stiffly from her armchair, Maggie left the room briefly, returning with a small oval-shaped wooden box that she wiped with a damp cloth. It was a souvenir from a road trip to the east coast that she and her husband had taken to celebrate his birthday. The trip included a number of historical sites, and they spent a chilly and blustery afternoon touring a Shaker village in rural Massachusetts. Almost as an afterthought, Maggie bought the box. As a rule, she didn't buy souvenirs, but the Shaker box was different. It had a utilitarian perfection, reflecting the patient craftsmanship of the inspirational community. As soon as they returned home, the box was pressed into service and thereafter delivered bread to their guests at countless dinner parties. In recent years she entertained less, and the box had been abandoned to gather dust on top of the kitchen dresser.

Bending over the coffee table, Maggie placed the stack of letters into the box.

"What would you like to do next?" Isobel asked.

"I'm not sure. Maybe I'll just sit here for a while and think."

⁓

*I never thought what it was like for Mummy and Daddy when I left. I was wrapped up in my own adventure and didn't think about them. Hindsight can be painful. It certainly shows you your flaws. They must have been heartbroken when I left. To have your child emigrate to America was still a terrible thing in Ireland back then, a reminder of the Famine years when every family was torn apart. Did they hope that my going to America was just a passing phase, that I'd come home after the year in Amherst?*

*I picture them sitting side by side in the car as they drove home from the airport, Daddy weeping silently, Mummy holding herself stiffly upright, looking out the side window, searching for any distraction. From now on, the house would be truly empty.*

*My letters would have been the highlight of their week. I imagine Daddy coming home from work of an evening and Mummy telling him, "There's a letter from Maggie!" as soon as he came in the door, knowing that it would put him into a good humor. He'd take it from her and place it on the dining room table, where he could look at it, postponing the pleasure. After his tea he'd open the folds and read it through slowly, savoring each piece of news, memorizing the names of my new friends, trying to picture the places I described. For the rest of that week, the letter would be read and reread by both of them, talked about over dinner, the stories in it passed on to friends and neighbors. All that time in Amherst, we never once spoke on the phone. It seems so strange now, but in those days the phone was considered an expensive tool to be used only in emergencies. Letters were our only conversation.*

*They deserved so much more. They came from large families, packed with aunts and uncles, cousins and grandparents, everyone living within a couple of hour's driving distance. A clan. Their lives should have been filled with family, their house echoing with gleeful squeals from boisterous grandchildren after Sunday dinners. The sort of families they grew up in, the families their friends enjoyed. I robbed them of that.*

*When my sister died in the accident, they were devastated. But at least they still had me. Sure, I was up in Dublin at University, but I came home as often as I could. I tried so hard to fill the gap she left, but it was exhausting. I couldn't make up for her.*

*What did they say when people asked when was I coming home? Because that's what people in Ireland always ask when a child has emigrated. "Will she be home for Christmas?" They must have grown to hate that question.*

*I can hear my father's soft voice as he answers. "Ah, sure she's happy where she is." My mother would add quickly, by way of justification, "She has a great career over there." The interrogation might end there but the emptiness they felt would never end. I did that to them.*

# Chapter 16

With the aid of a magnifying glass, Maggie had managed to
decipher the first letter. It was a bit of an anticlimax, she thought,
as she folded the aerogramme and placed it on the opposite
side of the box to the rest of the letters. The descriptions were
exactly as she remembered, from her arrival in Amherst to
finding a place to live. The tone of the letter was upbeat, and try
as she might, she could detect no hint of loneliness or regret.
Of course, the younger Maggie would have tried to make things
sound positive for her parents. Even so, the letter came across
as genuinely cheerful. Maybe she was deluding herself. She
read the letter again, this time aloud. Her voice sounded false,
its inflection carrying the reassurances of an old lady, not those
of a young emigrant. Opening the second letter, she held the
magnifying glass up to the first line and began to read, this time
in silence. Her eyes rushed ahead, scanning the lines, searching
for something—she wasn't sure what. She realized that she was
trying to read between the lines, searching for emotions she had
held back from her parents all those years ago.

Her gaze travelled around the room, coming to rest on
the photograph of her mother. Theirs had been a challenging

relationship, especially while she was a university student in Dublin. Somehow, she felt that she never managed to live up to her mother's expectations. Thinking back on it now, she never asked what those expectations might have been. She stared at the picture, taken at her mother's graduation from university. Did my mother have the same misgivings about fulfilling her parents' dreams? she wondered. Were all mothers and daughters condemned to suffer these misunderstandings? At least in her mother's case, she had redeemed herself by returning to the family fold, marrying, having children and living a conventional life. Still, if given the opportunity, Maggie wondered, would her mother have emigrated and escaped?

"All the questions I never asked...." Maggie said softly under her breath.

She glanced over at the rest of the zip lock bags, still laid out neatly on the bench. These letters were like a diary, although not as truthful as a diary generally is. What did people do with their diaries when they got old? she wondered. Did they burn them? If they knew they were going to die soon, they might want to erase any record of their life's indiscretions, lest anyone find out what they were really like. Maggie didn't care what people thought about her any more, but there was a certain attraction in destroying one's personal papers just before death. And she *was* going to die. How soon was not clear.

She thought back to Dr. Carney's visit, while she was still in hospital. When she read the label stitched on his white coat— Oncology—she knew his visit was not a routine courtesy. As soon as he said he wanted to discuss her recent CT scans, she knew something ominous was coming. She remembered his words exactly: "We've noticed some changes since the scans taken after your colon surgery." Over the past year, she too had noticed some changes: new pains and a persistent feeling of discomfort in her abdomen. Up to now she'd been willing to dismiss these symptoms, finding reasonable excuses for each one, but they were becoming impossible to ignore or rationalize. Dr. Carney had visited her one last time, on the morning of her discharge. He was persistent, and in an effort to get rid of him, she agreed that she would make an appointment with him in three months. "By that time, I'll be ready for you," she had said, with a knowing look. Neither of them smiled. Those three months were almost over, and she still hadn't decided what she was going to do.

It is a beautiful day outside, the sort of day that should not be wasted, Maggie thought, especially if you have cancer. She decided to take a walk to the edge of the prairie and see how far along the path she could go without tiring herself out. From her armchair in the living room, she had eyed that inviting ribbon of green for the past few weeks. Vic was diligent in keeping the fire break mowed.

She took a pair of hiking poles from the porch, crammed an old straw hat on her head and made her way down the gravel driveway, past the barn, to the mowed path. Despite twinges of pain in her wrist and ankle, for the first time in three months she felt invigorated. Her ribs hardly hurt, even with deep breaths. Since the burn, the prairie had greened out completely, and everywhere she looked plants were springing up from the fertile soil in competitive chaos. That was the wonderful thing about a prairie: Its success didn't depend on straight lines or orderly rows. Birds, butterflies and insects had returned, and there was a pleasant hum in the air, interrupted by an occasional chirp of an insect or the sound of beating wings. A pair of sandhill cranes flew overhead, contrasting with the white contrails high in the blue sky.

A twinge of pain in her right ankle reminded her that she would need to pace herself on these daily jaunts. Years earlier, Vic's father had built some rustic benches for her, placing them at key viewpoints around her property. The design was simple and familiar to anyone who knew of the Wisconsin conservationist, Aldo Leopold. Resting her hiking poles against the back of the nearest bench, she sat down for a few minutes, letting her mind wander. The surface of the pond shuddered irregularly as a breeze passed by. The sun felt good, spilling over the brim of her hat and warming her shoulders. Turning her face towards the sun, she pulled off the hat, and closed her eyes. After all, she thought, it is unlikely I'm going to die of skin cancer.

She was interrupted by someone shouting her name. It came from the direction of the Firhouse, and turning, she watched as Isobel made her way down the path towards the bench. Oliver trundled along gamely behind her, a plastic bag tied around his bandaged leg to prevent it from getting dirty. Since their awkward conversation a few days before Oliver's accident, Maggie had avoided asking Isobel about her plans. Over the past couple of weeks, she noticed how well the girl tended to the dog's injuries. Perhaps veterinary medicine wasn't as irresponsible a career change as she had previously thought. After all, children and animals had many similarities, and at least with animals you didn't have to interact with their parents. Even if things didn't work out for Isobel in veterinary medicine, she could probably go back to school counselling. If that happened, it would take the girl a decade or more to recover financially. Maggie realized that she was looking at the situation as a parent might and checked herself. If the subject came up again, she would try to be more supportive.

Isobel sat beside her on the bench.

"I could see you from the Firhouse, Maggie. You're walking much better...better than Oliver, I'd say."

Maggie chuckled. "It was such a lovely day; I couldn't stay inside. Besides, I wanted to see how far I could walk. In a few weeks I should be able to make it all the way around the prairie."

They chatted amicably for a few minutes, Isobel bringing Maggie up to date on her latest sales accomplishments. Someone was interested in the library shelving, but they wanted it broken down into manageable segments. Isobel had negotiated a good price but needed help with the disassembly.

"The thing is, they're awkward. I really need two pairs of hands to do the job," she said, "and I don't want you to try to help me, 'cause I know you'll say you can." She gave Maggie a mock stern look.

"Why don't I call Vic and see if he can come over to help you. He works during the day, so it would have to be an evening or weekend. Would you be able to stay late one evening? I'm happy to pay you overtime, and for once, you could eat the dinner you so nicely prepare for me. Maybe Vic would appreciate a good meal too."

"Vic's the guy who mows the fire breaks, isn't he?"

"I forgot, you haven't met him yet. You'll like him."

For some reason, Maggie *wanted* Isobel to like Vic. The two young people were, in their own way, essential to her current living situation.

"Vic's been coming here forever. His father did a lot of work on the cabin over the years. He built the Firhouse too."

Isobel looked over at Maggie, her eyebrows raised.

"Yeah. Carl was a really skilled carpenter. Vic used to cycle over after school and help his Dad or come down here to fish. The family lived farther up the valley. Then the parents got divorced, sold the house and Vic went to live with his mother in town. That was a rough time for him and he sort of went off the rails." Maggie paused, shaking her head from side to side.

"Carl asked us if we could help—come up with some work to keep the lad busy after school. He got in with a bad crowd and his parents were terrified he'd end up in jail. It was Alan who came up with the idea of having Vic stain the barn. It was a huge job that took up all of the summer, but it seemed to work. Carl says we turned Vic's life around. I give all the credit to Alan. He used to spend a lot of time with the boy, talking to him, but more importantly, listening. Things hadn't been good at home for a couple of years, and it was a nasty divorce. Poor kid. He needed a different sort of father at the time, I suppose, and Alan was just that. He was such a lovely man."

Maggie paused for a moment. She could feel Isobel looking at her, waiting for the rest of the story. She continued.

"It all worked out in the end. Vic straightened out, graduated from high school and went to Michigan Tech to do a degree in construction engineering. He's got his own company now and seems to be doing well. Fortunately, he's never too busy to help me out. I'll call him when I get back to the house and see which evening works best for both of you."

"Sounds like a plan. I'm looking forward to meeting him," said Isobel.

As they walked back towards the cabin, Maggie stopped abruptly and turned to Isobel.

"I've been thinking: I'd like you to read the letters to me, the ones from Amherst."

The idea had come to Maggie the previous evening, and the more she thought about it, the more it appealed to her. Her eyesight was still not back to normal, and as the day progressed, her double vision became more pronounced, making reading an exhausting challenge. She couldn't imagine poring over each line with a magnifying glass. Isobel would be perfect. After all, those letters were written by a girl around her age. They needed a young voice to make them come alive.

Isobel looked at Maggie, a quizzical expression on her face.

"But those letters are private. Maybe there are things in them you'd rather I didn't know about. Like personal stuff."

Maggie laughed. "Look, if I was willing to tell my parents..." Her voice trailed off. "Don't worry. There's nothing in those letters that will shock you. You'll probably find them very boring. At any rate, I'll enjoy them more when I don't have to close one eye or struggle with a magnifying glass."

# Chapter 17

They sat together on the screen porch, Maggie in her favorite rocking chair and Isobel in an old love seat with faded green cushions. The girl had placed the tea tray on a low table beside Maggie where she could reach it easily. She poured a mug for each of them and Maggie helped herself to a slice of cake. Isobel looked at Maggie with a questioning tilt of her head before extracting the first envelope from the Shaker box. Opening the folded blue aerogramme, she began to read.

"Dear Mummy and Daddy, there is so much to tell you...."

Isobel read well, with a clear voice and an easy cadence. As Maggie had hoped, listening to the girl's voice elicited a far more colorful tapestry than when she had read the same letter. Memory is such a strange business, she thought. It can be triggered by any of the senses: sight, sound, smell, taste, touch, yet each of these portals accesses those memories differently, generating a plethora of overlapping stories, each with its own flavor and nuance.

As the words washed over her, she closed her eyes and allowed her mind to drift.

~

*It's no wonder I couldn't wait to leave Ireland. Still, it was a shock to step off the plane and realize that I was completely on my own. Two hundred million people and I didn't know one of them. In those first few days, literally nobody knew who I was, what I was doing, where I had come from or where I was going. Nobody cared. My new anonymity felt wonderful and at the same time terrifying.*

*That was the trouble with Ireland: everyone knew what you were up to, and inevitably it would get back to your parents. I was always hiding something from them, afraid that if they found out, they would tell me to stop. Maybe it was a holdover from the nuns in boarding school. The first word out of a nun's mouth was always "Stop that!" True, Daddy gave me a fair bit of leeway because he was a bit of a terror himself in his youth. But Mummy was strict. In her world there were things you could do, and things that were beyond the pale. In my case that was fraternizing with a boy from the wrong side of the tracks, Seán Reilly.*

*We met in my first week at university. I was taking four science subjects, with a busy schedule of morning lectures and afternoon labs. We had assigned seating in lectures, with nuns, priests and girls in the front two rows and all the lads behind. Labs were different though. In chemistry lab we were seated eight to a bench, four on either side. I was the only girl at the bench—not too surprising in those days when so few women took science courses. The boy sitting beside me was tall and broad-shouldered, with a mop of tousled hair and blue eyes hiding behind wire-rimmed glasses.*

*"Hello, I'm Maggie O'Connor," I said. We didn't shake hands in those days. He nodded. "Seán Reilly's my name. So where do you hail from?" With just those few words, I could tell that he came from Dublin. The ones who came from "down the country," me included, had culchie accents that were all over the place, distinct enough that you could tell county Kerry from Donegal and Cork from Cavan. I wasn't used to boys, and his all-boys secondary school hadn't given*

*him much exposure to girls. Still, he knew a lot more about chemistry than I did, so I often asked for help writing up my lab notebook. It didn't take much. We were ripe, and sure enough, within a few weeks we were head over heels in love, that "truly, madly, deeply" first love that takes your breath away and fills every ounce of your being. After six years in a cloister, I was ready to break any rule, just so long as I could be with Seán.*

*We must have been seen together in the city, wrapped around each other. Sure enough, the next time I went home for the weekend, my mother asked casually, "Are you doing a line with anyone?" It was the expression people used for dating in those days. I must have blushed. She told me that a neighbor had seen me with a young man, and that we looked to be close. For the next hour she probed skillfully, inquiring as to his background, what his father did, where he lived, where had he gone to school. I could sense her growing disapproval. He didn't come from one of Dublin's wealthy suburbs. He hadn't gone to one of the better private schools like Castleknock or Belvedere. His father was a plumber. His parents lived with their seven children in a two-bedroom cottage on the far north side of the city. In her eyes he was altogether unsuitable for me, or as she put it, "the wrong sort." It didn't matter that he was clever and ambitious and going to university just like me. It just wasn't acceptable and that was that.*

*"I'm going to have to tell your father about this," my mother said one Sunday evening as she left me to the train that would take me back to Dublin.*

*"But I've done nothing, Mummy. Honestly. We haven't." I could hear my voice rising in panic.*

*"That's got nothing to do with it. It's just a matter of time."*

*We stood side by side on the chilly platform, away from the other passengers in case they might eavesdrop. She turned to face me.*

*"Mark my words: I know those Dublin gurriers. They're all the same. They just want to get into your knickers and then they're off.*

*Well, let me tell you: I didn't bring you up to throw yourself away on someone like that." Her lips pressed together in a tight thin line.*

*"We haven't done anything. Daddy will believe me, even if you don't."*

*She knew I loved my father more than her, and she chose her weapon carefully.*

*"I am going to tell him that you and that boy are having intimate relations. Your father will be devastated and so disappointed in you. He'll never let that boy cross our doorstep. It's up to you. Either you stop seeing him or I tell your father."*

*She turned on her heel and walked down the platform towards the car park. I ran after her, crying, pleading, but she ignored me and drove away.*

*Intimate relations. It sounds ridiculous now. But at the time it was considered a heinous crime, at least in the eyes of my parents and their friends. Good girls were chaste. Good girls did not let boys do anything more than kiss and hold hands. Under no circumstances would a good girl let a boy go any further. Otherwise, she'd get a "reputation" and that would ruin her chances of ever finding a suitable husband. As I think about it now, it reeks of Jane Austin, yet this was the 1960s. All the same, I understand now how terrified my mother must have been that I'd get pregnant. She'd be shamed and shunned in our village, saddled with me and my bastard child for the rest of her life. Even if Seán agreed to marry me, my mother would be linked with his family forever, and that would never do. In those days an abortion was out of the question. You couldn't even buy a condom in Ireland, instead smuggling them across the border with Northern Ireland like you would heroin or cocaine nowadays.*

*Of all the miseries in my life, the worst was breaking up with Seán. I broke his heart and mine too.*

~

"Maggie, are you awake?" There was a hint of alarm in Isobel's voice.

"Of course, I'm awake." Maggie sounded irritated.

Folding the aerogramme carefully, Isobel replaced it in the box.

"Would you like me to read another one?"

Maggie didn't respond immediately. When she spoke, her voice was subdued.

"No. That's enough of memories for one day."

# Chapter 18

From the front room, Maggie had a bird's eye view of the barn. Over the past weekend, she'd watched as Vic and his crew systematically removed the old shingles, collecting them into tarps they had spread on the ground and transferring the lot to a dumpster that would be hauled away at the end of the re-roofing project. Today, sheets of plywood were being hauled up to the roof, and she could hear the staccato sounds of a nail gun. Vic and his helpers worked methodically, rarely speaking, their heads bent to the task. They looked up briefly when Isobel's car arrived, and Vic waved to her when she got out. She waved back and continued walking up to the cabin, Oliver at her heels.

Over morning coffee Maggie and Isobel discussed the schedule for the upcoming week. Maggie had an appointment with her financial planner in Madison and, although she was comfortable driving to the local village, she felt less confident in city traffic. There were meals to plan, grocery lists to make, laundry to do and all the other chores that go along with running a household. Isobel had questions for Maggie about some of the large framed pictures that were propped against the bedroom wall in the Firhouse. To Isobel's untrained eye some of the paintings looked valuable, and even if they weren't, the frames were potentially saleable. Whereas Isobel went to the local post office regularly to ship smaller items, she often arranged for pick-ups. There were two scheduled for this week, and she planned to stay late on those evenings.

"The place is going to be busy," remarked Maggie, "what with Vic and his crew working at the barn."

"I noticed." said Isobel. "Those guys work hard. They got a lot of work done over the weekend."

"I've been bringing them cookies and lemonade; I think it motivates them." Maggie chuckled.

"How about I bake some cookies this morning? We can have some with our tea this afternoon...tea and letters." Isobel smiled, waiting for Maggie's nod of assent.

Oliver shifted his position on the rug under the kitchen table, alert to any movement Maggie might make. As soon as she pulled a plastic bag from the recycling container behind the fridge, he leapt up and hopped towards the back door. Maggie called his name and he returned reluctantly, submitting to her inexpert wrapping of his bandaged leg.

"Is it too much for you: walking Oliver every day?" Isobel asked.

Maggie shook her head. "No, not at all. I enjoy it, and he gets me moving."

Her walk with Oliver each morning was one of Maggie's favorite activities. With both of her hands fully occupied with hiking poles, she couldn't manage a leash, and at first, she had worried that he would run off. Isobel reassured her that Oliver was the sort of dog who didn't like to lose sight of his human. Now, walking along the prairie path, Oliver made short forays into the long grass, but within minutes returned and resumed his lopsided gait a few steps in front of Maggie, avoiding her poles. Each day they walked a little further, their leisurely pace giving Maggie a chance to appreciate the diversity of her land. What had once been homogeneous corn fields were now a patchwork of distinct soils, each with its own microclimate, flora and fauna. Walking up a slight incline, to her right she could see a stand of reed canary grass in the wet and shady area below. To her left were tufts of tall bluestem grass interspersed with an occasional bull thistle. Walking a little farther, Maggie stopped to admire the swathes of wild bergamot that colonized the drier, sunny areas. Here and there a tall stem of mullein emerged from the sea of purple. It was magnificent. She had taken to carrying a well-worn field guide to the wildflowers of Wisconsin in her pocket and stopped at each bench along the path to look up some new discovery. Her favorite bench stood in a shady spot, directly across the prairie from the cabin. From here she could see the barn, nestled securely at the base of the sandstone bluffs with the Firhouse partially hidden behind it, the pond to her left, and the pine woods and the tree-covered hillside in the distance. This was where she found solace each day, closing her eyes and allowing the sounds and smells of the land to envelop her.

Her meditation was interrupted by the sound of a nail gun coming from the barn. Looking up at the sun, she estimated it was almost noon. She had almost made it to the halfway point, a cause for celebration. Calling to Oliver, she turned and retraced her steps.

A rich smell of baking escaped from the cabin as she opened the door. A batch of oatmeal and coconut cookies were cooling on the kitchen counter.

Maggie gestured towards the cookies. "I can take these down to the guys, if you like. They usually take their lunch break around now." She added, "I'll be sure to tell Vic they were your idea."

Isobel blushed and Maggie pretended not to notice. She wondered whether Isobel had taken a fancy to Vic. They seemed to get along well, ever since that first time when he helped her break down the library shelving. The three of them had dinner together afterwards and Vic seemed quite taken by Isobel's cooking skills. Since then Maggie had noticed that Vic came to mow earlier in the evenings, usually coinciding with when Isobel finished work. Perhaps she was imagining an attraction, but Maggie wasn't above a bit of match-making. As far as she knew, neither of them was in a serious relationship.

The guys were sitting on the grass under a pine tree, their lunch pails open.

"Good timing," said Vic, as Maggie placed the plate of cookies on a nearby stack of shingles.

There was a mischievous glint in her eye as she said, "It was Isobel's idea. She made them. I'm just doing the delivery."

The mid-day hum of insects was interrupted by a volley of sharp sounds that echoed in the valley.

"That's not a nail gun, is it?" asked Maggie, looking up towards the roof.

"Nah. That's been going on all weekend," said one of the workmen nonchalantly. "I think one of your neighbors must be sighting in a gun, or maybe he's just target shooting."

He pointed to the hillside behind the barn. "I think it's coming from over there." He helped himself to a cookie.

"Tell Isobel, these are great cookies!"

As she chatted with Vic and his crew, the staccato sound of gun shots continued, each volley followed by a brief pause before resuming. By now she had worked out where they were coming from: Bill Breunig's property. She was certain he was doing this deliberately, telling her that he owned a gun and was entitled to use it as he pleased. She tried to push the thought aside. After all, he was within his rights. But this was intimidation, pure and simple.

# Chapter 19

Later that afternoon Isobel found Maggie on the porch. The box of letters was carefully positioned on the low table between them, Maggie's unspoken invitation to Isobel that she was ready to resume.

"You must have really enjoyed living in Amherst," Isobel said as she opened the folds of the aerogramme.

Maggie didn't answer. Instead, she sat back into her rocking chair and closed her eyes, inviting Isobel to begin reading. As Maggie listened to the log of her daily activities in Amherst, she couldn't help but marvel at the energy she had all those years ago. Busses were infrequent, and with no car, or even a bicycle, she hitchhiked everywhere. People who stopped to give her a ride went out of their way to help her, and she made friends easily, her Irish accent proving to be quite an asset in the Commonwealth of Massachusetts.

Every few minutes Isobel glanced over at Maggie, who despite an outward appearance of sleep, was listening attentively. Maggie often smiled and sometimes laughed aloud at a particular anecdote. Occasionally, she asked Isobel to repeat a sentence or to remind her of the date on the aerogramme. It seemed to

Maggie that Isobel too was enjoying this vicarious adventure into her past.

"Tell me about hitchhiking. Didn't you ever worry about... well, being raped?"

Isobel's question startled Maggie and brought her back to the present with a jolt.

She considered carefully before answering. After all, for Isobel's generation, hitchhiking was tantamount to asking to be sexually assaulted.

"Hitchhiking was so normal then. I'd been hitchhiking for years, not just in Ireland but all over Europe. Yes, there were a few times when I had to tell a driver to stop and let me out, but for the most part it was great. Mind you, in Greece my girlfriend and I used to toss a coin to see which of us would have to sit beside the driver and deal with his roving hands." She chuckled at the memory. "Ninety-nine percent of the time people were incredibly nice. I'd ask them about themselves and listen to their stories. You learn a lot when you're stuck in a car with a stranger for hours on end."

"Nobody hitchhikes nowadays," said Isobel shaking her head. Maggie could hear the self-righteousness in her voice.

"That's because your generation has been brought up on a diet of fear. From day one your parents coddle and protect you from everything: germs, falling off your bicycle, tripping on a step, getting out of a car, crossing the road... Then it moves on to strangers, bogey men. They don't warn you about the things that are really scary: climate change, corporate greed."

"But aren't you ever afraid of living out here on your own, Maggie?" The question was worded carefully.

Maggie looked directly at Isobel, making sure the girl made eye contact with her. Above all, she wanted to reassure this young woman that life should not be lived in fear.

"No," she said emphatically. "I *refuse* to be afraid. When I first moved out here, I wasn't married or even seeing anyone.

Friends would tell me I should have a gun in the house—just in case. I thought about it, but I didn't grow up with guns. I just couldn't see myself deliberately shooting someone. Instead, I decided to adopt the attitude that everyone who came up the driveway likely had a good reason. That philosophy has served me well. Most people are kind."

An image of Bill Breunig flashed through her mind, but Maggie ignored it.

~

Slowly, the Amherst letters had taken on a subtly different tone. Maggie could hear her younger self sounding more confident, more assertive, more adventurous. It was as if the recently-arrived immigrant had begun to leave her old life behind and turned to embrace the experiences her new life had to offer. Occasionally, Isobel interrupted the narrative, and Maggie enjoyed these digressions for they gave her an opportunity to think about the vast differences between Ireland and America in the sixties. It was hard to explain this to a child of the millennium; theirs had always been a fully connected, homogenous world.

"What was the big deal with pizza?" Isobel asked, looking over the top of the blue aerogramme in Maggie's direction, a puzzled expression on her face. A whole paragraph of the letter she was reading had been dedicated to this culinary miracle.

Maggie laughed. "I know it's hard for you to imagine a time without pizza, but honestly, I'd never eaten one. I hadn't even heard of it. The first pizza I ever had was in Amherst."

A look of astonishment came over Isobel's face. "You mean you didn't have pizza in Ireland? But Ireland is in Europe, and pizza is Italian. How come?"

"Ireland wasn't in Europe then, not really. This was before the EU, before McDonalds, before Starbucks. Life was very simple then. We didn't have many choices."

Maggie frowned as she tried to articulate why pizza had made such an impression.

"I think it was the shock of discovering that you could make a telephone call and within twenty minutes a hot pizza would turn up on your doorstep. In Ireland we had milk and bread delivered every day but not *hot* food. Nobody would have dreamed that something like that could happen in the future. When Jeff said he'd call out for a pizza, it was like a magic trick. I was gobsmacked."

Isobel continued to read, moving on to a paragraph about a potluck dinner that Maggie had been to with her new friends, graduate students in her department. This time it was Maggie who interrupted, at pains to help Isobel understand the chasm that existed between life in Ireland and America at that time.

"The whole concept of a potluck dinner was foreign to me. I had never even heard the word "potluck." In Ireland we used to get together with friends at a pub. I suppose our flats—apartments—were just too cold to think of entertaining. At least you'd be warm in a pub."

Maggie gave a chuckle. "On the way home, if we had some spare cash, we'd stop at a chipper, a fish and chip shop. Fish and chips were wonderful! You'd be salivating as you stood in the queue, sucking in the smells, and when you were finally handed your order, the whole thing wrapped in newspaper..." She inhaled deeply as if she were tasting the meal.

"Those fish and chips were the best. You'd be stinking of vinegar, and your hands would be greasy, but your belly would be smiling."

"Did you go back to Ireland often?" Isobel asked.

It took Maggie a while to reply and by then her tone had changed.

"I've not been back to Ireland in a long time. I'm not counting my parents' funerals. Those trips were as brief as I could make them."

Isobel waited. She was accustomed to these periods of silence when Maggie wandered back into her own thoughts.

~

*I've had a love-hate relationship with going back to Ireland all my life. After that first time, I didn't go back for almost five years. The thing is, I always felt that I had to compensate somehow for leaving my parents, for emigrating. And I couldn't. Nothing could do that. I couldn't face them, so I stayed away. After the first Christmas when I promised I'd come home and changed my mind, it became easier and easier not to go back. I missed Ireland though. Tír grá— it's like an ache in your bones. It eats at you and there's only one way to rid yourself of it. After a few years living in Wisconsin, I thought I was ready.*

*It was Christmas. I remember sitting at the bar in the international terminal at O'Hare Airport for an hour or two before my flight, nursing a glass of wine, dreading the days to come. The arrivals hall at Dublin airport was a scene of joyful chaos. I read somewhere that a million people come home to Ireland for Christmas. I scanned the waiting crowds and saw my father's face. He was by himself and for a moment I worried that something had happened to Mummy. He didn't see me at first, then his eyes lit up. I could see the tears starting as he wrapped me in the familiar hug that I had missed so much.*

*"There you are! You're looking grand. Your mother has been fussing around like mad for the past week. She'll be so pleased to see you. C'mon now, give me your bags and we'll get going."*

*And as I followed him to the car, he turned every minute or so to look at me, as if to make sure I really was there, that it wasn't a dream.*

*It's true what they say about Ireland being green. On the drive home, I couldn't help staring out the window at the range of that single color. At least forty shades. Fields looked tiny by comparison with Wisconsin, filled with grazing cows and sheep, something I had forgotten was normal in winter. Daddy chatted about people I used to know, but I couldn't connect. Five years is a long time. It wasn't that I had lost interest as much as realizing none of those people really mattered in my life any more. I didn't belong.*

*My mother was waiting at the front door to greet me. For the rest of the visit I'd come and go by the back door, but this arrival was special.*

*"Here you are at last. You're looking well."*

*We hugged awkwardly, and she ushered me inside more like a guest than her daughter. But I was her daughter, and she had to remind me.*

*"You've lost a little weight. It suits you. But I don't like that haircut. It makes your face look thin."*

*Dinner that evening was beef stew with boiled potatoes and cabbage. I can almost taste it now—that and the apple tart that followed used to be my favorites when I lived in Dublin and would go home for Sunday dinner. They were so happy to have me home. That evening I claimed jet-lag and went to bed early. Nothing had changed in my bedroom. I climbed into the bed I had slept in all of my life, pulled the covers up over my head and counted the days until I could leave.*

# Chapter 20

Maggie lay in bed staring at the ceiling. There was no hope of getting to sleep. She shifted uncomfortably every few minutes, trying to find a position where the pain in her lower back and abdomen wasn't so severe. Her mind was in turmoil with memories battling to the surface. She should have stopped Isobel reading the letters when she had the chance and gone back to her tidy, sanitized version of that time in Amherst. Instead, she had allowed the girl to open a tiny crack in the eggshell, and now it was leaking uncontrollably.

That afternoon, Maggie had listened with pleasure to Isobel's enthusiastic young voice as she read a letter written in late March. Spring had finally arrived in Amherst, and the young Maggie had bought a second-hand bicycle. A professor in the Zoology Department Gordon Marshall suggested she might enjoy the pottery class he was teaching, and as she couldn't think of a good excuse without sounding rude, she agreed. In the letter she gushed about the class, devoting precious paragraphs to describing it in detail. Twice a week the group met at the local community center, which was close enough that she could cycle there from her lab. The other students in the class were an interesting mix of university and non-university types, "town and gown" as they would have said back in Dublin. When the class ended, the instructor threw a party at his house and invited everyone to come. It was a potluck, but he would be providing the drinks.

$$\sim$$

*I remember that party as if it were yesterday. The house, a ramshackle old place in the country, was several miles from Amherst so I hitched a lift. A large crowd was milling around in the kitchen when I arrived, and I recognized a few of their faces. But the majority must have been friends and neighbors of Gordon, people I'd never met before. I got a glass of wine and sat on a tall stool in a corner of the kitchen, just watching. I was just about to sneak away when Gordon called for everyone's attention. The sauna was fired up and ready, he said, pointing in the direction of the garden. I'd never been in a sauna before and was curious. All the same, somewhere in the back of my mind a tiny alarm bell was ringing. Sure enough, when Gordon said something about leaving your clothes on the bench outside and grabbing a towel, I remembered. You were naked in a sauna. I thought about it for a few minutes, but in the end, I put on my coat and followed the others into the garden. After all, it would be another new experience, and besides, nobody in Ireland was ever going to know that I took my clothes off in front of a pile of strangers.*

*Gordon led the way, carrying a paraffin lantern so that we could see the path. After a hundred feet or so, it angled downhill towards a stream. I could hear it burbling over the excited chatter of voices. Walking another fifty feet, the smell of wood smoke was getting stronger. The path ended abruptly and we were in clearing by the riverbank with the sauna in front of us, its chimney pumping out smoke into the crisp air. Illuminated by a paraffin lantern on a pole near the entrance, the building was little more than a wooden shed. On one side of the building, a row of rough pegs stuck out from the wall, with clothes hanging from some of them. A pile of towels was stacked neatly at one end of a long wooden bench.*

*Everyone seemed to know what to do. People began undressing as if it were the most natural thing in the world. One by one, they hung their clothes on a peg, grabbed a towel and disappeared through a small wooden door on the opposite side of the sauna. I waited until everyone had gone inside and began to undress. It felt so strange, taking off my clothes in the middle of a forest, but it was freezing, so I didn't waste any more time thinking about it. I opened the door. It was dark and I couldn't see where I was going. I hesitated, even as a wave of dry heat swept over my body.*

*"Close the bloody door!" someone shouted, and I pushed it shut quickly behind me.*

*My eyes gradually adjusted to the gloom. I was in a tiny space, no more than ten by eight feet, with a boxy iron stove occupying one corner. Facing it were two tiers of wooden benches, like bleachers in a gymnasium.*

*"There's a space here," a male voice said, waving towards a gap between two shapes on the lower bench. Again, I hesitated and the same voice added, "put your towel underneath your butt or you'll burn your ass off." I did what he said.*

*It was a surprisingly intimate, yet anonymous, space. The walls and ceiling were covered with wood except for a single, large skylight in the roof through which I could see stars. Beside the stove there was a wooden bucket, and every so often someone would dip a ladle into it and sprinkle water onto the pile of stones on top of the stove. When that happened, a brief blast of hot moist air passed me and wafted up to the upper bleacher where people gasped their appreciation.*

*The conversation was scintillating. It was as if all verbal inhibitions fell away with peoples' clothes, and the talk was non-stop. The topics ranged widely, with words like "algorithm," "neoclassical," "theoretical shift," "biodiversity" floating around in the darkness. This was the most thrilling thing I had done in America. Here I was, thousands of miles from home, feeling like a sophisticated worldly adult in this group of fascinating people. Someone started to massage my shoulders. Whoever it was, their hands were firm but at the same time gentle. It felt incredible and for a minute I closed my eyes and just gave in to the pleasure. Someone brought a bucket of snow in, and this was passed around, with people taking handfuls and rubbing it over their bodies. I rubbed some snow over my breasts and the shock of the cold snow on my hot skin was like nothing I had ever experienced.*

*I began to feel a little light-headed.*

*"Which direction is the stream?" I asked, standing up and wrapping the towel around my body.*

*"I'll show you," came the voice of my anonymous masseur. He took hold of my hand, led me out of the sauna and we ran downhill to the stream.*

*"The best spot is over here," he said, pulling me towards where the bank sloped gently to a natural pool. The water was freezing and I gasped in shock, sure that my heart was going to stop.*

*"Yeah. It'd freeze the balls off a brass monkey," he said in a broad Yorkshire accent.*

*"I'm Tim. Who are you, then?"*

This is where she should have stopped, told Isobel to put away the letters, and burned all of them later that evening. But instead she had allowed the girl to continue reading. And now it was too late.

*It was Tim's idea to go to Montreal, but I was more than willing. Maybe I hoped that the weekend together in Canada would move things to the next stage. Tim reminded me of fellows I knew in Ireland, easy to get along with, full of charm and banter. I missed that. In the four months I'd been in Amherst, I still hadn't heard from my boyfriend back in Ireland. It was time to move on.*

*Instead, I got pregnant.*

*I've buried that fact for nearly sixty years. Nobody knows about it, not even my current doctor. The people who knew back then... well, they're either dead or I've lost touch with them. Besides, what would they remember? That they once knew a stupid Irish girl who got pregnant?*

*I am amazed at how well I've managed to forget it. Not just suppress the memory but erase it. And I'm not sure why I'm allowing myself to remember it now. Why do I need to open that Pandora box, pull out all the pieces and examine them one by one.*

*As I listened to Isobel reading those letters today, it was as if I was watching a movie about myself, knowing that something bad was about to happen. Yet, even as I was thinking that, another part of my mind—the sensible part—was reassuring me that the movie has a happy ending. I've had a great life.*

*After the weekend in Montreal, I knew that Tim was just a fling. His postdoc was coming to an end and he had a faculty job lined up back in England. He would be leaving Amherst in August, and he wasn't the sort of fellow for a long-distance relationship.*

*It wasn't as if I was stupid about birth control. I'd been on the pill in Ireland and brought a couple of extra month's supply with me to America. But with no boyfriend in the picture, I hadn't got around to renewing the prescription. For some reason I didn't menstruate when I was taking the pill, so I never noticed that my period was late. The little bit of nausea I felt every so often I put down to foods that I wasn't accustomed to eating. My breasts were tender, but I blamed Tim for that.*

*I must have been ten weeks pregnant when it finally dawned on me what was going on. I got two letters that day, one from my mother and the other from my best friend in Ireland. Catherine and I emerged from Catholic boarding school at the age of seventeen fundamentally ignorant about sex. We guarded our virginity judiciously for a few years, but it was an uphill battle. When the pill became available in Ireland, she and I found a young doctor who had divested himself of his Catholic scruples and was willing to help us control our periods, as he euphemistically phrased it. Catherine got married, and when I left Ireland, she was trying to start a family. The first line of her letter was a single word: "Pregnant!!!!" The rest of the letter was filled with details of every symptom she was experiencing: nausea, tender breasts, mood swings, fatigue. My mouth went dry as a horrible idea started to form in my brain. Going back over the timeline, the weekend in Montreal, it all fell into place. My hands were trembling as I slid Catherine's letter back into its envelope and put it on the counter. Beside it lay the letter from my mother, unopened, but already shouting at me. I ran to the bathroom and vomited.*

# Chapter 21

Rain thrummed on the skylights of the living room and lashed against the windows. The sky pulsed with lighting flashes, followed almost immediately by loud cracks of thunder. At least the barn is secure, Maggie thought. With a new roof, it had the air of a tramp who has just been given a hand-me-down expensive overcoat. She felt a tremendous sense of accomplishment. It was a magnificent structure, even if it looked somewhat disheveled underneath the pristine shingles. Since her accident, Maggie had felt a growing sense of urgency; there were so many projects that needed to be completed around the place, and time was running out. She asked Vic to find someone who could paint the board and batten siding. With a cheeky grin, he said it might be difficult to find someone as cheap as the last person who did the job. Maggie was quick to remind him that she wouldn't be providing lunches.

Summer storms had always terrified Maggie's dog, but Oliver seemed indifferent to the spectacle, content to lie quietly on the carpet between Isobel and Maggie's feet. Isobel had just finished reading a letter in which Maggie was explaining to her parents where her salary came from. It sounded as if she was trying to reassure them that, despite her fellowship ending in August, she would get paid through the end of the year.

Maggie had forgotten about the terms of her fellowship, that she left Ireland with no more than eight months of a guaranteed pay check. Had they known it at the time, her parents would never have allowed her to emigrate. They came from a generation that craved security, having lived through the Depression and the Second World War. "Get a job with a pension," was the advice she got from her mother when she graduated from college. Instead, she enrolled in a PhD program, postponing the coveted job-with-a-pension yet again.

Isobel looked up from reading the aerogramme. "Did you know what you were going to do when you finished your postdoc?"

The question took Maggie aback, and she considered for a few minutes before replying. Once again, here was the dilemma: How to phrase her answer so that it might help Isobel with her own future? Since their emotional conversation several weeks ago, Maggie had not asked Isobel about her plans for the fall or if she was still determined to become a veterinarian. She rubbed her thumb back and forth across the scar on her wrist before replying, choosing her words carefully.

"The thing is, when I left Ireland, I knew I had a safety net. No matter what happened, I could always go home."

She was surprised to see tears welling up in Isobel's eyes. The girl brushed them away with her fingers and fumbled in her pocket for a tissue. Her hand reappeared, empty. She sniffled and straightened her shoulders.

"Sorry Maggie. I don't know what's wrong with me today. I must be getting my period."

Maggie waited.

In a strangled voice Isobel said, "The thing is...I don't have a home like that anymore. Not in Canada or New Zealand.... I've got nowhere to go."

She balled her hands into tight fists and used them to wipe away the cascade of tears that was now flowing down her face.

Maggie looked at the sobbing girl and tried to understand her anguish. She had felt something like this once, but it had been so long ago. In a soft voice she said, "It'll be all right. I promise. It happens to everyone eventually. You learn to keep home in your heart, I suppose. It doesn't have to be a place."

Isobel nodded. She had composed herself and now looked down at the aerogramme, searching for her place.

Maggie's voice took on a more forthright tone. "Look. I had no intention of going back to Ireland with my tail between my legs. When I left, I knew I'd get paid until the end of August, so I started to look around for some other source of funding. That would have been about the time I wrote that letter, towards the end of April. I was starting to come up with a back-up plan."

She looked at Isobel pointedly, emphasizing each word. "Everyone should always have a back-up plan."

Isobel returned her gaze evenly. "So, did it work out? Your back-up plan, I mean."

"Well, I'm here now, amn't I?"

 

~

 

*Back-up plans. What a joke. Still, you learn to make them when you discover you're pregnant, alone and in a foreign country.*

*I thought I was pregnant once before, at university in Dublin. When I left boarding school, I didn't know much about sex because the nuns tore those pages out of our science textbooks. Eventually, I got around to losing my virginity, though it took a few years. When it finally happened, he withdrew before ejaculating. Coitus interruptus. The Latin name sounded so reassuring, but I knew it was a risky business. No pill, no condoms, but we kept doing it. All the same, I couldn't believe I was that unlucky. When I missed my period, I wanted to die, just like the thousands of other unmarried*

*Irish girls who made the same discovery every year. My boyfriend knew about the underground railroad to England to get an abortion. I'd get the 46A bus from Dublin to Dún Laoghaire, take the overnight ferry to Holyhead on the Welsh coast and get a connecting train to London. Someone would meet me at Euston Station, bring me to the clinic and stay with me for the next two days. All I had to do was come up with a plausible lie for my parents as to why I wouldn't be home for the weekend. My boyfriend's brother offered to loan us the money, 300 pounds sterling. It was all so straightforward that I've no memory at all of being worried. In the end, it was a false alarm. But I knew the way. My back-up plan.*

*This time there was no underground railroad. I found where the student health office was located on campus and went there the next day at lunchtime. The waiting room was littered with pamphlets about unprotected sex, depression and suicide. In those days there wasn't much literature about drugs. I asked to see a nurse, and after a few minutes, was shown into a small examination room. The nurse came in and before she had a chance to speak, I blurted out, "I think I'm pregnant" and burst into tears. She listened as I described the symptoms, did a brief physical exam, and agreed that it was possible. I would need to take a pregnancy test, and she made an appointment for me at a clinic in Northampton that afternoon. Back at my lab, I made some excuse and left. This time I took the bus; it took a lot longer than hitchhiking, but I didn't feel like talking.*

*Two days later, I went back to the student health office to get the results. The nurse was surprisingly gentle when she told me that the test was positive. With over forty thousand students at the university, she must have been accustomed to delivering this news. I said I wanted to get an abortion. Her reply came as a shock. "It's not clear how far along you are," she said. "You may be past the first trimester, and abortion is only available up to twelve weeks in the Commonwealth of Massachusetts. You'll need to get an ultrasound. Springfield is the nearest hospital where they do it. I'll try to get you in as quickly as possible."*

*She left the room to make the call while I tried to think rationally. It had never crossed my mind that I might not be able to get an abortion. This was America after all: the country where everything was possible. Little did I know. My mind was racing, calculating and recalculating the number of weeks between Montreal and when I could get an appointment in Springfield. The nurse returned with a date, five days later. This time I borrowed Jeff's car.*

*The Obstetrics and Gynecology unit at the Springfield hospital reminded me of the hospital in my home town in Ireland. It felt Catholic and clean and orderly, with glossy photographs of smiling mothers and pudgy-faced babies on the walls. I didn't smile, and the dark circles under my eyes must have given it away. Or the absence of a wedding ring. Another examination room, another nurse, followed by the ultrasound technician. They didn't even bother to take my vital signs, just asked me to pull down my pants. The technician rubbed jelly over my abdomen and went to work, his face a mask of inscrutability. Five minutes later he set the probe aside and gave me a towel to clean myself. Then he told me that I was in the second trimester, around fourteen weeks of gestation.*

*Until that moment, I hadn't allowed myself to think past the ultrasound. I began to sob uncontrollably.*

*"Oh God, Oh God, what am I going to do?"*

*The nurse said I should wait, and a doctor would come to see me soon. For the next hour I was unable to think beyond the fact that I had ruined my life. I wanted to die.*

*The door opened abruptly and an older man with thin greying hair and a dour face came in. He came close, too close for comfort, and looked down at me. I could see him thinking... judging... His look said everything: I was an irresponsible slut who deserved everything that was coming to me.*

*"You think you can come over here from Ireland, have your fun and just walk away? Well, you can go back where you came from and take your bastard with you. Do you even know who the father is?"*

*Before I could say anything, he jabbed his finger at me.*

*"You have sinned in the eyes of God. Indeed, you have sinned twice over. I'm told you want an abortion. Well, God has seen fit to save that child in your womb."*

*"I don't want the baby," I said, tears streaming down my face. "It'll ruin my life."*

*"Children are a gift from God. How dare you go against his wishes."*

*He was shouting now, his face getting redder.*

*I stood up to face him. My voice sounded shaky as I said, "I'm not going back to Ireland. I'm going to have the baby here and give it up for adoption."*

*He looked me up and down as if I were a piece of chattel. His eyes were cold and vengeful as he spat out, "I assure you we will find somebody better suited to be a mother."*

# Chapter 22

"Where are we now? June? July?" Maggie asked.

Isobel turned the blue aerogramme over and checked the postmark. "July 15th," she announced.

She relaxed back into the hammock on the screen porch, pushing an outstretched toe against the floor to maintain a gentle momentum. The persistent hum of insects filled the air, punctuated by a horse whinnying at the stables across the road. In the distance, a lawnmower droned interminably. Maggie glanced down at Oliver. His new favorite place to sit was at the edge of the screen porch, where, from a height, he could survey the driveway and beyond it, the pond and prairie—his domain.

Isobel began to read. "Dear Mummy and Daddy…"

The tone of this letter was different from the previous ones, almost businesslike. It described a discussion she had with the chairman of the department about the possibility of teaching in the fall semester when her fellowship came to an end. He suggested that she teach Introductory Zoology, an evening class that met twice per week. She wrote that she was delighted to get this opportunity—it would look good on her curriculum vitae. But it was going to take a lot of time. Each class consisted of a lecture followed by a two-hour laboratory, which, she explained to her parents, meant that she would need to spend as many hours preparing in advance as teaching. At the same time, she wanted to continue working on her research project. It was important to get a publication from this year in America, especially when she applied for her next position.

Isobel read the next sentence. "I'm sorry, but I think you should cancel your September visit. I feel awful about this, but I just won't have any time to spend with you if you come to Amherst. I'll be stressed and won't be able to do my best at teaching or research, let alone show you around." In the next paragraph, Maggie wrote that she needed to send an application to the Immigration Office for a different visa, as the one in her passport did not allow her to teach. Unfortunately, it might take up to six months to get the new visa approved, during which she could not leave the United States. She would not be coming home for Christmas. She knew they would be disappointed, but there was nothing she could do about it.

Isobel looked over the blue sheet of paper at Maggie, her forehead furrowed. "If you ask me, your work-life balance shifted—towards work, I mean. Did something happen?"

"Why do you say that? Maggie's response was sharp.

"Well, it's just that you sound different in this letter, more serious or something. You're not writing about doing fun things, like pot luck dinners and pottery classes."

Maggie considered what Isobel had just said. She was right. The happy-go-lucky voice of the previous months was gone.

"I suppose reality happened. My fellowship was coming to an end, and I needed to make some money...."

If Isobel could hear the change in her voice, her parents must have too. They would have pored over that letter, and the previous ones, looking for any hint. But what would they have imagined? Nowadays it would be drugs or rape or getting in trouble with the law. But in those days...? Did they talk about it amongst themselves, share their disappointment at not seeing their daughter for another six months or more? Maggie could imagine her father reassuring her mother, telling her that it was how America worked: you had to make sacrifices to get on. But her mother wasn't so easily taken in. She was astute and knew her daughter well. She'd never say it to Maggie's father but she would have wondered was her daughter pregnant.

All at once the pleasure of the summer afternoon drained away, replaced by a profound feeling of sadness and loss. Her whole life felt worthless; all the good things she had done over the years since that time amounted to nothing. Looking down at the scar on her wrist, Maggie began to massage it.

"You know, when you are old, you get to look back at your life and take stock. The bottom line is you can't have it all. You always give up something." She sighed.

"Why can't you have it all?" Isobel asked, sounding like a petulant child.

Maggie shook her head slowly from side to side and her mouth tightened into a thin line.

"Nobody gets it all," she said dully.

Isobel persisted. "But *you* seem to have managed."

She looked at Maggie for confirmation. "You had a great career, a happy marriage. You've got a beautiful place here. People who care about you. You seem pretty healthy...well, except for the accident. What more could you want?"

Maggie realized she had no answer for Isobel, not unless she was willing to tell the truth. She looked down at the box of letters. Two almost-equal sized stacks faced each other: before and after.

"I was pregnant when I wrote that last letter," she said, pointing to the box.

Maggie hadn't planned to tell Isobel but the words slipped out. She listened to the sound of them as they drifted off into the afternoon. Such a long time ago, she thought. And what did it matter now to tell the truth? She heard the sharp intake of breath and looked up. Isobel's eyes were wide with shock. Before she had a chance to say anything, Maggie raised her hand to silence the girl. She would answer questions later but now she wanted to say the words she had kept to herself for over fifty years.

"I got pregnant the weekend I went to Montreal. When I found out, it was too late to get an abortion. The baby came that Christmas...and I gave it up for adoption."

Maggie felt breathless, light-headed, almost giddy. She had finally confessed. She looked at Isobel, who still had a stunned expression on her face.

She continued. "So, you were right. Something did change. You are the first person I've ever admitted this to."

She waited for some response, but Isobel said nothing.

"Once it was over, I decided to pretend it never happened. I left Amherst shortly afterwards and went to Germany. Eventually, I came to believe my own lie. Up to now, that is."

Isobel's expression was impossible to read.

"Was it a boy or a girl?"

"A girl. They took her away immediately, and I never saw her again."

Isobel began to cry silently, the tears rolling down her cheeks and dripping onto her shirt.

Maggie shrugged and spread her hands wide, the palms upturned in a gesture of resignation.

"There was nothing else I could do."

Isobel continued to weep silently.

"What are you crying about? I'm sure she had a happy..."

With a strangled voice Isobel shouted at Maggie. "You have no idea what it's like to be abandoned!" She spat the words out, her eyes blazing with anger.

Maggie was taken aback by the outburst.

"Look. I gave her up for adoption. She wasn't *abandoned*."

The word hung in the air between them, waiting for Maggie to take ownership of it.

Isobel got up from the hammock and wiped her wet cheeks with the back of her hand.

"I'll get your dinner ready," she said quietly, turning her back on Maggie and walking towards the kitchen.

# Chapter 23

Isobel didn't arrive the following morning at her usual time. Maggie was a little surprised, for the girl always called if she was going to be delayed. Today they planned to start on the next project: decluttering Maggie's cabin. Isobel's transformation of the Firhouse had been a relatively painless process, and Maggie hoped the same miracle could be achieved with her fifty-year accumulation of treasures. The weather had become hot and humid, so they were going to start in the basement, a root cellar carved into the sandstone hillside that was always cool in summer. Since the accident Maggie had avoided the basement as much as possible, and she looked forward to the opportunity to erase painful memories with something constructive. The afternoon would be punctuated by Isobel's now-familiar questions: What is this? When did you last use it? What would you do if it disappeared? Would it be useful to someone else?

She considered calling Isobel's cell phone but became distracted by the e-mail she was writing. An ex-student of hers, now a professor at a large university on the west coast, wanted some advice about mentoring one of his own graduate students. Maggie wrote authoritatively on the topic, pleased to be asked for her opinion and confident that her advice was valuable. She had always liked that part of her job, mentoring the scientists of the future. It was past noon when she finally pressed the "send" key. Glancing to the left of the computer screen, she noticed a message from Isobel in her inbox. Something must have come up. She clicked on the e-mail and began to read.

"Maggie, I think it's best if I don't work for you anymore. I'll be starting classes soon and won't have extra time. The Firhouse project is finished, and you're able to drive now and manage around the house. I've updated the spreadsheets and attached them. You can e-mail me if there is anything I've missed. Isobel."

The letter was stilted, as if longer sentences had been chopped up, leaving just the bare essentials. Nonetheless, Isobel's message was unambiguous. Stunned, Maggie stared at the computer screen for several minutes. She thought about calling the girl, but what would she say? Please come back. I'm sorry. But sorry for what? She struggled to recall the last conversation they had. It had been about work-life balance and the impossibility of anyone "having it all." There were no red flags there. But afterwards she had told Isobel about getting pregnant and giving up the child for adoption. That was when Isobel had started to cry, and more or less accused Maggie of abandoning her baby.

"I'm the one who has been abandoned," Maggie said aloud, slamming the lid of the computer. With growing irritation, she got up from her chair, marched into the kitchen and yanked open the door of the refrigerator. Each Friday she and Isobel planned dinners for the following week, with Isobel shopping for groceries in Madison before she came to the cabin on Mondays. The refrigerator shelves were stacked neatly with enough food for the rest of the week. Shutting the refrigerator door abruptly, Maggie looked around the kitchen, hoping to latch onto some unfinished task, a sign that the girl had been sloppy. With the exception of last night's dinner dishes, everything was spotless and in its place. She continued to look for something into which she could channel her anger. The laundry had been done the previous Friday, the house vacuumed, the kitchen floor washed. Everything was in order. What about money? Surely there was still some unfinished accounting. But with the exception of paying Isobel for the previous day's work, nothing was owed. Maggie made a mental note to send a check. There would be no letter enclosed, no pleasantries. If Isobel wanted to cut off communication, so be it.

"It's her loss," Maggie muttered. "I can manage just fine without her."

The phone rang, and for a moment Maggie hoped she would hear Isobel's voice leaving a message to say she was sorry, that she had changed her mind and would be coming to work tomorrow. At the end of four rings, she heard the usual anonymous click, but nobody left a message. The day stretched ahead of her with no purpose. It was too hot to go for a walk around the prairie. Any other day she and Oliver would have already taken their walk. By now she and Isobel would be sitting on the screen porch, the girl reading a letter aloud, breaking off every so often to ask Maggie to explain something. Or they would be poring over a spread sheet together, laughing at the possibility that someone might actually want to buy the object in question.

All the joy had drained from the day. Isobel's rejection hurt her to the core. Opening her computer, she read the e-mail again, searching for any hint as to why she had chosen to leave so abruptly. She remembered how Isobel had become upset when she told her about the pregnancy. But that was *my* issue, Maggie thought. If anyone should have cried, it should have been me. The girl was right about one thing: she could manage by herself now. She still hesitated before going down to the basement, holding tightly to the railing and counting the thirteen steps aloud so as not to miss the last one. Her daily walks with Oliver had restored much of her previous strength, but more importantly, had helped her regain confidence. Besides, she reminded herself, the whole arrangement with Isobel had been temporary. Even so, she hadn't realized how dependent she had become on Isobel's cheerful presence around the place. It had started as a business arrangement, but over the past few months they had become friends, or so Maggie thought.

~

The week dragged by. It wasn't just Isobel's company, or the fact that she cooked and cleaned that made her absence so palpable. She had become indispensable to Maggie. She was a magician at anything to do with electronics, from upgrading software, to backing up files, to making the television work. Maggie had always kept a "to-do" list for the cabin, and over the past weeks, Isobel had systematically ticked off each item. She changed the batteries in the remote controls for the TV, made sure the flashlight beside Maggie's bed worked and tested the smoke alarms. The girl was methodical, going as far as to draw up a spreadsheet with a maintenance schedule for both houses on Maggie's computer.

Each day Maggie was reminded of her own shortcomings. In the past she could have unscrewed the water filter cartridge, but now she no longer had the strength. She had to ask one of her neighbors to carry bags of water softener salt to the basement from her car. Once there, she emptied the bags one scoop at a time. Each failure was one more reminder of how dependent she had become on the girl. After breakfast she sat at the kitchen table staring blankly into space. The thought of taking a solitary walk around the prairie held little appeal, and she had to force herself to go outside. She went through the motions of preparing a meal each afternoon, just as she would have done with Isobel but took little pleasure in eating it.

Maggie recognized that she was sinking into a deep depression. It had been the same when she was diagnosed with cancer and again when her husband died. On each of those occasions her doctor had recommended that she see a therapist, but she declined, believing firmly that time took care of most problems. This was different: She didn't have the luxury of time to get over this achingly sad separation. Isobel had come to represent many things in her life, but above all, the girl had become the grandchild she never had.

She tried to be analytical about the situation. What would a grandparent do if a favorite grandchild withdrew their affection? It had happened to friends of hers, and while it hurt, they distracted themselves by lavishing their affection on their other grandchildren who appreciated it. For the first time in days, Maggie had a plan. She might not have grandchildren, but she was rich in students. She decided that every day she would spend an hour or so writing to one of her ex-students. Letter-writing with friends had been a big part of Maggie's life, but recently their numbers were dwindling. In contrast, her ex-students were numerous, and she felt confident they would enjoy receiving a hand-written letter. By now her wrist was fully healed, and although her writing looked a little shaky, it was legible.

The telephone rang. Maggie lifted the hand set quickly and put it to her ear. It wasn't Isobel, and she suppressed an urge to slam the phone down without listening any further.

A familiar voice said, "Maggie. Is that you? It's Indra Hari."

"Hello Indra." Her tone was neutral.

"How are you doing, Maggie? It's been a while since we talked."

Maggie sighed audibly into the telephone. "I think I know why you are calling, Indra. I suppose Dr. Carney asked you, since I've been ignoring the messages his office keeps sending me."

Over the past twenty-five years, Maggie's primary care doctor had become a treasured friend. Originally from Calcutta, she had followed her physician husband to the United States where they both found jobs in Madison. The city was a good choice for them, with its cosmopolitan community and excellent schools. Their two children were now attending Ivy League universities, one studying law and the other medicine. Maggie had worried that Indra might retire soon, but the exorbitant fees at these two universities ensured that she would be working for several more years.

"Yes. Dr. Carney has been in touch. He's a very good oncologist, and I'd like you to follow up with him. I'm making it easy for you. I made an appointment for your CT scan, Maggie. It's next Thursday at eleven. That should give you enough time to organize a ride if you need one. It's at the hospital. You'll get a reminder on MyChart. And afterwards, I want you to go to the lab for a blood draw. We'll talk some more when the results come back." Her voice was stern. "You *know* this is important."

Maggie didn't answer immediately.

"Did you hear all of that, Maggie?"

"I'll be there. I promise."

"Good. We'll talk later then," Indra said with a satisfied note in her voice and hung up.

Maggie had been expecting this call. Indra was like a bloodhound, following up on every symptom even when her patients didn't, *especially* when her patients didn't. Many of these were elderly, and some of them genuinely forgetful. Others were like Maggie, avoiding the future. She had little doubt that the results of the CT scan were going to be ominous. Her weight had been dropping steadily since before the accident. With Isobel's cooking, she had barely managed to keep it steady, and now she could feel she was losing ground again. By the time she met with Indra, she'd be down another pound or two, and would get a scolding.

She eased herself into the rocking chair on the porch. She was accustomed to feeling stiff and sore, but the deep pain that filled her lower abdomen seemed to be present almost all the time now, and she could no longer pretend it was unimportant.

Looking over at the hammock, she remembered that it was Isobel who suggested hanging it here. The girl found it in a cupboard under the stairs while she was cleaning out the Firhouse and persuaded Maggie that it would be perfect on the porch in summer. Every day was going to bring a reminder of Isobel, Maggie realized, every day until the end. It wasn't just Isobel, though. The profound emptiness she felt now had its origin fifty-five years ago, when she left the hospital in Springfield.

# *Chapter 24*

Traffic was light on the highway as Maggie made her way in to Madison. School hadn't started yet, so the morning rush was much reduced. In a week or so, when the students returned from their summer break, things would be very different. It used to add fifteen minutes to her morning commute when she was still working, a daily irritant made tolerable only by listening to classical music on public radio. Today she drove in silence, thinking about what lay ahead. The results of her scan had come back, but Indra had insisted that they not discuss it over the telephone. Instead, she made an appointment for Maggie to meet with her and Dr. Carney.

As always, the hospital corridors were thronged with people. It was easy to identify the categories: the patients with worry written all over their faces and the staff with badges and business-like determination to get to where they needed to be. Maggie had spent many hours in this hospital over the years as a patient and a visitor. She knew her way around, despite its awkward lay-out, and found her way easily to the conference room where she was to meet with Indra. She knocked and opened the door tentatively, surprised to see so many people in the room. She recognized Dr. Carney, who stood up and shook her hand.

Her team had mushroomed. Indra introduced each of them with a brief description of their expertise. Besides the oncologist, there was a pulmonologist, rheumatologist, radiologist and hospitalist. The latter was a new title for Maggie, someone who could interpret and meld the disparate languages of the medical disciplines.

"You have an exceptional group of people who will be taking care of you," Indra said, looking across the round table at Maggie, who had taken a chair opposite.

"Now, let's review where we are." Turning to the radiologist, Indra asked, "Would you like to describe your radiological findings, Dr. Stang? Perhaps you could relate your findings to the scans that were taken when Maggie was admitted to the hospital last April."

For the next twenty minutes, each of specialists in turn gave their considered opinion as to Maggie's health or lack thereof. She already knew she was dying but understood that this was a process she had to submit to before her oncologist finally cut to the chase: Her cancer was advanced and her options limited. Nobody was willing to project a survival time, but it was clear that the index was months, not years. For now, she was managing but within weeks to months she would have considerably more pain. The treatment options were enumerated. The first line of defense was chemotherapy and various drug cocktails were available, each with their pros and cons. Dr. Carney went on to say that there might be a possibility of joining an ongoing clinical trial that was using a novel immunotherapy. The results of a recent clinical trial in Europe were promising. The rheumatologist and pulmonologist were particularly interested in side-effects and how they might be managed. The voices droned on and on. There was a time when Maggie would have found the discussion very interesting, asked a myriad of questions, even pushed back where appropriate. But she found herself almost indifferent to the conversation going on around her. At one point in the discussion someone must have asked her a question, for everyone in the room turned to look at her, waiting for an answer.

Without hesitation she said, "I'd like to think about this. I'll let you know what I decide."

Several of the white-coats started to talk at once, and she raised her hand to get their attention.

"Could I have a private word with Dr. Hari, please?" She looked around the table, meeting their surprised looks with a steely gaze.

Indra paused for a moment and then nodded. Turning to her colleagues, she spoke firmly, making it clear that the meeting was over.

"Thank you for coming here this morning. It's important to Maggie that we are all on the same page. I know you are very busy and anxious to get back to your other patients. I'll be in contact with you soon and we can go from there."

Maggie added a quiet "Thank you," as the white coats filed out of the conference room.

When the door closed, she turned to face Indra.

"Thank you for that." The two women were silent for a few moments.

Maggie spoke first. "I don't want to make any decision just now, but in all likelihood, I will do nothing. You have my living will on file. If you read it, you'll know that I don't want any heroic interventions at the end of my life. Between now and then, I really don't know what I want. I'll call you as soon as I have a plan. I'd like some advice on managing my symptoms when they start to get worse. I know there's going to be pain, nausea, shortness of breath, and likely a lot worse. But I'm fine for the present. I can manage with Ibuprofen and Tylenol...and alcohol." She gave a little laugh. "There's no point in going tee-total now, is there?"

Indra made a wry face. She came around the table, sat beside Maggie and took her hands.

"I re-read your directives earlier this morning. I promise I won't let you suffer, not now and not at the end. We can talk some more in a few days. Actually, we can talk at any time. You have my home number. Call me any time you want, day or night. But right now, the most critical thing is that you spend the time you have doing whatever is most important to you."

There were tears in Indra's eyes and Maggie felt small and frail as her doctor hugged her tenderly.

~

When Maggie got back to the cabin, she made a cup of tea and took it to the screen porch. So this is it, she thought, the real beginning of the end. She closed her eyes and for a moment wished that everything might end right now. She wasn't afraid of death. But dying was a miserable waste of time. And then there was the cabin, the land, all of her stuff. Would she be able to sort it all out in the next few months? Would she need to recruit a bevy of nurses, or should she consider moving to Cherrywood immediately? The questions tumbled around in her brain, leaving her exhausted.

What about suicide? Was that a possibility? In winter it was easy: You just got very drunk and wandered off into the woods, and by the time anyone came looking for you, it would be too late. Death from hypothermia was meant to be relatively painless. Mid-August presented a very different challenge. With the new laws in Wisconsin, she could walk into the local hardware store tomorrow and buy a handgun, no questions asked. But she knew she could never pull the trigger, no matter how bad things got. Some poor unfortunate would have to clean up the mess. Nor could she see hanging herself, at least not in the cabin—the ceilings were far too low. The barn was a possibility, but she didn't want to spoil the building for Vic. He'd probably be the one to discover her body and forever after carry that traumatic memory. Carbon monoxide poisoning was an old favorite in the 50s and 60s, but Maggie wasn't sure if unleaded gasoline still worked. Besides, she didn't have a garage. Her doctor was unlikely to over-prescribe sleeping pills or opioids at this time. But people still managed to find the right drugs. That was something she could look into. Like everything she had done throughout her life, she would approach this final challenge with logic and organization. At least for the present, *she*, not death, was in control.

With a sigh, she stood up and straightened her shoulders. She took her hiking poles and stepped out of the screen porch on to the grassy path leading towards the prairie. The late afternoon sun was still warm, but there was a hint of fall in the air. Looking up, she noticed that a few leaves at the tips of the maple trees were beginning to turn yellow. It struck her that she might not be able to do this for much longer—go for a walk. All the more reason to enjoy it today. At the first bench she paused, then sat down. For a few minutes she surveyed her land: the rippling expanse of tall prairie grasses and beyond it, sunlight shimmering on the surface of the pond. The air smelled of warm pines. Closing her eyes she could almost hear the snuffling sound of a dog. She smiled, remembering how Oliver would leap into the air and look around feverishly to get his bearings. She missed that ridiculous animal and Isobel too. But now was not the time to look to the past. From now on, every moment of the present had to be savored.

Continuing towards the pond, she stopped to look back at the cabin and barn. It was such a comforting sight. She wondered whether her predecessors, those pioneer settlers of the mid-1800s, felt the same way as they approached the end of their lives. More likely, had they been given the chance, they would have preferred a warm, comfortable apartment in the city, not a ramshackle cabin in the middle of nowhere. She walked on, her hiking poles making small indentations in the mowed grass. Rounding the farthest corner of her land, she looked back towards the barn, the roof of which was just visible above the prairie grass. There was a figure in the distance. It wasn't clear to Maggie whether they were on her land or Bill Breunig's, but she had no alternative but to walk in that direction. Coming closer she was relieved to see that it wasn't Bill. This person was short and thin, with a full head of hair. He held a small grey box-like device in his hand, which he looked at frequently, every so often pausing to write something on a pad of paper.

"Hello. Can I help you?" Maggie asked, when she was a few yards from the man.

He jumped in alarm, not having heard her approach.

"Thanks. I'm just taking some measurements. I don't think I'm trespassing." He spoke politely, as if he was accustomed to explaining what he did.

"No. I think you are on Bill's land, although they abut around here."

"Actually, I believe the county owns this piece." He gestured to an invisible line in the scrubby ground.

"What are you doing?" asked Maggie, her curiosity aroused.

"I'm a surveyor. I've been hired by Mr. Breunig, who has applied for a right of way through the county land."

Maggie was taken aback. "You mean Bill wants to put a road through here?"

"I believe so. It would come off the end of the gravel road over there." He pointed in the direction of Maggie's barn.

"But...but Bill already has access to his land from Old Settlers Road. Why would he want to come in this way?"

"I don't know. Maybe it's where he plans to put in a driveway to the development."

For a moment Maggie thought her legs were going to fold under her. Clutching at her poles, she steadied herself.

"Are you all right?" the man asked, sounding alarmed. "I have some water back at my car. I can go and get it."

"I'm okay, I'm fine. I just need to sit down for a while."

The man looked around, as if searching for a bench. Turning back to face her, he shrugged his shoulders.

"What do you mean, a development?" Maggie asked. Her voice was sharp.

"As far as I know, Mr. Breunig is planning to build six houses here."

Maggie felt as if someone had hit her with a sledgehammer.

The man continued nonchalantly. "He's hoping to break ground before winter."

"Do you know the name of the person in the county office who is dealing with this?"

"Yeah. His name is John Miller. I have his phone number back at the car. Do you want me to get it?"

"Yes. I want that number."

As she trudged back to the cabin, a piece of paper with a telephone number on it clutched in her hand, she thought of the line from *Hamlet*: "When sorrows come, they come not single spies, but in battalions."

# Chapter 25

"That bastard," Maggie shouted as she slammed down the phone. It was so much more satisfying to talk aloud than bottle these thoughts inside. She had spent the previous half hour talking with John Miller at the county offices in Madison. He had been reasonably helpful but guarded as to the outcome of Bill's application for a right-of-way. Bill had approached the county a couple of months earlier, requesting to buy the piece of land in question. He explained why he wanted it: to access his property from the gravel road shared by Maggie and several of her neighbors. He said that when he bought his land, his realtor led him to believe he would be able to buy the small sliver owned by the county, as it was too small to ever be approved for planning permission and therefore of no significant value.

Trying to control her fury, Maggie had pointed out that the county couldn't just pick and choose a buyer. By law they were required to have an open sale. Furthermore, they were required to notify the owners of adjacent parcels of land, and she had not been notified. Mr. Miller was initially taken aback by Maggie's vehemence, but when she described her recent interactions with Bill, that he had intimidated and threatened her, the man's attitude changed. He told her the county had not yet made any decision; they would be considering Bill's application in the coming weeks, and yes, she could lodge an objection to the right-of-way through county land, especially as it was adjacent to her property line. Maggie studied the plat map carefully. There were several choices for a right-of-way, but a worst-case scenario could have it pass within thirty feet of the Firhouse. She was certain this would be Bill's first choice.

One part of her wanted to curl up and crawl into her imminent grave. But that would only give Bill the satisfaction of getting his way. Her will had not been altered since after her husband's death. Four cousins in Ireland, now well into their 70s, would inherit everything. They all had children and grandchildren, and as nobody wanted to move to a log cabin in the wilds of Wisconsin, the property would be sold quickly. Bill would get it in the end.

"We'll see about that," she said. She remembered Indra's advice to 'do whatever is most important to you.' Thwarting Bill Breunig wasn't a very glamorous final project, but there was a certain satisfaction in coming up with a plan that would make it impossible for him to get his way. She didn't know any lawyers who dealt with property in Madison, but Alan's cousin had practiced law in the city, and he would surely be willing to help her find the right person for the job, someone who knew all the ins and outs of being an obstruction. There was no time to lose; she picked up the phone.

~

Vic came by that evening to mow the fire breaks. When he had put the mower back in the barn, she stepped out onto the deck and called to him to come up to the cabin. He pulled open the screen door a minute later, stepped inside and leaned down to give her a hug.

"Get yourself a beer from the fridge, and while you're at it, pour me a glass of wine. There's an open bottle in the refrigerator and you know where to find a glass."

He was back in a couple of minutes and handed her a glass of chardonnay. Taking a mouthful of cold beer from his bottle, he sat down with a satisfied sigh.

"How've you been, Maggie?"

"So-so," she answered indifferently. Listening to herself, the words sounded pathetic. She added quickly, "I'm grand," nodding her head for emphasis.

"Are you managing okay these days?" There was a pause before he added, "I know Isobel isn't coming around anymore."

He shifted awkwardly in his chair and for a moment looked away. She wondered how he found out. Neighbors, no doubt. They knew everything, although in this case they probably didn't know the "why." Neither did she.

"Is there anything I can do?" he asked. "I admit I'm not good in the cooking line," he smiled knowingly, "and maybe not too good at spreadsheets, but I can do all the other stuff."

"Thanks, Vic. You already do enough for me. I appreciate the offer, but you've got lots on your plate. I promise that if I really need something, I'll call you. Besides, I'm able to drive these days, and Julie and the other neighbors look in on me regularly."

They chatted for a while about Maggie's neighbors, Vic's business, the goings-on in the valley.

"There's something I need to talk to you about." Maggie's voice had taken on a serious tone.

She told him the whole story about Bill Breunig; his initial offer to buy her out, his threats and intimidation, and the right of way. She finished by telling him about the proposed housing development. Vic listened without interruption, his brow becoming more furrowed with every minute.

"I'm so sorry to hear this, Maggie, but I'm not surprised. He's a bad apple. Men like that think they're entitled to do anything they want."

There was a cold, hard edge to Vic's voice that Maggie had never heard before.

"Do you know something about him that I don't?" she asked.

"There's rumors. They say he did something like this in the Dells...bought a piece of land cheaply because it was landlocked, managed to get a right of way and then bribed the local planning office for a building permit. Looks like he's trying to do the same thing here."

Seeing the stricken look on Maggie's face, Vic added quickly, "I don't think the town board here would be so easy to bribe. I know a few of the folks on it and they're decent people. They don't want us to become another Wisconsin Dells, that's for sure."

He took a long pull on his beer.

"I'm of the same mind as you, Maggie—keep things as they are. I love this valley, and if I ever manage to buy a place here, I'll be sure to run for the town board. You can't be on the board unless you're a home owner. That's going to take me a few more years. I've already got a loan for the business, and I'm still paying back my student loans."

"Well, I have to do something. I can't just sit around and wait for it to happen. I refuse to have Bill Breunig speeding up and down my driveway, let alone a housing development in my backyard. Over my dead body. I'm going to get the best lawyer I can find in Madison and file objection after objection after objection. I don't care what it costs. In the meantime, I want you to talk to your friends on the town board."

As she listened to her outburst, Maggie could feel her energy returning. Indra was right: She had found a purpose.

"I've been thinking about the Firhouse.... I should rent it out. I think it would be prudent to have someone living there," she added.

Vic nodded. "You're probably right, especially if you plan

to go head to head with Bill. I'll ask around and see if anyone I know might be interested."

They stayed on the porch watching the sun slip behind the western hillside. As the temperature began to drop, Vic stood up to leave.

"You know I'd do anything for you, Maggie," Vic said softly. He looked down at the floor, his cheeks reddening. She thought he might cry and quickly stood up to give him an awkward hug.

"Thanks Vic. I know that."

He nodded and turned to leave. She watched him walk to his truck and was surprised when he didn't get in. Instead, he walked around the side of the barn in the direction of the Firhouse. Ten minutes later he reappeared, got into the truck and drove off. His detour might have been curiosity, but it was more likely a security check, she thought.

# Chapter 26

It was the Labor Day weekend, that unique American punctuation mark that brings an end to summer. Maggie had declined an invitation to a picnic in Madison hosted by old friends from her university days. Normally, she would have enjoyed the opportunity to catch up with colleagues, who she saw infrequently since retiring from the university. But since her diagnosis, she was beginning to take a more parsimonious approach to time.

On that morning's circumnavigation of the prairie, she had disturbed a deer with two fawns, all of which immediately disappeared into the tall grass. Watching their energetic leaps, she marveled at how effortlessly they moved, their white tails twitching at her approach. Every day, nature presented her with a surprise. She wasn't expecting any visitors today, and so the car that made its way up the driveway was another surprise. From where she stood, she couldn't quite make out the model but at least it wasn't Bill Breunig's SUV. A moment later, someone stepped out of the car, although at this distance it was impossible for Maggie to decide if it was a man or a woman. She was accustomed to people coming down her driveway by mistake, but this person didn't behave as if they were lost. They walked directly up to the cabin, and a few minutes later, she saw them heading towards the Firhouse. Her own car was parked by the barn, so whomever it was knew that she was somewhere around. She quickened her pace, curiosity giving her renewed energy after the long walk.

Suddenly, a familiar brown shape came rushing down the path towards her. Oliver's tail wagged furiously, and when he reached Maggie, he zoomed around in ever-decreasing circles, finally stopping directly in front of her. Free of his cast and bandages, he sat back on his haunches and looked up at her. She could see his body quivering with anticipation, and she lowered herself gingerly to pet him. Squirming into her arms, he licked her face with his pink tongue. She laughed aloud, turning her head from side to side, trying to avoid his wet kisses.

"Oliver! What are you doing here?" She almost expected a reply.

When she got to her feet with the aid of one of her poles and looked around, Isobel was standing a few feet away, watching the encounter. The girl's face betrayed a host of conflicting emotions ranging from guilt to embarrassment. She said nothing at first, just looked at Maggie, and then at Oliver who trotted confidently in the direction of the prairie.

"I think he's expecting you to take him for a walk," Isobel said, a careful smile on her face.

"Well, he's too late. I'm finished. I'm ready for my cup of tea."

Maggie didn't mean to sound waspish but couldn't help herself. She was still hurting from Isobel's rejection and needed to make sure the girl was aware of this. Isobel looked suitably chagrined and kept her gaze lowered by way of an apology. Maggie softened.

"You can join me if you like."

With a gush of relief Isobel said, "I'd love to. Thank you."

They walked to the cabin in silence, each busy with her

own thoughts and questions. In the kitchen Isobel stood uncomfortably by the counter, waiting for Maggie to break the ice, while Oliver settled himself under the kitchen table with a sigh.

Maggie busied herself with filling the kettle and putting it on the stove.

"I brought a cake," said Isobel. "It's in the car. I'll go and get it."

Oliver made no attempt to follow her as she opened the kitchen door and stepped outside. She returned a few minutes later carrying a small cardboard box bearing the logo of a popular Madison bakery.

"That was very kind of you," said Maggie, making an effort to sound welcoming. She was wary, not sure why Isobel had decided to come unannounced as opposed to telephoning first. Maybe she didn't even know. Maybe she was waiting to see how Maggie would respond to the surprise visit. They sat at the kitchen table both recognizing the awkwardness of the moment, not sure as to how to get past it.

"Maggie, I'm so sorry," Isobel finally blurted out. "I don't know what came over me that day. I suppose I was feeling sorry for myself. You've been so kind all the time that I've worked here. I feel terrible."

Her voice wavered and Maggie was afraid she was going to cry.

"Look," Maggie said. "I understand, or at least I think I do. You're all alone here and you're unsure as to what's going to happen next, especially as you want to change direction and try something new. It's a big risk."

Isobel met her gaze and Maggie could see that some of what she said rang true.

She put a gnarled hand on the young girl's slender one and said reassuringly, "It's going to be all right."

"You're right. I am scared about the future, but that isn't the whole reason I reacted the way I did." She took a deep breath. "You see, I was adopted."

Maggie could see the effort the girl was taking not to cry, squeezing her hands together tightly in her lap.

"Hearing that you gave your daughter up for adoption really upset me." Isobel sighed. "I'm okay now, though. I'm seeing the therapist I used to go to in college and it's helping a lot. I thought I had worked through everything but apparently not."

"Oh Isobel..." Maggie wanted to reach out and touch the girl but was afraid her overture might be rejected.

"It's a long story," Isobel sighed again. "When my parents moved to New Zealand, I fell apart. All I could think was, they had abandoned me. My grades tanked, and I didn't know what to do next. If I lost my scholarship...I had no home to go back to. It was my tennis coach who finally came to the rescue. She spoke to my professors and arranged for me to see a therapist. Things got back on track, and I managed to finish my degree on time." Isobel made a wry expression. "So you see, the whole thing about adoption...I just couldn't deal with it again."

"I had no idea." Maggie didn't know what else to say. She got up and put her arms around the girl. She could feel Isobel's sobs.

When they eventually subsided, she asked gently, "Do you know anything about your birth parents?"

"Well, like I told you, Mom's originally from New Zealand and my Dad's from Serbia. They met in Toronto and got married. I was a few months old when they adopted me from Bosnia. I was born there. But they never told me how I got from Bosnia to Toronto or who my birth parents were. Nothing. Any time I asked, they just clammed up. I've spent so much time thinking about the possibilities, whether Dad knew my birth parents...I just don't know. He left Serbia before the war. I asked him about that once, the timing and all, but he said he's not my real father. I'm not sure if I believe him."

Isobel wiped the tears from her cheeks and bent down to

stroke Oliver. The dog licked her salty fingers and lay back on the carpet with a satisfied sigh.

"A couple of years ago, I started to look for my birth parents. All I had was a date and a place, and I wasn't even sure if those were accurate. Did you know, the university has a department of Slavic studies? One of the professors there was great—he spoke the language fluently and did his best to help. But in the end, we got nowhere. So many records were destroyed during the war and afterwards too. I guess I'll never find out now. My last chance is DNA. I sent off a sample to ancestry.com. Oh, I'm Eastern European all right. No doubt about that. Maybe someday I'll get an e-mail asking if I'm related to such and such a person from Bosnia. I might have a family after all. Who knows."

They talked for well over an hour, Isobel bringing Maggie up to date on all of her plans for her new career. She had signed up for three courses, each of which was required for application to veterinary school. Sensibly, the girl had met with an admissions advisor at the school to see how she could strengthen her application. To her surprise, the fact that she was coming from a career as a school counselor was viewed positively. Nonetheless, with no experience in large animal veterinary medicine, the advisor thought it would be prudent to spend some months observing that type of practice. The veterinary clinic in Lodi, a nearby village, was willing to take her on as a volunteer. Her plan was to get a letter of recommendation from them in time to include it with her application.

"I have something else I want to ask you about, Maggie."

Maggie could hear the slight tremor in the girl's voice.

"Vic told me that you were thinking of renting the Firhouse."

For a moment Maggie was taken aback. When they last spoke, Vic had given her no indication that he was in touch with Isobel.

"You were talking to Vic?"

"Yeah. I've seen him a few times."

It was said casually, but Maggie detected a hint in Isobel's voice of something more. Before she could probe further, Isobel continued.

"Would you let me rent it?" Isobel's voice cracked as she asked the question. Looking directly at Maggie, she swallowed hard and waited for a response.

Maggie was taken aback. This wasn't part of her plans, yet it might be a solution. After all, Isobel knew the place better than anyone else. The girl was fastidious, didn't smoke and was unlikely to be holding wild parties. Most of the day she would be gone, which suited Maggie just perfectly. Evenings and weekends were when she felt most vulnerable. She tried to come up with arguments against the proposal but none came to mind.

Oliver shifted his position under the table, reminding Maggie that she would have companionship during the day time too. The more she thought about it, the more the idea appealed. Of course, their relationship would change; Isobel would no longer be her personal assistant. Nevertheless, perhaps the girl could be persuaded to spend a few hours each week helping out at the cabin. If it didn't interfere with her school work, she might like the chance to make some extra money. There was one issue that troubled Maggie, the reason she initially wanted someone living at the Firhouse: Bill Breunig. She would have to tell Isobel about him.

"I think it could work," Maggie said finally.

Isobel's face lit up. "Oh Maggie, that's wonderful. I could leave Oliver here while I go to class. You wouldn't mind that, would you? I'm going to be working at the Lodi clinic on Fridays. That's not far from here, so the six-thirty start wouldn't be so bad. And I could still do some work for you...if you need it, that is." The words tumbled out of her mouth.

It was clear Isobel had given considerable thought to the proposal. Now she looked at Maggie, anxious to see whether she agreed.

"I'm happy to have Oliver with me during the day. He's good company." Maggie smiled down at the dog. "We can work out the rest of the details later. When do you think you'll want to move in?"

"As soon as possible. I start classes on Tuesday, and I'll be going to Lodi on Friday. Would the coming weekend work for you? Vic offered to help me move. I don't have much stuff. Everything will fit in his truck."

"Isobel, there's something you should know before you make a final decision." Maggie said in a concerned voice. "I have to be candid with you. One of the reasons I decided to rent the Firhouse is that I'm having a problem with my neighbor, Bill Breunig. His land abuts mine, and he's trying to force me to sell my place to him. I've refused in no uncertain terms. I'll never sell to him. Right now there's a legal dispute going on about a right-of-way that would run behind the Firhouse. Bill needs this so that he can put in a housing development. He's a nasty piece of work and I wouldn't put anything past him. His beef is with me, though, not you, so I doubt he'd give you any trouble. Still, you need to know about this before you decide."

Isobel's response surprised her.

"He's the big fat guy with the bald head?"

Maggie nodded.

"Don't worry. I'm not afraid of him. Oliver will take care of me." She leaned down and rubbed the dog's head.

Maggie pursed her lips, ready to scold the girl for her cavalier attitude, but Isobel shook her head. A smile hovered on her lips.

"I met him at the Firhouse one day. I was upstairs and didn't hear him knock, although I'm not sure he did—I think he just came in when he found the door unlocked. I was a bit taken aback: this weird, bald guy standing in the living room. I reacted pretty violently, I suppose, grabbing a knife from the kitchen and holding it up as if I was going to do something with it." She mimicked the gesture and laughed. "Oliver went berserk. He started barking, then went for the guy's ankle and bit him." She paused theatrically before continuing. "He didn't draw blood...at least I didn't see any. The guy was wearing shorts, so I'm sure I'd have noticed. He started to say something, like he was looking for you, and I screamed as loud as I could. He turned and ran down the stairs with Oliver behind him, barking crazily."

With an apologetic look, Isobel added, "I never told you. Sorry." She gave a shrug. "Then I forgot all about it."

Maggie couldn't help laughing. The image of Bill with Oliver's teeth clamped into his thick ankle, running in panic down the stairs was hilarious.

"That's the best story I've heard in years. Chased out of the Firhouse by a small dog—it's not something he'll be boasting about. And he can't complain either. He was trespassing. God, I hate that man! Well, in any case, just keep your wits about you."

"Don't worry. I'm well able to look after myself. But thanks for letting me know what's going on."

"Have you told that story to Vic?"

"Nah. But I will now," said Isobel with a mischievous smile.

# Chapter 27

Life settled back into a comfortable routine for Maggie once Isobel moved to the Firhouse. On mornings when Isobel had class or worked at the veterinary clinic, she dropped Oliver off at the cabin. Announcing her arrival at the kitchen door with a cheery "Good morning!" she waited for a response from Maggie who was usually still in bed. On hearing Maggie's voice, Oliver scooted past Isobel's legs, raced upstairs and jumped up onto the bed. In the past, Maggie would never have allowed this behavior, but these sorts of taboos no longer seemed important.

Regardless of the weather, Maggie took Oliver for a walk each morning after breakfast. With the coming of fall, the prairie grasses had mellowed into hues of pale green and gold punctuated by purple aster, mullein candles, and the occasional bull thistle. In the past she would have attempted to cut the heads off the invasive thistles, worried that their seeds would spread. But this too no longer seemed a worthwhile use of her time. Weren't these immigrants entitled to survive and thrive in their new environment, as she had done?

For much of the day, Oliver was contented to sleep at Maggie's feet, but as the day drew to a close, he became increasingly alert, anticipating Isobel's return. As soon as he heard the crunch of tires on gravel, he rushed to the kitchen door and whined impatiently until Maggie opened the door, whereupon he ran to meet Isobel's car.

On some evenings, Isobel joined Maggie at the cabin for a glass of wine before returning to the Firhouse to make her own dinner. She worked long hours, and Maggie often sent the girl home with a care package. Within a few weeks of the new living arrangement, Maggie insisted on cooking dinner for Isobel each Friday. Gradually, Vic became a regular at the table. He came by more often now, even though the fire breaks no longer needed to be mowed. A few times she noticed his truck parked down by the barn but no sign of him. He could have been busy with any of the small chores he routinely did for her around the place but most likely he was with Isobel at the Firhouse.

These were some of the loveliest days of her life, Maggie thought. As she puzzled over the source of her happiness, it came down to one thing: having what amounted to a family around her. The realization shocked, for she had spent the past fifty-five years sure in the knowledge that she was devoid of any maternal instincts. At no time in those years had she heard the faintest tick of a biological clock. In contrast, she professed to disliking small children and resented the ridiculous amount of attention they received from their parents and grandparents. Her own parents were adherents of the credo that children should be seen and not heard, and Maggie felt inordinately peeved that her generation of parents seemed to have turned their back on that mantra. Yet, here she was at eighty years of age, fussing over a couple of young people whom anyone would have thought, had they seen the Friday evening gathering, must be related to her.

The evenings are getting cooler and this might be the last time we can all eat outside on the screen porch, she thought, as she set the table for dinner that Friday afternoon. Pausing to look out across the prairie to the ponds, she inhaled deeply. In the valley each season had its own magic but fall was special, bringing welcome relief from the humidity and heat of summer, and filling the air with a crisp nutty smell that infused energy into any outdoor activity. Despite the relentless aches and pains, Maggie was surprised at how well she felt. This would be her last fall in the valley. Nonetheless, it was as if cancer had paused momentarily, giving her the gift of a few good months.

Isobel had offered several times to resume reading the Amherst letters, but up to now Maggie had demurred. They had stopped at a critical juncture: the young Maggie was pregnant, hiding the fact from her parents and facing the prospect of having to carry the child to term. What would be the point of reading further? The remaining letters would be a fabrication, designed to keep her parents in ignorance. Even now she could almost pretend that none of that had ever happened. But having said the words, "I had a child" out loud and admitted this fact to Isobel, there was no going back.

Each time Maggie found herself thinking back to that time in Amherst, she balked at the next question: What would have happened had she kept the baby and gone back to Ireland? The country was a pitiless place for unmarried mothers in those days. Many parents banished their pregnant daughters to mother and baby homes run by religious orders, who believed they were doing the Lord's work by allowing illegitimate babies to succumb to neglect. If a baby survived, it was taken from the mother, by force if necessary, and given up for adoption. Many of these adoptions were illegal, with falsified birth certificates that deprived the birth mother of any legal recourse. The wayward mother was then incarcerated in a Magdalene Laundry until she had paid moral restitution to the church.

Lara. That was the name she chose, the name on the baby's birth certificate. Likely it had been changed, and Maggie wondered what the baby's adoptive parents had chosen. Her own name, Margaret O'Connor, was listed on the birth certificate, but not Tim's. Father unknown seemed a safer alternative, even if it suggested that she was not just careless about sex but promiscuous. Giving the baby up for adoption had been the right decision, of that she had no doubt. But Pandora's box had delivered something else. A horrible thought had wormed its way into her brain: she had deprived her parents of their chance to enjoy a family as they grew old.

~

"Have you read any more of them?" said Isobel, gesturing towards the box of letters. It was a Monday in mid-October, and she had dropped into the cabin after work to collect Oliver. Maggie hadn't seen her in several days as she and Vic had spent the weekend up north at his father's cabin.

"No," said Maggie. "I'll get back to them. I just need to be in the right mood."

Isobel persisted. "I've got time this Sunday, if you like. Shall I come over?"

"Let me think about it," Maggie said, anxious to change the subject. "Tell me about going out on call with the vet last Friday. How did it go?"

There was excitement in Isobel's voice as she described her day at the Lodi clinic. She spent the morning with a bovine veterinarian doing pregnancy checks on two hundred dairy cows at a local dairy. It was physically demanding dirty work, yet Isobel sounded rhapsodic as she described how the ultrasound images from a probe inserted into the cow's rectum were projected onto safety glasses the veterinarian was wearing.

"That way, he didn't have to mess up his computer. It was amazing. He let me try. Maggie, you've no idea what it feels like to be up to your shoulder in a cow's rectum. It's warm and...and your arm gets squeezed," she said, laughing at the memory.

In the afternoon Isobel shadowed an equine veterinarian,

Shirley, who happened to be married to the morning's vet. They made house calls to horse owners in a three-county radius, clocking up almost two hundred miles. Isobel was quick to point out that Shirley checked in with the clinic before and after every client visit and not just for book-keeping purposes. A lone female veterinarian, especially a young attractive woman, could expect some unwanted attention at these remote barns. Shirley did have a companion with her in the truck, a border collie named Tui, who sat in the passenger seat and eyed Isobel resentfully when ordered into the back of the truck.

Shirley had grown up in the area and seemed to know everything about her clients, many of whom she had gone to school with.

"We went to a barn that was owned by someone called Breunig, so I asked Shirley if it was Bill. I was kind of curious, especially after what happened at the Firhouse. Wouldn't it have been funny if it was his horse we went to see?"

With an anxious look, Maggie gave Isobel her full attention.

"It wasn't his horse, but there are lots of Breunigs in this area, and they're all related to one another. Shirley told me she heard that Bill Breunig was planning a new housing development somewhere near Madison but that there were problems. Someone had lodged a formal objection, and it was probably going to have to go to court. At any rate, the development is on hold. What do you think of that, Maggie?" Isobel's eyes were shining.

"My lawyer has been very busy," said Maggie, nodding her head approvingly. "Let's hope she's successful."

# Chapter 28

By Sunday afternoon Maggie was beginning to regret her decision to go back to reading the letters. It must have been influenced by too much wine at dinner Friday evening, for why else would she choose to revisit the worst thing that had happened in her life? Isobel had been persuasive at dinner, insisting that she was curious to know what happened next in Maggie's immigrant life and renewing her offer to come by on Sunday. Now, as Maggie looked at the box of letters, she realized she had no memory of those final months in Amherst. It was a blank, as if that block of time had been surgically removed from her consciousness. For a moment she considered the possibility that she was getting dementia but dismissed the thought. Everything else in her mind seemed to be functioning well. She concluded that the memory lapse must be the result of a deliberate suppression that had, over time, altered her neural synapses.

Through the window, she caught sight of Isobel coming around the barn and walking towards the cabin, Oliver at her heels. By the time they reached the kitchen door, Maggie had already filled a water bowl for the dog. He trotted in confidently, his nails clicking on the linoleum, and looked up expectantly at

Maggie. She made a fuss of taking the tin of dog biscuits from the top of the refrigerator, opened the lid slowly and took out a Milkbone. Looking for all the world like a large meerkat, Oliver sat back on his haunches and took the proffered treat from her outstretched fingers with a delicate ease.

Isobel watched the interaction with amusement, muttering, "You know Maggie, you spoil him rotten."

The tea things were laid out on the kitchen table: two mugs, a small jug of milk and a loaf of home-made zucchini bread. At this time of year there was always a glut of zucchini, and Maggie was determined to keep up with the harvest of vegetables that Sally and John delivered to her door on a weekly basis. She measured a generous two teaspoons of leaves into the round blue tea pot and filled it with scalding water. They sat companionably, waiting for the tea to brew, as Oliver chewed at his Milkbone under the table.

There was an earnest tone to Isobel's voice when she spoke. "I really appreciate you looking after Oliver. He's not getting much attention from me these days, what with my classes and working at the clinic. I feel guilty every Friday when I have to drop him off so early."

She made a supplicative gesture with her hands. "I suppose I could just open the kitchen door and let him inside, but I know he'll run upstairs and wake you. If you like, I can leave him at the Firhouse and you could let him out later."

"It's no problem. Honestly. I don't sleep well these days, so I'm awake at that time of the morning in any case. Besides, he puts me in a good humor at the start of the day, and if I'm grouchy, he doesn't complain. Actually, he's the perfect companion." Maggie looked down at the dog affectionately.

"And that lasagna you sent home with me was a life-saver. I ate it almost every evening last week."

"Every evening? Nobody should have to eat my lasagna four nights in a row," Maggie said, shaking her head.

"Okay. I admit, it wasn't every night; Vic made dinner for me on Tuesday."

Maggie looked skeptical. As far as she was aware, Vic's idea of dinner started and ended with a piece of meat and a barbecue grill.

"Actually, he was pretty good. There was a salad with the grilled steak and frozen French fries. I think he's trying to keep me healthy. Well, maybe not—he got ice cream for dessert." Isobel giggled, adding, "And he's learning: there were fresh blueberries to go with the ice cream."

Maggie nodded her approval. "I'm impressed. I hope you told him how wonderful he is. That way, he might do it again." She gave Isobel a questioning look. "You two seem to be getting along pretty well."

A slow blush rose to the girl's cheeks.

"We are," Isobel agreed, "He's a really nice guy. The first in a long, long time."

Maggie raised her eyebrows.

"What I mean is, it's nice to meet someone the old-fashioned way. For once, I didn't have to meet him online." She frowned as she tried to explain. "It's different somehow..."

Maggie had read about dating sites but didn't know much about how they worked.

"Online dating sounds very strange, almost like a take-out menu at a restaurant. How do you actually go about finding someone online?"

"Well, you begin by posting your profile...and paying, of course. There's a questionnaire and a place to upload an image. Then you just hit 'send.' Within minutes you'll start to get pings, and by the time you sift through them, there could be dozens of responses. Most people just go by the selfies in the beginning. Then you start to narrow it down and actually read what they say about themselves. Everyone is into some sport, and they have to let you know how good they are at it. Then there's the bit about being in shape and working out regularly. Usually, they say they're not looking for a relationship, just casual dating, although a few admit they are looking for 'the one.' Candlelight dinners, walking on the beach...that sort of stuff."

Maggie couldn't help laughing at Isobel's cynical take on contemporary suitors. She was fascinated by the process, which bore no resemblance to her own experiences.

"What sort of boys did you choose after you had worked your way through the menu?" Maggie asked.

"Some were students. Others were young professionals; the corporate computer-savvy types, really into their own success. It was obvious they wanted to have sex on the first date, even if they said they didn't."

Maggie prompted Isobel to continue. "What happened after you posted your profile?"

"I met a lot of real losers. You'd go out for a date and spend the evening listening to them. They never seemed to be curious about me. It was weird at times, like they were the only person in the world."

"And Vic?"

Isobel paused to consider the question. "He listens to me. He's interested in what's happening in my life. He doesn't assume I'm going to do everything with him, like going out with his friends. Even if I'm not studying, sometimes I just want to stay home and read a book. In the beginning, I worried that he wouldn't have anything to talk about, especially with my friends. They're not really into hunting or fishing. But they all really like him."

Maggie could hear the cautious affection in her voice.

"Does he like your friends?"

"Yeah, he does, even though a lot of them are scientists. There's a few of them in business and he gets along really well with them.

"I almost forgot. Vic said to tell you that he can come by

tomorrow evening. He said you wanted to talk to him about throwing a party."

She looked inquiringly at Maggie. "A party?"

"Yes, a winter solstice party. We used to have one every year when Alan was around."

Maggie looked out of the window in the direction of the pond. "It was always a brilliant party, with a massive bonfire down by the pond. Everyone came, and kids especially loved it. I remember overhearing one kid asking another, 'Will you be here next year when I'm old enough to light it?' The tradition is the youngest kid over the age of five gets to light the bonfire."

She smiled with pleasure at the memory.

"Well. This year I'm bringing back the tradition. It's my way of saying thank you to everyone in the valley."

# Chapter 29

Vic arrived as Maggie was clearing away the dishes from her evening meal. He accepted a beer, and they moved to the living room where they sat facing each other, warmed by the gas stove. Maggie got down to business immediately.

"I told Isobel that I wanted to talk to you about the solstice party. I admit that was a bit of a ruse. I have something much more important to discuss."

Vic looked puzzled, and she added reassuringly, "We're still on for the party, don't worry. But there's something else I want to talk to you about."

Maggie massaged her wrist as she searched for a way to move to the subject she really wanted to discuss.

"Vic, I know you love this place—the cabin, the barn, the prairie, the pond, everything." She made a sweeping gesture towards the darkened windows. With a wary look, Vic kept his gaze fixed on her face, waiting to see where this conversation was going.

"I've watched you ever since you came here with your father that first time and all the years since then. This place means a lot to you, almost as much as it does to me, I think.

You've played here, worked here, grown up here, and I think you might have fallen in love here too. You've taken care of the place, especially since Alan died, and made it so that I can continue to live here easily."

She sighed, took a deep breath and continued. "The thing is, I know you cannot afford to buy the place..."

A look of alarm crossed Vic's face and he opened his mouth to speak. Maggie put her hand up, indicating that she didn't want to be interrupted.

"I'm not about to sell...but the place will end up being sold when I die."

There was a stricken look on his face, and Maggie suppressed the urge to cradle the young man in her arms.

"Vic, I've got cancer and it's terminal. I've decided not to go through with any treatment. I'm eighty years of age and I'd rather enjoy my last few months of life. I'm feeling okay for now, but I know that's going to change. This will be my last solstice party."

Tears began to trickle down Vic's cheek and he brushed them away.

"After Alan died, I rewrote my will, leaving everything to my cousins in Ireland. I've been thinking about that recently. I don't know them at all, and there's only a few of them left. But I'm sure they'll get together and decide to sell this place as quickly as possible. None of them wants a settler's cabin in rural Wisconsin. They'll want their children and grandchildren to get a bit of cash, and the person who can do that for them is Bill Breunig." She gave a derisory snort.

"I've told you about his plans for a subdivision. Right now, I'm the only thing stopping him, and according to my lawyer, there's a good chance that I'll succeed. But when I die, everything will change. Even if he can't get planning permission for the houses, he'll demolish the cabin and build a McMansion for himself. After that, he'll cut down the pine trees. They're almost a hundred years old and will bring a good price. Needless to say, he'll plow the prairie under. It'll be put into corn and fertilized mercilessly, killing off all the bees and butterflies..."

Her voice trailed off. She looked out the window into the greying light, as if she could already see the destruction.

"So, I have a proposition for you. I am going to sell the place to you, lock stock and barrel, for one hundred dollars."

Vic's eyebrows shot upwards. He opened his mouth to speak but Maggie's hand came up again, warning him.

"Hear me out. I'll tell you when I'm finished."

Vic took a mouthful of beer and swallowed it with difficulty. He waited for Maggie to continue.

"There's one condition: I get to live here in the cabin for the rest of my life."

She couldn't help smiling as she added, "Don't worry. I'm not going to be like that French woman who lived to be one hundred and twenty. When she was ninety, her lawyer offered her a reverse mortgage. He was in his forties so I'm sure he thought it was a great bargain, only she outlived him in the end." Maggie chuckled.

"I'll be gone by this time next year. But between now and then, I don't want anything to change. For as long as I have, I want to be able to look at all the things I love, just the way they are."

Maggie heard the wistful note in her voice. Shifting in her armchair, she straightened her shoulders and continued, her tone now businesslike.

"On a more practical note, in case you are wondering about money, I'll look after the lawyer's fees, and I'll continue to pay the utilities. I'll pay the property taxes too. But when I die, you'll have to come up with those, and they're not cheap. All the same, you'll own a property worth half a million dollars, or thereabouts, so I'm sure the bank will be willing to give you a loan if you need it."

It was impossible to interpret the look on Vic's face, and by now Maggie was too exhausted to try.

"There are a few more things you need to know. I've talked to my lawyer about the objections I've filed over Bill Breunig's application. As the owner, you'll become the plaintiff in that battle. You'll have a lot more energy than me, particularly if it ends up going to court. I'll look after her fees until I'm gone. Now, the other issue is the Firhouse. As you know, Isobel is renting it from me, and that means that you'll become her landlord. She doesn't have a lease, but this is a critical year for her with a career change. I want her to be able to stay here until she's got her life sorted out: either getting into vet school or deciding to do something else. That's probably going to take her a year, so I want you to promise me that you'll let her stay until next September."

Maggie noticed a smile hovering at the corners of Vic's mouth.

"I know this seems an unnecessary promise right now, but things can change."

There was a brief silence as each of them allowed their thoughts to shift tentatively into the future.

"Another thing. Isobel doesn't know about my cancer, and I want to be the one to tell her. So please keep that to yourself for a few more days. I'll find the right time. She'll come to you when she hears so you'll know that I've told her."

Maggie continued in the same, businesslike voice. "You're bound to have a lot of questions, so I think the best thing is that you think about this proposal for a few days. Talk to your father. Talk to Isobel if you like. But in the end, it's your decision. You'll be the one living here," Maggie made a gesture towards the inside of the cabin with her hand, "and I'll be gone. Well...maybe my ghost will be hanging around for a while."

Her features softened and she smiled as she reached for her glass of wine.

# Chapter 30

Lying awake in bed later that night, Maggie went back over the day in her mind. The talk with Vic had gone more or less the way she expected. She wondered who he would tell first: Isobel or his father? It was late when she and Vic finished talking. Immediately after he left the cabin, she heard his truck going down the driveway, so he had probably decided it was too late to disturb Isobel.

Now that the first part of her plan was in place, she felt an enormous sense of relief. Vic had already accepted her offer, even as she insisted he think it over carefully. But there were no downsides, at least none that she or her lawyers had identified. And whereas in the past she had felt a little guilty asking Vic to fix something at the cabin, now all those irritations were no longer her problem. She wouldn't have to downsize or throw out anything. When she died, Vic would take care of it. All of a sudden everything had become so simple. Everything except dying. That was the next project. Meanwhile there was a solstice party to organize.

Her increasingly sleepless nights were frequently occupied by resurrecting pieces of the past fifty years at the cabin. This night she tried to distract herself by thinking about the first solstice party. Vic had reminded her of some of the details. His memory of that first party, twenty-three years earlier, was surprisingly vivid. He was barely five years old, he said, when his father asked if he would like to go to a party at the "Irish lady's place."

"The chance to go to a party with my Dad was a big deal in those days," Vic had told her.

"It was dark, and I remember a long driveway with huge trees on either side. It felt like something out of a movie, and when I saw the cabin covered in snow, all I could think of was *Snow White and the Seven Dwarves*." He chuckled.

"Remember, I was the youngest child at the party that year. I couldn't believe it when you said that I was going to light the bonfire. Me. I was terrified that I'd fail. But it all worked. I remember the whoosh as it caught and exploded into flame. I think Dad must have been standing behind me and pulled me back. People began to clap and congratulate me. Ah, Maggie...it was best thing that had happened in my life up to then!"

Maggie shifted her position, grunting with the pain. She dreaded the upcoming conversation with Isobel.

~

Isobel had spent almost an hour describing to Maggie every detail of her day at the Lodi clinic. A Belgian mare had delivered a perfect foal after a difficult few hours, and Isobel had been on hand for the whole event. As the girl prattled on, Maggie nodded and smiled, but she wasn't really listening.

"So, how about you, Maggie? Did you get the invitations done? I can drop them off in people's mailboxes whenever. I'm really looking forward to the party, and Vic is acting like it's the biggest thing to happen in the valley since...well, since the time he lit the bonfire. He's told me that story at least three times now."

Maggie began. "There's no easy way to tell you this. The thing is...I have cancer and it's quite advanced. The last scans showed multiple lesions on my liver and my lungs. I've decided not to do anything...no chemo this time. I don't want to be miserable for my last months. I want to enjoy what's left of my life here, at the cabin."

Maggie watched Isobel's face crumple as the reality of her statement dawned.

"But you can't..." she howled, "you can't die, not now..."

Tears streamed down her face and the words came out in hiccups.

"Just when everything was beginning to go right with my life...living here...feeling like I had a family...being able to talk to you about everything.... It's just not fair. I lose everyone. First my parents and now you," she wailed.

Maggie watched impassively as Isobel cried her eyes out. There was absolutely nothing she could do or say that could make this any easier for the girl. Oliver paced around the kitchen, ignored by Isobel until Maggie gathered him up in her arms and settled him on her lap. She stroked the dog rhythmically.

Isobel's sobs finally subsided. She looked up at Maggie, her eyes searching for some hope. Maggie just nodded, her expression inscrutable.

"Vic is going to be devastated. You've no idea how important you are to him."

"I've told Vic already. I asked him not to say anything to you or anyone else for that matter. I wanted to tell you myself."

She pushed Oliver from her lap, went over to Isobel and took the girl's hands in hers.

"Things are not going to change for a while." Her voice was reassuring. "I expect I'll just slow down, do less, get more tired, and then...well, then it will be over. I'm not afraid of dying."

She looked down at the dog. "Oliver will have to get used to shorter walks, I'm afraid. But not just yet."

In a heartbroken voice, Isobel said, "Maggie, what can I do for you? There must be something..." Her voice trailed off.

"Nothing. You've done it already."

# Chapter 31

Winter solstice fell on a Friday, and Vic took the day off work to make sure everything was ready for the party the following day. The weather was crisp and cold, with a few inches of snow already lingering on the grass. He busied himself with arranging the Leopold benches near the bonfire: a stockade of stacked branches encircling a mound of densely compacted brush. The foundation was a base of huge soft-wood logs arranged for maximum oxygenation such that they would burn out completely. The final touch had been to pile tinder-dry pine cones just inside the stockade. A single sheet of newspaper and a match would get the fire started—an easy task for any five-year-old.

People began to arrive at dusk. Over the next hour, a procession of figures walked up to the cabin from where they had parked by the barn, carrying bottles and casseroles, and plates and baskets of food. Over the years the potluck had been honed and perfected, and by now certain people were identified with their party offerings. One of Maggie's neighbors in the adjoining valley reared goats and always brought a round or two of her most popular cheeses. Another friend was a successful chocolatier in Madison who made mouth-watering dark chocolate truffles. Even neighbors who thrived on store-bought food were apt to bring a summer sausage from their recent deer kill, if only to boast about it. Home-baked pies were plentiful, and for those who had no time to cook, a last-minute purchase of vanilla ice cream was always a safe bet. Unlike Thanksgiving or Christmas, Maggie actually enjoyed cooking a turkey for this occasion. She had all day to prepare it, and as people came through the kitchen door, they were met with the comforting aroma of roast turkey. The cabin thrummed with noise and excited activity for a short while as the various dishes were laid out on the kitchen counter and dining table. People served themselves and moved to the living room, the study, the front room, the stairs, the bedroom—wherever they could find a place in the small crowded cabin. Maggie moved from group to group, catching up with old friends and meeting newcomers—for someone always brought a stranger to share in the experience. Kids ran around excitedly, fascinated by a house where nothing was straight: walls of made of rough-hewn logs, sloping floors, crooked doorways, low ceilings.

Maggie was accosted by a small boy with a solemn expression who tugged at her sleeve insistently.

"Maggie! Maggie! I'm five. Can I light the bonfire?"

She demurred, saying, "Let's ask your Mom and Dad, shall we?"

She called for silence and asked for the younger children to gather around her. Each child was asked to announce their age. In the past, the process of identifying the youngest child had occasionally resulted in tears. Fortunately, the bonfire was big enough that, if necessary, two or three ignition points could be assigned, for in their excitement, each child believed that they were responsible for the totality. This year the young boy with the solemn expression was indeed five, and when nobody else came forward, he was given a ceremonial lighter wand and sent off to get his snowsuit.

"Vic, will you go with Max and show him what to do, please," Maggie asked. She took the little boy's hand in hers and pointed towards Vic. "He did it when he was five, you know. He lit the bonfire that year."

Vic gave Maggie a nod and turned to the little boy, asking "Are you ready, Max?"

Bundled into his snowsuit, Max followed Vic and his parents outside. Just before the door closed, he turned to look back at Maggie and asked, "Aren't you coming?"

"I'm going to watch you from the porch," she replied with a reassuring smile. Seeing the disappointment on his face, she added, "It's a bit too cold for me outside, and I can see it perfectly from here. You'll come back and tell me about it afterwards, won't you?" The boy nodded solemnly and turned to follow his parents.

From the screen porch Maggie heard the whoosh that announced ignition. Flames leapt into the air, easily forty feet high. She saw a ring of figures stepping back from the bonfire as the searing heat spread outwards. Kids jumped around excitedly, dashing forwards towards the flames only to beat a hasty retreat, all the while squealing with bravado and fear. Their parents watched, transfixed, as their precious offspring displayed their true primal instincts.

Maggie found Isobel in the kitchen, clearing plates and rinsing glasses. Pouring herself a glass of wine, she said, "Why don't you leave all of that until later and go down to the bonfire?"

"I thought I could get started on these," Isobel replied.

"It's a party! We'll get around to it later. Come down to the bonfire with me." When Isobel looked reluctant, Maggie continued, "You can make sure I don't stray from the path." That brought a smile to Isobel's face. "And bring a refill for Vic. He'll be needing it."

Down by the bonfire, Maggie wandered amongst her guests, listening to their conversations and catching up with people she hadn't seen in the house. Children played in the firelight, while the adults stood around in groups, chatting to one another, sipping on beer or wine or just staring into the flames that leapt upward and disintegrated in the night sky.

Maggie stepped away from the bonfire and strolled into the middle of the prairie, her coat brushing against the dry stalks. She stopped, and in the sudden silence heard an owl hoot and soon afterwards the distinct howling of coyotes farther up the valley. The sky was clear, and even with the background glare of light from the bonfire she could make out Cassiopeia, a huge 'W' shape in the sky. She looked back towards the bonfire with a sense of wonder and appreciation. Everything important to her was here. She could make out Vic's silhouette against the glow, one arm resting on an asphalt rake, the other raising a bottle to his lips. Beside him stood Isobel, a slender form leaning in towards his bulk. Maggie smiled to herself. They made a good-looking couple.

Out of the corner of her eye she saw a dark shape emerge from the woods. The figure, wearing a parka with the hood pulled up, made its way slowly towards her, as if the person had been watching her movements. When the figure was barely ten feet away, the light from the bonfire reflected off the hooded face, and with a jolt of alarm she recognized Bill Breunig.

"Well. Fancy meeting you here," Bill said, pulling the hood back. He walked towards her, stopping barely a foot from where she stood. She recognized this move: an invasion of personal space designed to intimidate. She didn't look up at him. Instead, she turned towards the bonfire, which now seemed to be a long way off. She could feel the tightness in her neck and shoulders as she tried to breathe normally and stay calm.

Something about the shape of his head, the reflected glow from the bonfire, his stealthy movement towards her, triggered a memory. This was the figure she saw in the woods the night of the prairie fire, the night she fell down the stairs.

"I never got an invitation to the party, Maggie," he said with a sneer. "That's a bit rude, don't you think, especially for your neighbor."

"It was you, wasn't it? You were there that night—the night of the prairie burn. You started that second fire!"

"What if it was me? You'll never prove it."

She began to walk away, but Bill grabbed her wrist roughly. He squeezed it hard causing her to wince. It was the wrist she had broken a few months earlier.

We haven't finished our chat yet, Maggie," he said menacingly, bending her arm and forcing her to turn around to face him.

"Let go of my wrist," she said.

Although she tried to instill her voice with authority, the words came out sounding weak and plaintive. She looked towards the bonfire, desperate to find someone who might be watching them, but the fiery spectacle had captured everyone's attention and nobody noticed the two figures far off in the prairie.

"I'm just making sure you don't fall, Maggie." His voice was soft, and he sounded almost reasonable. "It's dangerous out here in the snow, you know. You could trip and bang your head. And then what would happen?"

He bent down until his face was level with hers, and she could smell the alcohol and cigarettes on his breath.

"I suppose you'd freeze to death," he said. His tone, a mixture of menace and mock sadness, galled her, and for a split second she considered spitting in his face. She pulled against his grip, but he held her wrist tightly. A cold, clammy feeling started to rise in her chest. Was it possible? Would he dare?

The wheedling voice was back. "Look, Maggie, I'm only trying to help you out. When the right of way is approved, nobody'll want to buy your place. You'll won't be able to give it away."

Maggie shifted her weight to her right leg as she swung the hiking pole around, lashing it upward at Bill's head. He sprang backwards, releasing his hold on her wrist. His hand came up to the side of his face.

"You bitch!' he screamed at her. "You fucking bitch."

The tip of the hiking pole had caught in his stocking cap, wrenching it from his head and leaving behind a long bloody scratch above his right ear. Before he had a chance to recover, Maggie began to run towards the bonfire. She could hear Bill's heavy breathing and the sound of his body as it thrashed through the dry grass behind her. He was going to catch up.

She stopped abruptly and turned to face him.

"You're too late, Bill," she shouted, "I've already sold the place!"

He was level with her now, his breath coming in short gasps, but he didn't make any attempt to grab her.

"You're lying," he snarled.

Maggie stood her ground. She looked him directly in the eye and shook her head slowly from side to side. "It's the truth. It's gone," she said triumphantly.

"I'd have heard if it was sold," he said. A hint of doubt entered his voice. "Who did you sell it to?"

"You'll find out eventually. But no matter what you do, it will *never* be yours."

She turned her back on him and began to walk towards the bonfire. Someone shouted her name and waved. She waved back and continued to walk slowly towards her guests, putting Bill Breunig out of her mind forever.

# Chapter 32

For Maggie the perfect Christmas day was one spent alone, with a bottle of champagne, cheese and crackers and a good book. When her husband was alive, it was different, for he loved to entertain. The guest list varied from year to year, but he tried to invite people who otherwise might be left out: visiting students and professors, the partner whose spouse had to work at the hospital over the holiday, a neighbor who lived alone. The Christmas after he died, Maggie received several dinner invitations from neighbors and friends. Reluctantly, she accepted an invitation to go to a neighbor's house, reasoning that at least she didn't have to travel far. The couple, whom she didn't know very well, did their best to include her in their family celebration as their grandchildren ran around the house screaming uncontrollably. Seated with the adults at dinner, the meal revolved around these children, with no possibility of Maggie having an adult conversation. After that, she resolved never to accept a Christmas dinner invitation again.

Isobel came by the day after Christmas with some cold turkey breast, which she put in Maggie's fridge before coming to join her in the front room. A single letter remained on one side of the Shaker box. Several times in the previous weeks Isobel had asked Maggie if she wanted it read aloud to her, but each time Maggie declined. Now Isobel gestured to the box.

"What do you think? Would you like to finish the story?"

Isobel watched Maggie intently, noting that she was massaging her wrist. Maggie picked up the blue aerogramme and brought it to her nose, inhaling deeply. She stared at the address for a long time, delicately stroking the raised type with her middle finger. Slowly, she unfolded the sheet of paper and focused her gaze on the date typed in the upper right-hand corner.

"I wrote this letter the day I came home from the hospital. It would have been around now, actually. It was just after Christmas...fifty-five years ago. She was born on Christmas Day."

For several minutes the only sound in the room was a gentle hiss from the gas stove.

"I wonder what I wrote about that week," Maggie said, folding the letter and returning it to the box. "Whatever it was, none of it happened," she said shaking her head.

"Tell me what *did* happen," Isobel said gently.

Maggie thought about what she was going to say next. This was going to be a confession and she wanted to tell the truth. But truth had become a slippery commodity over the years. She was going to have to listen critically to her own voice describing what happened all those years ago. This was her last chance. She took a deep breath and began.

"I was feeling sorry for myself, had been for months. But I was especially low coming up to Christmas. 'Gravid' is such a good word to describe the whole business. Towards the end I felt like a bloated seal, stretched and ready to burst. I just wanted the whole thing to be over with so I could get on with my life.

"Nancy—she was my roommate at the time—didn't go home for Christmas. Being Jewish I suppose it wasn't an important celebration for her or her family. Looking back on it though, I think she must have stayed in Amherst for me. There were a couple of people I could have called to take me to the hospital;

even my boss would have done it. But when the contractions started on Christmas Eve, Nancy piled me into the back of her car and drove to the hospital in Springfield. They admitted me, and I told her to go, although she would have stayed if I had asked her. When she left, I remember feeling more alone than ever in my life. But at the same time, I didn't want anyone I knew to be there—to be a witness. If nobody saw it, maybe I could pretend it never happened.

"I was still in labor on Christmas morning when the doctor did his rounds. I had never seen this doctor before. He looked at my chart and listened to what the nurse had to say. Maybe he was irritated at having to work that day, or maybe the first doctor had said something to him about me. I just remember he had no kind words for me. None. There was a really nice Philippine nurse on the ward. She stroked my hand and told me not to worry. It had never occurred to me that there could be complications with the delivery."

Maggie paused for a moment, as if listening to a distant voice.

"You know, I cannot remember the feeling of giving birth... of the baby actually coming out. I remember an indescribable sense of breaking apart, but it's not a memory of pain per se. They say the pain of childbirth is forgotten quickly, otherwise nobody would have another child. It must be true. The next thing I remember is hearing a woman's voice saying, 'It's a girl, a healthy baby girl.' People were fussing somewhere beyond my line of sight, and then I heard a high-pitched wail.

"I never saw the baby. Maybe it was hospital policy in those days, to minimize the emotional loss, or maybe they did it just to expedite the adoption process. I left the hospital two days later. During those two days, I hardly spoke. The Philippine nurse came by often. I remember her telling me she had two children at home in the Philippines, being reared by their grandparents. She hadn't seen them in several years. 'You get used to it,' she said.

"They needed a name for the birth certificate. I called her Lara. I'd seen the movie, Dr. Zhivago, when I was a student in Ireland and liked that name. I'm sure they changed it. After all, it's not a Catholic name, and she was going to be adopted by a 'good Catholic couple,' or so they said.

"A week later Nancy brought me to the bus stop on the town square in Amherst. I was going to Germany where I could begin all over again. It was almost a year to the day that I had stepped down from the bus and into my first day in America. I was wearing the same coat and carrying the same suitcase, but that girl was gone forever. Driving away from the town square, I wiped away a small patch of condensation on the window and peered out at all those places I had come to know, and love, and eventually hate.

"I landed in Munich and took a train to Seewiesen—it's a small town in Bavaria. I spent the next three years working at the Max Planck Institute for Behavioral Physiology. The director was an old friend of my boss in Amherst; that's how I got the position. The institute was a very self-contained place. The postdocs and students lived above the labs, and there was a cafeteria on site so we didn't need to go into the village. I worked all the time—there wasn't much else to do there. It paid off because I ended up publishing several research papers that made quite an impact. When it came time to find a permanent job, I decided that I wanted to come back to America. I was ready by then."

Maggie clasped her hands together, as if in prayer. She had finished telling her story and felt utterly drained. Had it been the truth? Perhaps. She realized that she would never really know. As her historian husband used to say: "If it's not written down, it's as if it never happened."

"Did you miss her? Your baby?"

Maggie sighed. "Honestly, I don't know. I didn't have any image of her, just that one cry. But she left something behind in me, something I didn't know was there…until the letters. I miss her now."

"Did you ever try to find her?"

Maggie shook her head. "No."

"And your parents? Did you go back to Ireland?"

For a moment Maggie was taken aback by the question, but then realized that from Isobel's perspective, she hadn't seen or spoken to her parents during that year in Amherst.

"I waited for a few months—until I was sure that I wouldn't break down when I saw them. Also, I needed my body to look the same as when I left, and that took a couple of months. I went home for a few days in March, around St. Patrick's Day, as I knew there would be a lot of distraction with all the celebrations. I remember my mother asked if I wanted to go along with her to mass. I said 'No,' that I didn't believe in mass any more. I remember her pinning a little sprig of shamrock on my jacket when she left for the church. She said she would say a prayer for me. She called me her little changeling."

"What's a changeling?"

"There's a myth in Ireland that sometimes the fairies come and take your child from the cradle. They put another one in its place, a changeling. It explains so many disappointments for parents—when their children grow up and aren't what they expected. My mother was right, though. I had changed."

As if he sensed a shift in the conversation, Oliver uncurled himself from his position in front of the gas stove and stood up. He stretched lazily, and his name tag rattled as he shook vigorously. He looked first to Isobel and then to Maggie before trotting towards the kitchen. The sky had darkened and it was time for his evening walk. Maggie winced as she stood up, not able to suppress a grunt of pain. Isobel stood up quickly and took a step towards Maggie who waved her away.

"I'm fine. I'm just stiff from sitting so long. Nothing to worry about, I promise."

Maggie's face softened, and she put her hand on Isobel's arm.

"Thank you for encouraging me to finally tell the whole story of what happened in Amherst. I realize now that I needed to do it...for my own sake."

# Chapter 33

Maggie found it hard to stay active, despite Vic's efforts at keep-ing the driveway clear of snow. He plowed it obsessively, and each morning either he or Isobel spread a mixture of sand and salt on the concrete pad by the kitchen door to melt any ice that might have formed during the night. Vic had even plowed the path that led towards the pond and around the prairie so that Maggie could continue her daily walks with Oliver. But it was challenging. She tried strapping on snowshoes but bending over to secure the bindings was difficult and painful. Searching the internet she found a pair of spiked cleats that she could attach to the soles of her winter boots. Armed with ski poles, she tried these out on the icy driveway and was delighted to find that they worked as advertised. Her daily walks resumed, and to her amusement it was Oliver who was inclined to lose his footing, despite having the twin luxuries of youth and three good legs.

Isobel and Vic had just returned from a ten-day vacation in the Florida Keys, looking tanned and relaxed. Winter was a relatively easy time for Vic to get away, although he had been busy in January with a big indoor remodeling project. No longer taking university courses, Isobel was working four days a week at a research laboratory on campus. She still spent one day at the Lodi veterinary clinic, now Wednesday instead of Friday. As a result, she volunteered to make dinner on Friday evenings, taking over from Maggie, who hadn't objected. Maggie's appetite was much reduced, and Isobel struggled to come up with ideas for nourishing meals that also made good leftovers.

"I've been thinking about going to Ireland," Maggie said casually one Friday evening in late February as they were eating dinner.

The three of them were sitting around the kitchen table, finishing the last of an excellent apple pie Isobel had baked. Having delivered her bombshell, Maggie tried to interpret the look that Isobel and Vic exchanged across the table. Regardless of what they thought, she was determined to follow through with the plan. She couldn't remember where the idea came from or exactly when she started to think about it seriously. Initially, it had been no more than a nostalgic whim. Then, on New Year's Day, with little prospect of seeing out the incoming year, Maggie had asked herself what it was that she wanted most, right now. It was obvious: to go home to Ireland. The big question was, could she hang on until spring and be healthy enough to make the journey? Winters were very depressing in Ireland: cold and dark, but spring arrived earlier there than in Wisconsin.

"Are you sure that's a good idea?" said Isobel, a cautious expression on her face as she looked from Vic to Maggie.

"That's wonderful," said Vic with genuine delight. "When are you thinking of going?"

"And for how long?" Isobel chimed in.

"Actually, I have a flight in just over a week. I was hoping one of you might be able to take me to the airport."

They both looked surprised.

Before either of them had a chance to press her for more information, Maggie added, "I don't know how long I'll be away for. Two to three weeks, I imagine." She let the thought sink in as she got up and began to clear dishes from the table.

"I can take you to the airport," Vic said, jumping up to help. "Just let me know the day and time and I'm on it."

Maggie noticed the look of concern on Isobel's face. Their eyes met and she said reassuringly, "I'll be fine, Isobel. I've done this before."

"But what if something happens while you're there?"

With a note of exasperation in her voice, Maggie said, "Oh, for heaven's sake! It's a first world country. They have hospitals and doctors, same as here. Actually, now that I think of it, one of my cousins is a doctor in Dublin, or used to be. I'll be grand."

Maggie understood the girl's concerns. She too had weighed the pros and cons of this trip. One part of her wanted to stay at the cabin, secure and cosseted. Yet, the winter was dragging her down, and she knew that if she didn't escape from it now, she'd never see spring. A memory of fields of daffodils, their heads waving lazily in a light breeze, suddenly came to mind and she smiled, secure in the knowledge that she had made the right decision.

"Where will you stay?" Isobel persisted.

"I'll be staying at the Shelbourne Hotel in Dublin for a few days. After that I'm not sure."

Isobel opened her mouth to say something but changed her mind. She glanced over at Vic, whose forehead creased into a disapproving frown as he returned her gaze. Turning back to Maggie, she smiled reluctantly and said, "I think it's a wonderful idea, Maggie. Let me know if there's anything I can do."

～

Maggie was unusually quiet on the drive to the airport. She had chosen the day deliberately, knowing that Isobel was working and wouldn't be able to come along with them. For some reason that she couldn't fully articulate, she didn't want to say goodbye to both of them, together, at the Madison airport. It had a finality to it that she wasn't quite ready for.

The dominant color of the wintry landscape through which they drove was brown, interspersed with patches of dirty snow. Everything had a jaded look, as if the previous three months had sapped every ounce of energy from the land. Spring was still several weeks away, although in the last week she had watched the outdoor thermometer climb above zero on her midday walk to the mailbox with Oliver. Huge piles of manure steamed quietly in the corners of dairy farms, waiting for the muddy fields, already covered in a thick layer of dark brown, to dry out. Maggie was looking forward to green...the lush green patchwork of fields that every visitor to Ireland remarked upon. An image came to mind of the four-lane highway from the airport into Dublin city, lined with daffodils. That was a long time ago, almost twenty years, so maybe the daffodil plantings would be gone by now. But at least the fields would still be green.

When they reached the airport, Vic pulled his truck into the drop-off area at the main entrance. He helped her down from the cab and set her roller bag beside her.

"You've got everything you need?" he asked, bending down to give her a hug.

"I have my passport and credit card," she said, tapping her purse. "And if there's anything I've forgotten, I'll buy it in Ireland."

He looked at her fondly. "We'll miss you, you know. The place won't be the same without you."

She smiled with pleasure. He meant the compliment sincerely.

"Two to three weeks, you said?" You'll let us know when you are coming back and we'll pick you up. Doesn't matter when, day or night. One of us will be here. And we'll look after the place while you're gone, so you don't need to worry."

She nodded. "Thank you. I'll miss you both." She took a few steps towards the entrance but changed her mind and came back to where Vic was standing.

"I almost forgot. Isobel will be hearing about her vet school application soon." She hesitated. "If it's a rejection, she's going to need all the support you can give her. It's not the end of the world but she'll feel like it is."

Vic nodded. "I know. But she can apply again next year. And thanks to you, she has a good back-up plan. She's almost certain she'll be accepted into the Public Health program. You gave her great advice, Maggie."

"And she listened to me? Wonder of wonders." Maggie chuckled.

"I'll hang around here for a few minutes until I know you've checked in. Isobel will want to know that you got off safely."

"I know she's worried about me, but I'll be fine. And if anything does happen, just call my lawyer. She'll sort it out."

She could feel Vic's eyes on her, trying to interpret her last comment, as she turned and walked slowly but decisively towards the terminal entrance.

# Chapter 34

The flight from Madison to Chicago took barely thirty minutes. Maggie had given herself a generous amount of time to change terminals at O'Hare airport, and as the overhead tram sped towards the international terminal, she recognized the familiar Aer Lingus logo on one of the airplanes parked on the ramp. At the sight of the bright green shamrock, she felt her eyes begin to tear up and looked around furtively, hoping that her fellow passengers didn't notice. It didn't seem to matter how many years had passed or how many times she had made this trip, the same emotions always surfaced: longing and apprehension, familiarity and dread.

With a brisk shake of her head, Maggie looked around for the Aer Lingus lounge. For the first time in her life, she was traveling on a Business Class ticket with all the attendant luxuries. The refrain 'If not now, when?' seemed particularly apt, and on this trip especially, she decided she would deny herself nothing. After a pleasant couple of hours in the lounge, during which time she watched people and planes coming and going, she made her way to the departure gate. At the entrance to the cabin, she was directed to the left, escorted to her seat by a green-uniformed steward and offered a glass of champagne. It seemed ridiculous to have withheld this luxury until her final flight, but a lifetime of financial caution was difficult to jettison. She accepted the glass of champagne and settled comfortably back into her spacious seat. She had thought carefully about what to take on board: a real book, her iPad, and most important of all, anti-inflammatory pills for the inevitable pain and stiffness she would experience.

The announcement that they were beginning their descent and would be landing at Dublin Airport in thirty minutes came as a surprise. She realized that she must have fallen asleep after the meal, an excellent and beautifully presented dinner accompanied by a surprisingly good wine. Opening the window shade, she saw that the sky was brightening a little. They were approaching the Irish coast, and she scrutinized the topography, trying to identify exactly where they made landfall. Despite having to learn to draw the outline of the country at school, the myriad inlets, beaches and villages along the coast made it almost impossible to decide which county they were flying over. Searching for a landmark, she recognized Ben Bulben, the table-shaped mountain in County Sligo that was forever associated with the poet William Butler Yeats. One of his poems in particular she had always liked and now found herself silently mouthing the words.

> *When you are old and grey and full of sleep,*
> *And nodding by the fire, take down this book,*
> *And slowly read, and dream of the soft look*
> *Your eyes had once, and of their shadows deep;*

She remembered all four verses and felt inordinately pleased with herself.

There was a gentle bump as they touched down at Dublin airport and almost immediately a voice over the intercom announced *"Céad Míle Fáilte a Baile Átha Cliath.* Welcome to Dublin." She was home.

Prying herself out of the seat, Maggie felt every bone in her body complain loudly. Seeing her discomfort, a stewardess asked had she requested a wheelchair, and if so, would she mind waiting until the other passengers had deplaned.

She smiled at the young woman. "No. I'm able to walk, thanks. Just a bit slow to get going after sitting for so long."

"I understand," came the woman's reply. "Take your time. Are you here on holiday?"

"Yes, for a few weeks. It's been a while since I've been back, though. Almost twenty years."

"Oh, you'll notice a lot of changes," the stewardess said, "But sure, it's still Ireland."

She gave a chuckle and they both laughed. She must have caught the remnants of Maggie's Irish accent for she asked, "When did you first leave?"

"Fifty-five years ago," Maggie said with a tiny shrug.

"Well, welcome home. I hope you have a lovely stay."

~

Ireland had indeed changed. The arrivals hall in the new terminal building was thronged with people, despite the early hour. There were at least a dozen taxi and limousine drivers waiting for their passengers, each holding up a name card. Maggie noticed a well-dressed middle-aged man scrutinizing the arriving guests, and for a moment she wondered if he was a member of the national security police. He made eye contact, and with a lift of his eyebrows, he held up a computer tablet. Her name was there in big bold letters. She made her way towards him through the crowds, smiling with relief.

"I'm Maggie O'Connor," she said.

He shook her hand. "Welcome to Ireland. If you'll follow me, we can go down in the elevator."

She noted the slight hint of a Dublin accent in his voice as he took her bag and led the way. At the curbside, he opened the door of a large black Mercedes sedan.

"You'll be tired after the long flight for sure, so I'll take you straight to the hotel. But if there's anything you want to see on the way, just let me know. Otherwise, our next stop is the Shelbourne."

The Shelbourne Hotel was an indisputable Dublin icon. Everyone of importance who visited the city passed through its doors. All her life Maggie had wanted to stay there, but up to now had never been able to justify the extravagance. This time was different, however, and she had made a reservation for two weeks with the possibility of staying longer. Although there were more luxurious rooms available on the lower floors, she had requested a room on the fourth floor facing St. Stephen's Green. Now, standing at the window, she looked down into the park, already busy with people making their way to work. Reluctantly, she pulled the heavy drapes closed, lay down on the bed and with a sigh of relief closed her eyes.

Waking a few hours later from a dreamless sleep, it took her a few minutes to remember where she was. The muffled noise of city traffic was unfamiliar, and for an anxious moment she thought she was back in Cherrywood. With her next intake of breath, however, she was reassured. Instead of institutional cleanliness, the room smelled vaguely of lavender, with a hint of the sea. Still with her eyes closed, she revisited the previous twenty-four hours. It seemed impossible to believe...she was finally here.

A glance at the bedside clock showed that it was mid-afternoon. Pulling back the drapes, she looked out at the city. It was already beginning to get dark, and traffic was backed up around the Green with buses, cars and taxis jostling for position where three lanes narrowed to two. She pursed her lips; it seemed that there was always construction around this square.

Just as quickly as that thought arose, another displaced it. A distant memory of cycling around the Green late at night, she and another bicyclist, lazily pedaling in the middle of the road. Who was it she had been with that evening? She sighed. Like so many fragments of memory that drifted through her thoughts these days, that particular detail would never be resurrected.

She wasn't hungry but nonetheless made her way downstairs for afternoon tea. In the Lord Mayor's Lounge, she was shown to an armchair by a small table in one of the bay windows that looked out on the hotel entrance where liveried porters greeted guests. Sipping at a cup of Darjeeling tea, Maggie let her mind drift back to a magical afternoon in her childhood when she and her sister had afternoon tea in this lounge. Her mother's aunt was visiting from the west of Ireland and had suggested that the girls join her for the treat. Whether Maggie's mother was not invited or had chosen to do some shopping instead, it was just the two little girls who were escorted into the Lord Mayor's Lounge by a uniformed porter. Dressed in their Sunday clothes and cautioned to be on their best behavior, they approached the grand old lady and sat on the edge of their cushioned, brocaded chairs facing her. Next, with some ceremony, a waiter wheeled a shiny trolley to their table, laden with cakes, pastries, tarts, trifles and a huge bowl of whipped cream. The great aunt said they could choose anything they wanted, and not just one dessert, but two or three, or all of them if they liked. At first, they were too well brought up to accept, but with encouragement from the old lady, they accepted. No dessert trolley since had equaled that childhood hedonistic experience.

Despite the magnificent room: white linen tablecloth, silver teapot and bone china, and the finger sandwiches, scones and bite-sized cakes on a three-tiered silver platter—Maggie felt disappointed and wondered if the journey had been a mistake.

# Chapter 35

Maggie woke in the middle of the night and listened to the quiet hum of the room, interrupted occasionally by the sound of a car on the street below. A church clock chimed four times and in the distance two more bells joined the chorus, their sounds overlapping harmoniously. She lay in bed, unable to sleep, her mind churning. Why had she come to Ireland? Was she expecting some sort of spiritual healing? The hours passed slowly, draining her emotionally as she struggled for answers. Finally, she counted eight chimes. Pushing those questions aside for the moment, she took stock of how her body felt this morning. Overall, it wasn't so bad: the usual pains in the usual places. Fortunately, nothing new. Her doctor had warned about taking pain pills on an empty stomach, so she showered quickly and went downstairs to breakfast.

For the first time in decades, Maggie had absolutely no idea what she was going to do. If she were still at the cabin in Wisconsin, it would be time to walk to the mailbox with Oliver. Later in the day Isobel would come by to collect the dog, and they might have a cup of tea together or a glass of wine. Instead, here she was, alone in a strange hotel, anonymous and invisible.

She sat down on an armchair in the corner of the hotel lobby and picked up a copy of the Irish Times. The news failed to keep her attention, and she folded the newspaper and returned it to the table.

The lobby was a microcosm of contemporary Irish society. After an hour of anthropological scrutiny, and with her pain significantly diminished, she decided to take a walk. The doorman saluted her smartly, identifying her correctly as a guest by the dark green hotel umbrella she was carrying. Undecided initially as to where to go, she crossed the road and went through one of the small wrought-iron gates that opened into St. Stephens Green. Within seconds of entering the park, the noise and bustle of the city disappeared as if by magic, and she found herself strolling along familiar pathways lined by tall deciduous trees. The manicured gardens were filled with daffodils and tulips, corralled behind neat privet hedges. Leaves drifted on the surface of the pond, ignored by the ducks that glided along effortlessly. The old-fashioned park benches with their wrought-iron arm rests and slatted wooden seats were as popular as ever: two middle-aged women engaged in intense discussion, their heads almost touching; an old man staring into space; a young mother holding a paper bag as her child threw handfuls of stale bread at the flock of pigeons at their feet. In the past she had spent many hours sitting on these same benches: in love, heartbroken, daydreaming...

By now a light drizzle was falling, and she sheltered under her umbrella, considering where to go next. It was far too early to go back to the hotel, but she felt chilled to the bone. Turning the corner, she saw a sign, Glandore Hotel, and decided to escape the damp for a couple of hours with a cup of tea. The building looked vaguely familiar, but it was only when she looked to the structure's flanking it that she realized this was Loreto Hall, the Catholic residence where she had stayed during her first year at university.

Her spirits lifted a little as she walked into the hotel. The building was transformed. A log fire warmed the comfortable sitting room on one side of the lobby, a well-proportioned Georgian reception room with an ornate plaster ceiling from which hung a Waterford crystal chandelier. This must have been the nuns' parlor, she thought, and chuckled, but in her time the room had always been frigid. Boyfriends who came to the residence hall to collect their dates were shown into the parlor by a wizened nun, who left them there under the stern gaze of a portrait of the foundress of the Loreto Order. While they waited, they must have wondered whether their planned liaison was worthwhile. Eventually, their date would appear, and the two young lovers could escape for a few, unsupervised hours. The corners of her mouth twitched in amusement as she remembered those trysts. Curfew was at seven p.m. on weekdays and ten p.m. on weekends, and the nuns were unforgiving when it came to locking the massive oak door. Many times she had arrived back at the residence hall out of breath, apologizing profusely to the presiding nun and blaming the bus for being late, whereas it had been the long drawn out, passionate kiss at the corner of the park with Seán Reilly that was the actual cause of her breathlessness.

It was getting dark when Maggie left the Glandore. People huddled at bus stops along Harcourt Street, and lights were beginning to come on in the windows of the Georgian terrace houses. Looking upwards, she remembered that she had once rented a flat in this neighborhood, and how she used to trudge up the three flights of stairs with heavy grocery bags. That was the year after Loreto Hall, when she lived with two other girls from her home town. They had shared everything, including a chilly bedroom with three single beds, not unlike the dormitory in the residence hall. Now, sixty years later, she noticed that many of the buildings had been converted into stylish hotels with elegant Georgian facades that exuded luxury.

By the time Maggie arrived back at the Shelbourne, she was

exhausted. The room felt cozy, and rather than dressing for dinner, she ordered room service and a bottle of expensive white wine, muttering to herself, "If not now, when?" It was still too early to try to sleep. Without thinking, she opened the leather-bound folder on the desk. The heavy, cream-colored hotel stationary felt smooth under her hand and for some reason, she felt an urge to write to Isobel. The ballpoint pen fitted comfortably in her arthritic fingers. She set the glass of wine beside her on the desk, and taking a sip, began to write:

*Dear Isobel,*

*I thought about you today, imagined you sitting across from me here in the hotel, a pot of tea between us, chatting like we do at the cabin.*

*Why did I come? If I'm honest, I thought this trip would heal me. Of what, you might ask? For starters, the burden of guilt that comes from being an emigrant. Is it just the Irish that feel this way? It's bred in the bone for us, a visceral tether to the country. Coming back here was meant to bring my life full circle: home, my real home. Only now that I'm here, I almost wish I was back at the cabin in Wisconsin.*

She set down the pen with a sigh. She'd try again tomorrow, try to be searingly honest in a letter she would never mail.

For the next several days, Maggie became a flaneur, wandering around the city aimlessly, experiencing Dublin in a way that would have been impossible when she was younger. For an hour each morning and evening she sat in the hotel lobby, a newspaper opened on her lap, watching the coming and goings. It was a fascinating and ever-changing window on Ireland. By the third day, many of the hotel staff greeted her by name: Doctor or Professor O'Connor. She made an effort to learn most of their names and reciprocated these greetings warmly. The staff were attentive to her needs, stopping by regularly to offer coffee or tea, a glass of wine or a cocktail. She had spoken to the concierge several times and learned his name was Johnny. A man in his 50s, he hailed from the north side of Dublin and knew the city intimately. If he wasn't busy with other guests, often he would come over to where she sat and chat for a few minutes. Inevitably, she had questions about a place she had seen the previous day, and generally he had the answer at his fingertips. But if not, he'd seek it out and deliver the information to her the following morning.

After dinner each evening, she took a glass of wine to her room and continued writing to Isobel. The tone of the letter changed day by day. In the beginning the letter was little more than a travelogue, recounting the places she had been that day, with little personal reflection. The Dublin city bus tour stopped outside the Shelbourne, and on a whim she stepped aboard the old-fashioned double-decker for a three-hour tour. Instead of the scratched metal benches she remembered from her student days, comfortable upholstered seats were spaced generously along each side of the center aisle. Gone were the women with their tightly-tied headscarves and bags of groceries. Gone too, the steamed-up windows, floors littered with cigarette butts and the ever-present smell of wet wool. From her vantage point upstairs, Maggie watched the city going about its business, allowing her memory free rein, noting with curiosity which pieces of her past were dredged up. As they passed through the Phoenix Park, she considered contacting one of her cousins who lived in the nearby suburb of Blanchardstown but immediately dismissed the thought. This trip was all about her, and she didn't want to complicate it.

As the days went by, her letter to Isobel took on a more contemplative tone. Whereas she had started out wanting to take Isobel on a journey through the city with her, now she wandered alone. A few years earlier, she had heard an interview with the Irish writer Colm Tóibín, one of her favorites. Responding to a question as to why so many of his stories were set in the small town where he grew up, his answer resonated with her: "You can recover time." That phrase became her mantra. Her *Ulysses*-like wanderings around Dublin were an opportunity to recover her past, examine every facet of it in a new light and recognize how wonderful it had all been.

# Chapter 36

One evening before dinner at the hotel, Maggie positioned herself in a quiet corner of the lobby and waited for an opportunity to talk with the concierge. He smiled warmly at her as she approached the desk, greeting her by name. Taking the proffered chair, she sat down and began to explain her dilemma. She needed to hire a car and a driver for four days to travel to the west. However, the prospect of sharing such a small space with a complete stranger for that length of time was disconcerting. Did he know of anyone suitable? Johnny listened sympathetically, asked a few questions and finally said to leave it with him. He had someone in mind but would need to make a couple of phone calls. He would let her know as soon as possible.

When she woke the following morning, she saw that there was an envelope tucked under her door. The note was from Johnny, who proposed that she spend a few hours that day with a driver he knew well. The man in question, an older individual now semi-retired from the chauffeur business, might be persuaded to take on a special client providing suitable arrangements could be made. If Maggie was agreeable, the driver would be available from ten onward. All she had to do was call the desk and let Johnny know at what time she would like the car.

Stepping out of the elevator into the lobby later that morning, Maggie saw an older man in conversation with the concierge. Johnny noticed her immediately and touched the other man on the elbow, guiding his gaze towards his client. With a broad smile and a gesture of his hand, he introduced the driver to Maggie.

"Dr. O'Connor, this is Peter Quigley. You'll be in good hands with him, I give you my word. He's a good driver, and he knows Dublin well. You'll have a grand time."

Peter Quigley held out his hand to Maggie and gave her a firm but gentle handshake. He was between sixty-five and seventy, she guessed, with a healthy head of grey hair and a carefully trimmed grey beard. A shade under six feet, he was dressed in brown slacks and shoes, and wore a tweed jacket over a charcoal woolen sweater. He looked completely at ease with himself, the hotel and life in general. She noticed the crows' feet in the corners of his eyes, a testament to his frequent and genuine smile.

They said their goodbyes to the concierge and walked towards the exit. Maggie couldn't help but notice the distinct limp; Peter favored his right leg. She speculated as to whether he was on a waiting list for knee replacement surgery, or perhaps he had had a car accident, or maybe it was a deformity from birth. She assumed he would be driving an automatic, so it hardly mattered. She was curious nonetheless and wondered if she would find out over the course of the next few days. A gust of cold biting wind put the thought out of her mind and she hurried to follow Peter, who despite his limp, moved quickly down the steps towards the car, a spotless, black Peugeot sedan idling at the curbside. He opened the rear door, and she felt the warmth pouring out of the vehicle into the damp air. She hesitated. If she was going to spend the next several days in this man's company, she didn't want to treat him like a chauffeur.

"I'd prefer to sit in the front, if you don't mind," she said, adding by way of clarification, "It's easier for me to hear you."

Peter nodded. He walked around to the passenger door, opened it carefully and waited until she had settled herself before closing it gently behind her. He got into the driver's seat, buckled himself in and, before moving away, turned to her. His question was surprisingly direct.

"And now, tell me, what shall I call you? I know your name is Professor Maggie O'Connor. Should I call you Doctor or Professor?"

His voice was educated, and Maggie detected a northern Irish accent. It didn't have the harsh notes of Belfast. Instead, she heard the softness of County Donegal.

"Maggie," she answered without hesitation. "Maggie is just fine."

He smiled and nodded his approval. "Maggie it is then."

"And how about you, Mr. Quigley? Should I call you Peter?"

"You can call me anything you like," he answered with a laugh, his eyes crinkling up, "but Peter is grand."

With that, he eased the car away from the curb and merged expertly with the traffic flowing around St. Stephen's Green. Maggie was a little surprised that he hadn't asked where she would like to go. But as he was at her disposal for the next several hours, it hardly mattered. He would drive and she would look outside and they would talk. By the end of the day she'd know if he was the right person to take her to the west of Ireland.

~

After breakfast the following morning, Maggie read the pages she had written to Isobel the night before. The day with Peter Quigley had been an unexpected journey back in time, crammed with memories of her boarding school and college years. Her descriptions were vivid, and the emotions each place elicited were equally telling. Writing to Isobel, Maggie realized, had become a form of therapy. For a moment she considered, if for some reason she mailed the letter, would Isobel try to read between the lines as she herself had done with the Amherst letters? Maggie lingered on that notion, that people read letters for information, for descriptions of places and events, not for hidden meanings. Could her parents have read her letters from Amherst strictly at face value, never considering that anything was amiss? It was an earth-shattering idea, and for a moment Maggie felt breathless. If that was the case, perhaps the years of accumulated guilt and estrangement had been founded on a misconception.

She got up from her desk and began to pace around the room, alternately rubbing at her wrist and wringing her hands. This new interpretation of her past felt like a tangled ball of wool, which needed time and patience to unravel. She gathered up her coat and purse, and almost ran from the room. She needed to get outside and walk, either for distraction or contemplation—she didn't know which.

Some years earlier Grafton Street had become a popular pedestrian walkway, with traffic diverted through the adjacent streets, to the dismay of taxi drivers and delivery vehicles. Few of the shops Maggie remembered from her childhood remained. Pubs were more resilient, and she was reassured by the familiar ornate signs that still hung outside a few of her student haunts. If familiar stores had disappeared, some things never changed. Rain or shine, the flower sellers on the corner of Chatham Street still plied their trade, and Bewleys Café continued to welcome tired mothers. Buskers entertained shoppers and tourists alike, arranging themselves along the length of the street: a group of singers, a troupe of Irish dancers, a young girl cradling a harp that she stroked lovingly. Maggie inserted herself into a large crowd arranged in a ragged semi-circle around five boys, barely in their teens, who would have blended easily into a Dickens novel.

Just past Bewleys Café, she turned left into a familiar narrow lane. A row of antique jewelry shops lined one side, their windows filled with the treasures of long dead generations. She slipped into a doorway partially hidden on the opposite side and entered a familiar building. St. Theresa's Church was one of the hidden gems of the city, a haven for believers and non-believers alike. Inside, the church was dark and hushed, and as she tiptoed towards one of the side altars, Maggie inhaled the cloying scent of recently-snuffed beeswax candles. There must have been a mass earlier, she surmised, and felt a small pang of remorse that she hadn't made the effort to attend. Catholic churches had an uncanny way of making one feel welcome, regardless of how long the lapse. She dropped some coins into a narrow slot beneath the altar in a side-chapel and listened to the clinking sound echoing around the small alcove. Helping herself to a votive candle from the box, she touched it to the flame of an adjacent candle and set it on an ornate metal bracket beneath a sad-eyed Virgin Mary. It was a comforting ritual. Now, watching the tiny flame flicker in the semi-darkness, she thought about its symbolism. You lit candles for people you cared about, alive or dead. This candle, she realized, was for herself.

She sat for a long time staring into space, her mind in chaos. Guilt. It was all about guilt. The guilt she felt towards her parents. Her abrupt withdrawal from them had been misdirected. *They* were never the problem—she was. They were the innocent victims of her selfishness. Now, after so many years of evasion, she desperately wanted to talk to them.

～

"Glasnevin Cemetery, please," Maggie said to the driver as she stepped into the taxi. He was a small, wiry man in his thirties with dark curly hair and a sallow complexion. He had a thick Dublin accent, leaving no doubt that he had grown up in the city.

"It'll be slow," he warned. "They're diggin' up all the old water pipes and replacin' them. Sure, we'll be payin' for the next twenty years."

Maggie wasn't in the humor to chat, so she tried to keep their conversation to a minimum.

"Are yiz here on holidays?" he asked.

"Sort of," she replied. "I used to be a student in Dublin a long time ago. I've lived in America for years now. This trip...home... is to look at some of the places I used to know. But everything has changed so much."

"But sure, the cemetery doesn't change much," he replied, with a delighted laugh.

After another thirty minutes, during which Maggie answered his questions as briefly as possible, the familiar tall round tower came into view as they paralleled the high stone wall surrounding the cemetery. He took the brightly-colored euro bill that she offered and returned several smaller bills.

"It's good that you've come back to pay your respects," he said, as she opened the door of the taxi and stepped out.

At the information desk in the modern building by the entrance gate, an efficient young woman typed the names of Maggie's parents into her computer. A minute later, she told Maggie their ashes were in the Garden of Remembrance and handed her a map on which she had marked the location of the memorial. Back outside in the sunshine, Maggie followed the red lines on the map, making her way along paved walkways between well-kept graves and neatly trimmed cypress trees. Multi-generational families strolled past, the babies strapped into buggies pushed by parents or grandparents, the smaller children running ahead. Elderly family members shuffled slowly behind or were pushed along in wheelchairs. A couple of cyclists passed her, going slowly. Initially, she was taken aback by their indifference to the solemnity of the place, but looking at her map, she saw that the cycle path connecting the Botanical Gardens with the Phoenix Park passed through the cemetery.

She came to a broad pathway bordered by a low privet hedge. Tall beech trees arched gracefully over the red bricks, shading them from the watery sunlight. Slabs of grey granite flanked the path on both sides, each of them angled such that the names engraved on their surface could be read easily. She peered at the names and dates etched on the first slab, north facing and encrusted in lichen. Someone had cleaned a small section, and leaning over it she made out the date: 1960. Continuing along the path, noting the years, eventually she found them, their names etched into the grey surface of a west-facing slab. She stood for a long time, staring at the small neat words, Michael and Anna O'Connor, her mind a blank. Looking around for somewhere to sit, she found a wooden bench under one of the large beech trees. Pulling her coat tightly around her, she sat down. Her gloved hands were tightly clasped, as if in prayer. She began to speak, her voice barely a whisper.

"I'm sorry it took me so long. I should have told you the truth a long time ago. Maybe I would have had a different life.

"If I close my eyes, I can see the three of us sitting around the kitchen table in the old house. You are so happy to have me home: your wonderful, clever daughter who has just spent a year in America. You are hoping that I'll find a good job in Ireland, get married, have a couple of kids and a house not too far away so we can all have Sunday dinners together. The years will pass happily enough, and your lives will be just like all of your friends, wrapped up in kids and grandkids. Eventually your health will give out, but you'll have family around you, right up to the very last minute.

"I ruined that dream. I was selfish, but I was also trying to protect you. What would have happened if you came to America that September and found your daughter six months pregnant? I can see it now: meeting you at the airport, watching your gaze drop to my swollen belly. There would be a shocked silence, neither of you daring to speak. Eventually, one of you would say, "Who's the father?" as if that was the critical question and that knowing the answer would solve everything. I'd see the alarm in your eyes as you realized that he might not even be white. I'd tell you the truth: an English postdoc, gone back to England and out of the picture. 'He doesn't even know.' A momentary fragment of relief—at least the baby wouldn't be black or brown or yellow. Eventually, one of you would gather up your courage and ask what I planned to do about it. By now a new fear would have surfaced in your minds: that I might want to keep the baby and bring it back to Ireland. Hearing that I was going to give it up for adoption in America would have been a huge relief. I'd see it on your faces. Nobody in Ireland need find out about this. Your respectability would remain unblemished. Even though I could have understood those feelings, I'd have hated you both for your predictable small-mindedness. There was no way any of us could have come out of this unscathed, so I did the only thing I could: push you away and try to protect myself. Did I do the right thing? I was certain then, but I'm less sure now."

Maggie pulled a handkerchief out of her pocket and wiped at her eyes. They had begun to tear, whether from the cold or the emotion? she didn't know. Her gaze drifted past the granite slabs to the endless rows of gravestones, as if searching for a reaction to her words. Shifting her position slightly, she resumed her confession.

"In Germany I shut off emotionally and buried myself in work. I didn't want to see you. I couldn't let you get close to me. I'd have weakened and confessed. I'd have sought your forgiveness; not for getting pregnant but for failing to give you the lives you had hoped for. My penance? The only acceptable atonement would have been to come back to Ireland. I couldn't do that.

"It's funny how you look at things differently as you grow older. The absolutes fade and you begin to notice the vast possibilities that lie in between. We could all have lived happily in those spaces. Instead, I hid behind the wall that I built between us in Amherst. I suppose I didn't know how to dismantle it, and by the time I could see how, it was too late. You were both gone. That's my biggest regret. Not the adoption, not a lifetime dedicated to career, not the guilt that I've carried like a cross. My biggest regret is that I never told you how much I loved you both and how grateful I am to have had you as my parents. You did everything right. I was the one who made mistakes.

"I never wanted a child, not then, not since. But it's funny how life turns out. I seem to have acquired a grandchild, or at least that's how it feels. Isobel has brought me so much pleasure over the past nine months. She reminds me of myself at that age. Maybe because of that, I know she's going to be just fine. I think about her and Vic and Oliver at the cabin in Mazomanie and it makes me happy.

"I'm sorry I hurt you. I know that all you ever wanted was for me to be happy. I wish you could see me now. Thank you for everything."

The cold had seeped into her bones, and Maggie winced as she braced to get up from the bench. Taking a handkerchief from her coat pocket, she wiped her eyes. With a final glance back at where her parents' names were etched, she walked slowly towards the entrance gate to find a taxi.

# Chapter 37

"It's a grand day to be going to the West," Peter Quigley said as he ushered Maggie to the car the following morning. Noticing the travel blanket she was carrying over her arm, he took it from her, tucking it around her legs once she was seated comfortably. It was a gloomy morning, but he reassured her that the weather forecast was for bright spells west of the Shannon. She looked over at him, her eyebrows raised skeptically, and they shared a laugh.

"It's Westport we're going to, isn't it? Do you know which road you want to take?" Peter asked, as he placed his smart phone into a cradle on the dashboard.

"It's where my grandparents came from," Maggie said, by way of explanation. "We used to go there a lot as children." She gestured to the smart phone. "Less than three hours? It's hard to believe. The journey seemed to take the whole day when I was a child."

"Three hours if we take the motorway, but we don't have to. Let's see. You'd have been starting from..." Peter mentioned the name of the town where Maggie had told him she was born.

"I remember driving through Kells and Longford...we always

stopped for lunch in Longford. It must have been the only hotel that served food in those days. There were other towns after that but I've forgotten their names. As we got closer to Westport, my sister and I would start to look for Croagh Patrick—you know, the mountain. The first one of us who spotted it got a sixpence."

"That settles it," said Peter. "We'll take the M2 to Slane and go on from there to Kells. We could stop in Longford for lunch, but I'd suggest another place. It's a wee pub on the Shannon River, and you'd be surprised at how good the food is there. In summer the place is alive with tourists off the cruise boats, but it'll be quiet this early in the year."

Peter was right about the pub. It was warm and welcoming, with a small turf fire smoldering in the grate in the back bar. They sat in the tiny dining room and enjoyed a delicious meal. Maggie wanted to find out more about Peter, but he was adept at steering the conversation away from himself, asking questions about her life instead.

"Is your sister still around?"

"No. She died while I was at university in Dublin. She was cycling home one evening and was hit by a car. It was dark and raining. It was nobody's fault, just an accident."

He nodded sympathetically. She gestured towards his leg. "Is that what happened to you? An accident?"

"No. Mine wasn't an accident. It was very deliberate. I was knee-capped in Derry during the Troubles." His hand went down to his knee and he massaged it tenderly. "They did a good repair job at the Royal in Belfast—they had a lot of experience with gun shots in those days. When I could walk again, I left Northern Ireland and spent almost ten years in Australia. When things quietened down, I came back. I've lived in Dublin ever since."

They sat in silence for a few minutes. Eventually, Maggie said, "There's something to be said for growing old. Tragedies don't hurt as much."

As they drove farther west, the landscape changed. Fields

were smaller, each enclosed by stone walls. Sheep replaced cattle, with new-born lambs trailing after their mothers, angling for milk. Peter generally had something interesting to say about each village or township they passed through. Like many of his countrymen, he was an excellent story teller and had an encyclopedic command of Irish history and geography.

"There's Croagh Patrick," said Peter, taking one hand off the steering wheel and pointing excitedly. "I think you owe me sixpence," he added with a laugh.

Following his finger, she caught a glimpse of the mountain, before it was obscured by a tall hedge. Around the next corner it came into view again, its perfect grey dome silhouetted against the sky. Maggie felt an intense ache in her heart, part yearning and part joy, at having finally come to the end of a long journey. Her eyes welled up with tears, and she let them slide down her cheeks unhindered.

Within an hour they arrived in Westport. The Wyatt Hotel wasn't as grand as the Shelbourne, but the staff were friendly and welcomed her warmly. Maggie assured Peter she would not need him for the rest of the evening, and they arranged to meet in the hotel lobby the following morning. Before dinner, she took a stroll along the mall, a tree-lined walk by the river. The town was quiet, the bustle of day-time crowds having dwindled to a few solitary figures hurrying home. A row of tall curved wrought-iron lamps hung over the path, making it easy for her to find her way. She leaned on the parapet of a low stone bridge that crossed the river. Random thoughts passed through her mind. Ireland had not been in her plans as recently as six weeks ago. Yet, here she was in Westport, where the damp air was infused with the smell of smoky turf fires. This elusive smell was part of her childhood, conjuring feelings of safety, family, love. She took a deep breath and licked her lips, tasting the sea. The heady combination spread though her like a balm, reaching into her soul.

~

The following morning Peter arrived promptly, looking a little tired, which Maggie attributed to a late night of drinking. On the drive west the previous day, he mentioned that he had friends in Westport whom he might try to look up if time allowed. Clearly, he had succeeded. The car was parked outside, its engine running.

"We're in luck with the weather," he said, looking up at the sky. "So what's the plan for today? Where would you like to go?"

Maggie knew exactly where she wanted to go. This plan had been conceived and crafted weeks earlier, every aspect of it carefully measured.

"I'd like to drive out the road towards Croagh Patrick," she said.

Peter raised his eyebrows and looked at her with a mixture of inquiry and skepticism.

"Don't worry," she said with a laugh, "We're not going to climb the Reek."

Known locally as the Reek, every year thousands of people climbed Croagh Patrick on the last Sunday in July. The pilgrimage, which commemorated St. Patrick's sojourn on top of the mountain for forty nights, had become one of those "must attend" events in Ireland, like the Galway Races and the Ploughing Championships.

"Did you ever climb it?" Peter asked.

"I've done it six times," Maggie replied, a hint of pride in her voice. "I was thirteen the first time—my father's idea. He wasn't religious, but he loved the rural pageantry: arriving at dusk, parking in some muddy field miles away, listening to the hawkers calling out 'Sticks for the Reek,' starting up the hill in the pitch dark." Maggie continued, her eyes bright with enthusiasm. "It was amazing experience. You were part of this great swath of humanity, all with a common purpose, but each person with their own reasons for doing the climb. Some people prayed out loud as they circled the statues along the way. Others were silent, stoic, even barefoot or on their knees. For some it was an opportunity to kiss and cuddle in some sheltered spot off the track under cover of darkness. Close to the top you'd see the lights of the kerosene lanterns hanging by shebeens, with people huddled nearby sipping cups of tea poured from blackened kettles slung over smoky peat fires. And then the dawn would break. I think that's the most authentic religious experience I've ever had: dawn coming up over Clew Bay and each one of the islands emerging from the sea fog, like stars."

"My God, Maggie. You're almost making me jealous," said Peter, the corners of his eyes creasing with mirth.

They took the quay road with its spectacular views of Clew Bay, and in the distance, Clare Island. Abruptly, Maggie put her hand on Peter's arm and pointed to the left as they drove by an imposing gate set back from the road. Tall stone pillars on either side of the entrance merged with a curved stone wall that extended for fifty feet in both directions.

"My grandparents used to live there," she said.

Peter looked at her. "Is that why you wanted to come here?" His voice was gentle.

She nodded. The road curved to the left and Maggie craned her neck to look back towards the house. Its location was magnificent, situated on a low hill that gave a commanding view of the bay. Behind the house loomed Croagh Patrick, silhouetted against the blue sky.

"Our parents used to leave us here for a few weeks every summer. I suppose it was a chance for them to get a proper holiday. We adored coming here. We were utterly spoiled by Granny and Granda, and we had loads of cousins of our own age to play with. When our parents came to collect us, we didn't want to go home."

She laughed, and the smile lingered on her face. Peter slowed the car down and checked in his rear-view mirror.

"Do you want to go back?" he asked.

"No, that's not necessary," Maggie said but without conviction.

"Oh, come on Maggie. Why don't we turn around and drive up to the place?" Peter's enthusiasm and curiosity were palpable. "What's the worst they can do? They'll hardly come out with a gun, and if they do, we'll just drive off. What do you say?"

Despite the look of disapproval on her face, she began to laugh. The specter of a gun-toting owner coming out of the house to challenge them was so ridiculous. That sort of thing might happen in America but never in the west of Ireland. Around the next bend the road widened, and Peter turned the car into a pull-out, strategically placed so that tourists could take in the stunning views of the bay and the mountain without creating a traffic jam. He stopped the car and looked inquiringly at Maggie.

"Okay. Let's go back," she said. She was rewarded by a mischievous grin from Peter as he turned the car around.

They drove through the gateway and up the long sweeping avenue. Maggie noticed weeds growing up through the gravel, and as they approached the house, she saw that the lawn hadn't been mown in some time. A porcelain sink lay awkwardly on its side at the base of the steps leading up to the front door. Parked, one behind the other, on the lower driveway leading to the kitchen and stables were three vans, each advertising their trade: plasterer, electrician, plumber.

"Why don't you wait here and I'll see what's going on," said Peter, getting out of the car.

Maggie could hear drilling and hammering coming from inside the house as Peter climbed the steps to the front door and disappeared inside. She got out of the car and walked back along the driveway a few paces to get a better view. Despite its shabbiness, the house was still impressive: a large, two story

Georgian-style building situated perfectly, with Achill and Clare islands visible in the distance. A dozen or so wide steps led up to the hall door, which was flanked by tall glass panes. Above the door, a window was inscribed with the name: Killadangan House. She walked back to the house and eased herself down on one of the lower steps. It was seventy-five years since she had last sat here. She still had a black and white photograph of her mother in exactly this spot, flanked by two little girls dressed in matching white pinafores. That photograph captured everything she felt about this place: childhood, security, love.

When he returned, Peter looked pleased. "I had a wee chat with the foreman. They've gutted the place, but he says we can take a look around if we want. He doesn't know any O'Connors, but the place has changed hands a good few times over the years. Now it's going to be an upscale B&B." He was clearly excited to go back inside.

He helped Maggie to her feet and took her elbow as she climbed the steps. Once inside, she provided a continuous narrative of her childhood memories as they peeked into each of the upstairs rooms. As children, they were rarely allowed upstairs into the formal sitting and dining rooms and never into her grandparent's bedroom. They continued down the stairs to the ground floor. The hammering and drilling had stopped and the house was now quiet, its thick stone walls muffling any noise from outside. It was lunch time and the workmen had taken a break, leaving their tools strewn around the kitchen. Maggie stood in the middle of the room, reconstructing it in her mind, adding furniture and people and layering on smells and sounds.

"If I could re-live one day of my life, it would be here in this room as a five-year-old child."

Peter cocked his head to one side. "Tell me more."

"There was a huge Aga stove along that wall." She pointed to an empty space below a stovepipe that stuck out from the wall.

She looked up towards the ceiling. "That's where the laundry was dried, on a wooden rack with a pulley to haul it up." With a chuckle, she added, "I've often wondered if any laundry ever fell into the pots on the stove." Turning slightly, her eyes roamed around the room. "There was a big wooden dresser against that wall. We'd sit at the kitchen table—it was covered in oilcloth—and Bridie would bring over an old sardine can filled with crayons. She'd give each of us a sheet of kitchen paper and tell us to stay out of her way because she was 'up to her ears.' But after a few minutes, she'd put a plate of homemade biscuits in the center of the table and a glass of milk by each of us."

Maggie's delight was palpable as she regaled Peter with these snippets of memory.

"It sounds magical," said Peter, a note of envy in his voice. "What age were ye when it ended?"

Maggie frowned. "I must have been about six; my sister would have been eight. Granny died. After that it all changed. I don't think Granda could bear to live here anymore."

They left by the kitchen door and walked around the house and through the stable yard before returning to the car. Peter waved at the workmen, who were sitting on some old rusted garden chairs eating their lunch. A couple of them waved back, and he shouted his thanks.

"Would ye be interested in a wee bit of lunch yourself?" Peter asked.

"A cup of tea and a scone would be perfect, thanks," Maggie said in a quiet voice.

"There's a place in Louisburgh that I've heard is good. We'll be there in less than ten minutes."

They got back into the car. As Peter made a wide turn in front of the house, Maggie took a final look. The visit had been a rare and unexpected gift.

~

It was mid-afternoon when they left the coffee shop and turned towards Westport. Over lunch Maggie told Peter she wanted to stop at Old Head, the beach where she had learned to swim as a child. They drove down a narrow winding laneway towards the pier. Only the locals came here when she was a child. Few people had cars in those days, and the laneway ended abruptly at the shoreline. To her surprise, there was now a paved parking lot and a public toilet.

She turned to Peter. "There's no need to come with me. I might just sit awhile and look at the water. I'll take the blanket in case I get chilled, and I've got a thermos of coffee from breakfast this morning."

Peter helped her out of the car and handed her the blanket. She gathered her purse and walked across the parking lot in the direction of the water. She walked along the shoreline, a few feet back from the foamy edge of the incoming tide. In the distance she could see Croagh Patrick, resplendent against a sky filled with perfect, puffy white clouds. The beach curved to the right and just before she lost sight of the car, she turned and waved. Peter waved back, then climbed into the car and pulled the door shut.

# Chapter 38

*It's funny how you choose the place for your own death. Of all the places I considered, the beach at Old Head felt perfect. I'd sit on the sand with my back against a rock, the smell of the sea everywhere around me, and take a long, last drink. It was easy to get the sodium pentobarbital powder mailed from India. I brought the blanket in case I got chilled, but with the dose of drug I planned to drink, I would asleep within minutes. Just to make it easier for everyone, there was an envelope in my purse marked "Suicide Note," with contact information for my lawyer in Wisconsin. I thought about putting a note in there for Peter by way of apology but decided against it in the end.*

*I walked along the beach until I was out of sight of the car, found a place to sit and wrapped the blanket around me. I let my mind go blank. A part of me knew what I was about to do, but it was as if I was watching that person from a distance.*

*It was a perfect spot: well sheltered, with a watery sun glistening off the sea. I watched the shorebirds for a little while. Oyster catchers are wonderful. They have this carefree approach to waves, dancing back and forth, dipping their long beaks into the newly wetted sand. They don't seem to worry. No back-up plans there.*

*I stared down at the thermos in my lap. Time passed. Little wisps of memories strayed into my head and I let them float away, not choosing to focus. I heard children laughing and looked around, but the beach was deserted. Closing my eyes, I saw my sister and me as children, laughing and playing in the sand next to Mummy and Daddy. We were here, in exactly this spot. It was such a rich, vivid, joyful memory. That's when I knew I couldn't do it, not here. I put the flask back in my purse, got up, and walked back towards the car.*

*Peter must have been asleep, for he jumped when I opened the passenger door. He started the engine immediately and turned the heat up full. I told him I was ready to go back to the hotel and that I wanted to go to Dublin the following day. He nodded, and we drove back along the road to Westport. He must have sensed that I didn't want to talk, for he didn't ask any more questions.*

~

That evening Maggie felt strangely elated. Everything about the day had been unexpected, and she needed some time to think about her decision. After dinner she went for a walk around the town. It had started to drizzle. The sound of traditional music drifted out into the evening air from one of the bars. To her surprise, she went in and ordered a hot Irish whiskey. There was hardly anyone in the place, but the musicians, a couple of fiddlers, a boy with uileann pipes and a girl with a bodhran, didn't seem to care. Neither did she.

The drive from Westport to Dublin the following day took a little over three hours. They spoke very little, Maggie watching the countryside slide by, lost in thought. When they arrived at the hotel, Peter came around to the passenger door and helped her to get out of the car.

The doorman greeted her warmly. "Welcome back to the Shelbourne, Dr. O'Connor."

Peter insisted on carrying her luggage to the Reception

desk, refusing the porter's help. He held his hand out to her and she took it on both of hers. He had been the perfect companion for this journey and she was sad to say goodbye. She handed him an envelope.

"Johnny took care of everything already," he protested, accepting the envelope with reluctance.

"Ah, but Johnny wasn't brought up by nuns," Maggie said with a laugh. "We were always told to write proper thank-you letters."

"Thank *you*, Maggie. It has been my great pleasure," said Peter.

She watched him limp across the lobby towards the main entrance. With a wave to Johnny, who was occupied with a guest, he stepped out into the street. She turned to the receptionist, whom she recognized, a charming Italian man who always bowed slightly as he pronounced her title.

"We have you in the same room as the last time, Professora O'Connor. Is that's okay with you?"

"That will be fine," she said, taking the key card from him. "I don't need any help with my bag, thank you all the same."

He bowed again.

～

With nothing else to fill the afternoon, she decided on a final walk around St. Stephen's Green. Without noticing or caring in which direction she wandered, she came to a small fountain with three life-sized female bronze statues in the center. The plaque at the base of the sculpture explained that the figures were called *Norns* in Norse mythology, but Maggie recognized them from a play she read at boarding school as the Greek Fates, goddesses who assigned a destiny to people at their birth: Clotho, the spinner; Lachises, with a measuring tape; and Atropos, with a small knife poised over the thick thread she held in her hand.

The two standing figures looked like mother and daughter, but it was the seated figure that captured Maggie's attention. Positioned slightly apart from the other two, the gaunt face of this old woman wore a melancholic expression, indifferent to the thread of life she held in her hands. Maggie was stunned by the realization that everything about her life was in that sculpture: youth, with its excitement and promise; middle-age, with its measured successes; and old age, with its acceptance of the approaching end.

She returned to her room, nodding to the young man at reception before taking the elevator. Sitting on the bed, she considered what she was going to do for the remainder of the afternoon. She took the flask and the suicide note from her purse and placed them on the bedside table. She was fairly certain the drug would still work. Nonetheless, it might be better to wait until later in the evening when there would be no fear of interruption. A quotation came to mind: "*To cease upon the midnight with no pain...*" She felt completely at peace with herself, her life and the decisions she had made along the way.

The phone rang, and she reached over to the bedside table to pick it up.

"Professora O'Connor?"

"Yes, this is she," Maggie said.

"I apologize. I forgot to tell you that there is a message for you here at Reception. I shall send it up immediately."

Maggie was perplexed. With the exception of the concierge and her driver, she hadn't spoken to anyone in Ireland. A few minutes later an envelope was delivered. Her name was printed on the front, and beneath it a note: Telephone message taken at four p.m. on Thursday, followed by a signature, presumably the person who had taken the message. Maggie opened the envelope and read:

*Isobel has found Lara. She wants to meet you.*

She turned the page over but it was blank. She stared at the two short sentences. She could almost hear Isobel's voice, carefully spelling out each word and insisting that the person taking the message repeat it back to her.

It was getting dark outside. For several minutes she sat, staring into space. She thought about the cabin, Isobel and Vic... her home. Picking up the telephone, she pressed the button for the concierge desk.

"Johnny, this is Maggie O'Connor. I need your help with a flight to the United States."

# Acknowledgments

First and foremost, enormous thanks go to my editor, Christine Keleny who has been a part of this project from the beginning. She has guided me with a gentle but firm hand, and with her help I have become a better writer. You always hear that writing is a lonely endeavor, and much of the time it is. But something I didn't anticipate was how enthusiastically friends, family and acquaintances become engaged. My beta readers, Janne Balsamo, Valerie Burland, Sandra Faust, Kim Lord-Plummer, Rex Owens, Donna Preis-Siede, William Ried, and Ledell Zellers have been wonderful — insightful, thoughtful, critical and timely. The 'Yoga Ladies' who gather at Mary Devitt's coffeehouse in Cross Plains have kept me smiling over the years as well as encouraging me to keep writing. Crossroads Coffeehouse is also where I first saw Gina Hecht's evocative painting, Pastoral, now hanging in my cabin as well as being on the cover of this novel. Valerie Biel and Peter Rhoades gave me excellent advice about how to pitch my novel. George Siede came to the rescue with the cover. I'm indebted to the Division of Continuing Studies at the University of Wisconsin-Madison for hosting two great writing conferences, Write by the Lake and the Writers Institute. My sister Valerie Behan-Pelletier has been on this writing journey with me for many years, and I can only hope for many more. Finally, I am eternally grateful to my husband, Tim Heggland. This book is dedicated to him and rightly so.

# *About the Author*

MARY BEHAN is a retired professor of neuroscience at University of Wisconsin – Madison. She devotes her time to writing fiction, memoir and short stories. Her first book, *Abbey Girls*, is a memoir she wrote with her sister, Valerie Behan, about their childhood in Ireland. She lives with her husband in the Driftless Area of Wisconsin in a historic log cabin overlooking a tallgrass prairie. Visit her at mvbehan.com.

§

If you enjoyed this book, please consider leaving a review on your favorite website.

~ Thank you